ESSENCE BESTSELLING AUTHOR
ANTHONY WHYTE

GHETTO GIRLS

D1059349

BACK IN
THE DAYS

WHERE
HIP HOP
LITERATURE
BEGINS

AUGUSTUS
PUBLISHING

© 2013 Augustus Publishing, Inc.
ISBN: 978-19358833-7-1

Novel by Anthony Whyte
Edited by Parijat Deasai
Creative Direction & Design by Jason Claiborne
Photography by BigAppleModels.com

Augustus Publishing paperback September 2013
www.augustuspublishing.com

ACKNOWLEDGEMENTS

I would like to extend my sincerest gratitude to all the people who have helped me to make the Ghetto Girls Series possible. Six books of adventure, took me a minute, and a lot of 3W's, but we did it. Thank you goes to Professor Susan Shapiro for all your help. Jason Claiborne, it's more than just biz, my brother. Thanks to Carl Weber, Lisette Matos, Tamiko Maldonado, Tracy Sherrod, Clarence Haynes, Parijat Desai, Shulamy Cassado, and Juliet White. Without your individual support this project would not be completed. Good looking out to Silky Black, and Show Biz— DITC 4ever. Thank you Jerry Lakatos, you've been like a father to me. Thanks to all the readers for your continued support. Thank you all. Your kindness was a tremendous help. Jah told me that my Guiding Star would always be there. Been about Black Art... I was Hip Hop Lit from the start...

RIP to my mother, Violet White and father, Ernest White, my nephew, O'brien Phillip Tapper, my ninja, William Alicea, and all my fallen warriors...

"She didn't know what she was doing! You don't have to take her, man!" Eric Ascot loudly pleaded.

Despite his protest, officers escorted Coco and Eric out of the crowded studio. Eric Ascot stared angrily at all the audio equipment the officers were removing from his famed recording studio. He had built the business legally from the ground up, and now the law was essentially shutting down his career.

His musical talent had brought many accolades, but ultimately this attention may have silenced a man who was making serious noise in the music industry. His protégé and new artist, Coco Harvey, had jumped to his aid, defending him against the sea of police officers that had rushed into the studio. The place was now not only cramped with equipment, but now seemed packed with police. Lead by the authorities, Coco and Eric Ascot were escorted out the building.

News hounds were already outside waiting, and sniffing for clues. When they spotted music's hot producer and his protégé, they greeted the pair with flashing light bulbs.

"Ascot, why are you and your artist under arrest?"

"Mr. Ascot can you tell us—"

Eric Ascot heard questions popping out of the mouths of different representatives of the media, but remained lockjaw-quiet. He translated his pain into a smirk. Meanwhile the officers seemed smug, posing for cameras with their prized capture. It was as if they had just won a championship.

"Does this have anything to do with his impending trial on those, ah, murder charges?" Sarcasm dripped from the mouth of the questioner.

"We have no comment at this time," said a lead officer, smiling mockingly.

Waving his hand, he commanded the sea of reporters to part, and the police brusquely guided Eric and Coco through. Questions were still being hurled, but Ascot remained tight-lipped. He was rushed into the back of a squad car, and watched as Coco was placed in another car.

"Why do you have to take the girl?" Eric asked. "She's a teenager for Christ's sake. C'mon, man, give her a break!"

Coco heard Eric pleading, but was caught up by still more paparazzi racing to the scene. They were taking pictures of her face. She ducked, trying not to stare directly into the lens of any of the cameras. But there were so many aimed at her, she would turn away from one and be caught by another.

"Don't y'all got anything else to cover, yo?"

"Coco, why are you under arrest?"

"Ask these officers that, yo. All I was doing was just standing up for my rights."

"Save it for the judge. So now you're just poor, ol' Orphan Annie, huh? Watch your head getting into the car!" An officer said, pushing Coco forward.

Handcuffed and sitting in the back of a police cruiser wasn't Coco's idea. She made a choice to intercede on behalf of Eric Ascot. He was a music producer and Deedee's uncle. Because of a random meeting with his niece on a fateful Friday night outside of a nightclub in the city, Coco became close to his niece, Deedee. Ascot's influence was all over her musical career, and Coco felt loyalty to him for helping her. Their destiny was sealed when she signed the agreement to work with him, giving Ascot the right to determine the direction of her musical career.

She sat inside the police cruiser trying to shield her face from the flashing lights. There was nothing promised to her, she knew that. Coco was compelled to jump into action without thinking of the actual consequences. She was comforted by the fact that what she had done was much deeper than music. There was a certain dislike for the police that she held, and remembered how they always seemed to be on the opposite side of her life. Never the one to fear anything, Coco was now facing the prospect of going to jail. Inwardly, she simmered. On the other hand, her face reflected an unusual calmness.

Deedee had introduced her to Eric Ascot, but Coco felt the bond growing beyond just music. She couldn't standby and watched when the police tried to physically overwhelmed Ascot in his studio. It was like a family member being attacked, and she felt the compulsion to do something about it. The singer- rapper sensation was second-guessing her decision. Coco's determination to step up and Ascot in whatever way she could, was her true crime. Shaking her head, Coco watched the commotion with the news seekers. Like piranhas at the smell of blood, they rushed in to get the sensationalism of the arrest. The police fed it to them with sirens blasting. In a flash of lights, the cruiser sped away. Coco knew this wouldn't be an easy ride.

She saw Deedee walking quickly with Kim and Tina. Then they disappeared from her view along with the paparazzi, and Coco was alone with her thoughts. The wailing of sirens receded to the background of her rumination. What started out as a good summer was suddenly taking a sharp left. She felt the handcuff on her wrist tightened when she twisted her body to gain some measure of comfort.

Glancing out of the window as the convoy of police cars pulled to a stop outside a city precinct, Coco kept thinking that riding to jail with Eric Ascot never was part of her plan. She had become closer to Deedee and Ascot. It was now far more than a business relationship. That was her reason for standing by Eric, and she would stick with it.

"Hey c'mon man, take it easy with the girl," Eric shouted.

Ignoring his plea, the officers shoved them both toward the precinct. Inside Coco was immediately taken by a female officer who led her to a cell downstairs.

"Where you taking me, yo? Don't I have any rights?"

"You have a right to remain silent and anything you say may be used against you in a court of law. So just shut your mouth and come with me."

She was thoroughly searched again, and the handcuffs were removed. Coco stood, enjoying the temporary freedom.

"So what y'all gonna do next, yo?"

"Look young lady, you're a real pretty girl, but all that 'yo' is totally not necessary. Inside here, I'm boss and you'll address me as Sergeant Ross or don't say nothing at all. But I don't respond to 'yo.' Those are your choices. I'm not your yo-yo."

Coco stayed silently while staring at the officer's mean face. She was a huge woman. Tall, with large hands that could easily smack Coco down, the officer examined the contents of Coco's wallet. Her eyes seemed riveted on Coco's fears. Thoughts resurfaced of all the stories she had heard about people suffering beat-downs while arrested invaded the teen's mind.

She was booked, and the officer was about to give Coco a released on recognizance notice. Then a man in dark pinstriped suit arrived on the scene. The officer not only became friendlier, but was also kissing up to everything the attorney said.

"Gentlemen, and lady," Max Roose said smiling. "I'm sure all this is not necessary. Let me acquaint you with some facts. Coco Harvey is an honor student who has already been accepted to Harvard. And she's in no way a threat nor will cause any harm to anyone including officers of the law. I'm sure we can excuse an emotional outburst from a scared teen. We've all been there..."

Max Roose delivered the necessary legal arguments. In an applauding action heard around the precinct, the ROR was unconditionally vacated and Coco was released. The fast-talking attorney walked with Coco upstairs to a waiting area.

"Please stick around here and wait for us," Max Roose said, walking away. "I was going to secure Mr. Ascot's release. He has something very important to say to you, young lady."

Coco sat on a wooden seat in a waiting area next to a couple of vending machines. While sitting around waiting, Coco was relieved to see Deedee walking toward her along with the attorney. Deedee hugged her. Then Coco saw Eric coming in their direction, fixing his clothes. He appeared calm, but there was a determined look on his face.

"Let's get out of here. I hate this place," he said. "Max, you handle the press people. I've got a car waiting to take me and my niece and Coco outta here."

"Okay, will do. But I'll remind you that dealing with the law is what you pay me to do. So next time please call me before you jump on any of the officers. As for you young lady, we'll get the charges dropped on grounds of past good behavior," Max Roose said, walking away.

Eric, Deedee and Coco walked behind him and slipped away

as the lawyer engaged the news people.

"What we have here is a simple case of over zealousness on the part of the law enforcement. My client was willing to cooperate and if a few questions were answered— we wouldn't all be standing outside central booking on this lovely Monday evening, and having this conversation..."

Cautiously, Eric Ascot guided Deedee and Coco through the buzzing paparazzi and to a waiting limousine. The driver slowly moved out, and in the background the crowd was soon congregated around the attorney.

"Damn yo!" Coco suddenly said. "They be getting the news with the quickness."

"Who...?"

"Them yo," Coco said, gesturing back to the newshounds fading away behind them.

"You know they got all kinds of connects," Deedee said.

"Like, really...? They be on the money, yo."

"Speaking of being on top things... Coco, it's cool that you wanna stand up for me, but please don't next time—if there's a next time. I'll tell you what I always tell my niece..." Eric said, looking at Coco.

"Leave grown folks' business alone and—" Deedee said, joining in.

"But I was—"

"There are no buts. Just let grown folks handle grown folks' biz, and that's final," Eric sternly interjected.

Coco was about to go on arguing. She thought better of it and decided she would heed the words of Eric Ascot. Coco nodded. He then focused all his attention on Deedee. She reached up and gave her uncle a hug and a kiss. He returned her embrace and Coco watched. She wanted to say something but she held her breath. She felt an awkward feeling arise, and needed to be alone.

"I'm good at the hospital. I'm gonna see madukes. You don't have to come with me, yo."

"I can't believe those fuckers shut me down," Eric blurted at the same time. "Driver, please make a stop at Harlem Hospital," he said, raising his voice. "I gotta sell that damn mansion," he whispered under his breath, shaking his head.

She thought they were all getting out of the limousine to visit her mother, so Coco stalled for a couple of beats. But she realized no one was making moves to exit the limousine with her. She was on her own.

"We're here, Coco," Deedee said, reminding her of the obvious.

"Good looking out, yo" Coco said, getting out the car.

"Say hello to your mom for us, Coco," Eric offered.

"A'ight, I will. See y'all," Coco said, looking at Eric then Deedee.

"Are you sure you don't want me to tag along, Coco? I mean it's no problem and you know your mother loves to see me. Maybe I could—"

"No, I'm good. I need to see her by myself anyway. But thanks for offering, Dee. I'll hit you up later, yo."

She opened the door and Coco's thoughts raced ahead. Earlier in the morning she had visited and her mother's condition was grave. Coco wished for a positive change, but felt a sinking feeling watching Deedee wave to her. The limousine pulled away and Coco looked across the street. Despite the discomforting thoughts, she bravely eased into her bop and crossed the busy street. We all have our problems, she concluded. The automatic doors opened and with lingering trepidation, Coco walked inside the hospital.

Hospital security waved Coco on, allowing her access. She bopped to the elevator door and went upstairs. She exited the elevator slowly, almost dragging herself to her mother's bed. Although Rachel Harvey seemed like she was resting, a look of discomfort registered on her face. Coco watched her mother for a few moments.

Tubes extended from her mouth and both arms, and several monitors were hooked to different parts of her body. Emaciated with dried lips, Rachel Harvey appeared even more unwell than the doctors had let on.

With tears clouding her vision, Coco reached for a glass of water, wet her hands, and wiped her mother's severely chapped lips. Then she pulled out lip balm, and closing her mother's lips, Coco applied the moisturizer.

"You may use Vaseline on her exposed skin. Apply it in a

circular motion, to the dry patches you see on her skin. That will help your mother feel comfortable."

Coco turned around and smirked when she saw that a nurse had been watching. She resented the intrusion, but Coco nodded politely. The nurse had a smile reeking of sympathy, and she spoke again before moving on.

"I'll be at the front desk just in case you need me."

One of the reasons she hated hospitals was the smell. A sigh escaped her pursed lips and Coco's focus returned to her ailing mother. She sat down in a soft chair next to the bed and stared blankly at the shell of her once-vibrant mother. Crack had eaten away the heart of Rachel Harvey and now she was infected with HIV. Coco's hands were clasped together. Her palms were sweaty and she wrung her hands trying to dry them. She wanted to remove herself from the chair but couldn't make herself stand. Coco buried her face inside her palms and sighed.

It seemed like just a short while ago that her mother was excited and enjoying Coco's graduation service. Everything seemed much better then. Now her mother wasn't breathing properly and everything looked bleak. Coco wished that she could snap her fingers and make things the way they were. It's only wishful thinking, Coco thought as she cried softly.

After some time, Coco arched her back and realized that she had been sitting with her face down for too long. The weight of her problems on her slender shoulders was almost unbearable. The situation with her mother had become worse than she had imagined. Her mother had been using drugs since Coco was a toddler, and Coco had tried dealing with it as best she could. Yet, there were always friends and neighbors to get high with. Her mother had blown all the money she had in a major way. Her ravenous habit consumed everything they owned including her family.

Growing up in a household without a father, Coco relied on

her instincts to guide her. She would need it all if her mother was no longer around. Loneliness steadily crept into her mind. She wasn't ready to lose the woman who was there for her, even if she was under the influence of crack.

Coco was well aware of her mother's drug of choice and the fact that she drank a lot. It was known inside and outside the neighborhood. Coco even knew the dealers her mother had purchased drugs from. It was early in childhood that Coco had seen her mother in the act of copping drugs. She had acted as if she didn't know what was happening, but later could no longer closed her eyes, and began to argue endlessly with her mother about her bad habits.

Staring at what remained of her mother, it dawned on Coco that this could possibly be the end. Coco quickly tried to dismiss the dismal thought. She reached for a small towel and tenderly wiped her mother's perspiration. Then while silently praying, Coco applied Vaseline on her mother's exposed skin in the manner the nurse had described.

"Oh God, please help my mother," she cried.

Her tears came as she sat in the quiet hospital with the hum of life-sustaining machinery buzzing her in the head. Later Coco felt the gentle nudging on her shoulder. She must have dozed off and Coco awoke as if from a dream. She peered up at the sympathetic smile waiting on the nurse's face.

"You've got to get some rest. And that chair might not be too good for your back. Maybe you should get home and get some rest. You'll be welcome back tomorrow."

Coco glanced at her mother then back at the nurse. Without saying anything, she nodded, and rose from her seat. She had been sitting in the same position for such a long time, her joints cracked when she stood. Coco stretched, yawned and planted a long kiss on her mother's dry lips. She then moistened her lips and her mothers. Coco struggled to leave her mother's side. Glancing at the nurse's face, she could tell what time it was—she couldn't stay. Slowly Coco walked away.

Street lights paved her way, reflecting from the blacktop and brightening her path. Coco was in her bop. The summer night's air greeted her. Coco lit a cigarette, took a couple drags, and stomped it out with her Gucci sneakers. Headphones in her ear, her hands in her pockets, Coco slowly walked home.

From the corner she heard the buzz and recognized their faces. Coco saw the same small crowd, the ones who never seemed to leave the front of the building. They were outside waiting like paparazzi when she arrived at her apartment building. Coco bopped through the hub of the crowd, and instantly became the topic of discussion.

"Whaddup Coco...? You were all over the news, my girl," a young kid said in between puffs on a blunt.

He took another puff and attempted to pass the smoldering weed to Coco. She was about to reach out and accept it, but paused and just stared at the boy's face.

"I'm a chill, yo."

"You turning into a star, huh Coco Puff?"

"Yeah, she all over the airwaves," another kid said, sucking on the blunt.

"Word, that new song banging on da radio, and girl you on da fuckin' TV news..." The first kid said. "You a real star now, huh Coco...?"

"Yeah, she slummin' with real niggas. Can't even hit the blunt and this good weed too," another joined in laughing.

"We not on your level, huh, Coco?"

"Nah, nah, you got it all twisted, yo. It's like this. First of all, I don't smoke anything when I ain't seen it being rolled. And second, I just came from visiting maducas and I ain't feeling too good about that situation. You feel me? So you see it ain't really like that, yo."

"Sorry to hear about your mom, Coco."

"Word, we totally forgot about that shit."

"Say hello to her when you visit her. We miss her."

Coco nodded and kept it moving. She was aware that the crowd was watching her going inside the building. Coco could hear the mumblings as they returned to their conversations.

"No wonder that crack bitch ain't been around—she in da hospital."

"Word, we miss that lil' cheddar she used to bring us."

Coco was walking up the stairs, and the same sentiments echoed throughout the entire hallway. Those people outside either missed the money she spent buying their crack or they were used to getting high with her mother. She knew that no one really cared for the right reasons. Coco stopped her thoughts and opened the door to her mother's apartment.

As she walked into the two-bedroom apartment, she felt the chill of loneliness invading her body and headed to the kitchen. The place seemed empty. There was no way she could survive this cold spell in life without her mother. Coco stared outside the window and saw the reason it was difficult for her mother to leave the drug game. Street hustlers and pitchers were everywhere relentlessly laying their hustle down.

Dealers were out stalking every potential customer on the corners and everyone entering the building. Any recovering addict was at the mercy of their greed. It was not a level playing field. Coco saw the users running between drug dealers who peddled their drug of choice. With her mother now in the hospital locked in a deadly battle for life, Coco grew blank.

Placing the headphones over her ears, she pulled out her pen and pad. She sat at the kitchen table, lit a cigarette, and gathered her thoughts. Inhaling and exhaling slowly, she tried to write the lyrics playing in her mind. Coco continued to smoke and soon put the cigarette out. She walked to the living room, turned on the television, and plopped down into the sofa.

"Fuck it," she said, turning on the television.

A cloud immediately crossed over Coco's face when she saw the program. It was another episode of *Sanford and Son.* Her mother was always watching the sitcom. Coco's thoughts were off and running again, and she couldn't stop them. The sitcom about the lives of a father and son reminded her of the fact that she had no father. With the exception of Eric Ascot there was no solid male figure. Her thoughts made her body shiver with tension. The combination of a warm summer night in a lonely apartment caused her to steam with a slow anger.

She had to do something. Coco got up and walked through the apartment to turn on the air conditioner. Thinking about her mother, she stood outside her bedroom door. Coco cautiously walked into her mother's bedroom as if Rachel was in the apartment. She looked at the clothes hanging everywhere, and began searching the room. She went into her mother's dresser drawers. While digging around, Coco found a bag. Inside there was a small glass pipe, residue, and a piece of rock.

She grabbed the bag, stomped to the kitchen window and looked at the bustling crowd in front of the building. She saw that most of the hustlers were men and most of the customers were women. Anger built to a crescendo inside her. Her sensitivity was about to choke the life from her, and Coco had to release it. An explosion went off inside her as she held the bag of drug paraphernalia works above her head.

"Here, you can have this back!" Coco shouted, raising the window, and tossing the bag out.

"Whaddafuck! Shit almost hit me!" Someone shouted.

"Who da fuck tossing shit out the window?" Another person shouted.

"That shit was coming from the third floor over there!" Someone said, pointing to the window where Coco stood.

"Hey yo, Coco. Is you going crazy, girl?"

There was no answer and the crowd continued to stare up at the window. They were anticipating something coming back, but nothing came.

"Yeah, that bitch getting crazier than her mother," someone remarked.

The small crowd had gathered then quickly went back to their hustle. Coco's furious expression turned to a cynical smile, and she went to her bedroom. Pacing, she returned to the living room, sighed, and sat back on the sofa. Turning up the music in her headphones, she muted the volume of the television and closed her eyes.

Her tears rolled while the antics of the sitcom provided laughter. Coco was devastated by the loss of companionship and the possibility of not ever regaining it. Her mother's condition weighed heavy on her and Coco couldn't help but think about it.

"Dear God, please don't take my mother..." Coco cried, praying.

In the following days, Coco visited her mother at the hospital like clockwork. There were no changes and Coco returned home after every visit deep in depression. She would pass the people hanging out in front of the building with the same determined expression. And they would look at her as if she was going crazy.

Besides daily conversation with Deedee, Coco was left to her sad and lonely thoughts. For a couple of weeks, daily visits to Harlem Hospital to see her mother were the only things occupying Coco's days. Her mother's condition deteriorated and tore into Coco's heart. Despite Coco's regular visits and daily prayers, Rachel Harvey's condition remained dismal. Coco remained resolute and had a bold exterior, but while alone she was a worried teenager. She smoked regularly, but kept telling herself that she would soon quit.

More weeks went by, and Coco awoke one morning to light a cigarette and walk into the bathroom. Glancing into the mirror above the sink, she told herself once again she had to give up all her bad habits. She had just sworn off doing all bad things when she heard her cell phone ringing. Coco sat on the toilet and thought about Deedee.

"That's the only person who could be calling me this early..."

Deedee awoke early in the morning, and automatically checked her cell phone. There was a missed call and voicemail from Rightchus. She shook her head, and smirked as she put the phone down. Deedee pulled out the package with the pregnancy kit, and stared blankly at her reflection in the oversized bathroom mirror.

Summer was moving rapidly, and the trial fast approaching. Eric woke up, showered and quickly got dressed in a lightweight dark-colored suit. He found Deedee sitting at the kitchen table as he rushed into the kitchen.

"Dee, good morning," he said, greeting with her a hug. "You're up early."

"Yeah..."

"You all right...? I mean, what's the matter? Can't sleep...?"

"Something like that," she answered in a matter-of-fact tone.

"I'm sure if you eat some breakfast that'll help."

"Maybe... I'll get to it. Uncle E, you're dressed and off already?" She asked, turning away from the huge television screen built into the wall.

"Yeah, it's gonna be one of those long days, Dee. I gotta meet with the attorney and find out what's going on with the studio equipment. These people are cramping me. Anyway I'll take care of it."

"Maybe you should wear a lighter color suit."

"Why you don't like my suit?"

"It's not that I don't like it. Maybe a lighter color will cheer up the day..."

"Oh...?"

"Yes, this one makes you look dark and gloomy."

"So you think I should change?"

"Not really since you seemed to be in a rush."

"Okay, this once I'll change."

Eric Ascot slipped out of his jacket as he walked away. Deedee burst into tears, and wiped them from her eyes before her uncle returned. Dressed in a lighter colored suit, Eric spun around for her and Deedee smiled.

"I like that better," she smiled.

"So what you do have planned for today?"

"Well... Ah, I think I'll drive over and see Coco later on or something."

"Remember no spending spree. Be careful, there are people watching your every move," Eric Ascot said, and turned to walk out the door.

"You be careful too Uncle E."

She watched the door close and knew there was security around. Eric, concerned about safety, had taken the bull by the horns, lining up a two-man security team downstairs. Her safety wasn't so much on Deedee's mind as the urge to shop. For once in her life Deedee faced the possibility of not being able to spend money freely. Her charge card and her ability to shop had been curtailed.

Her sadness seemed to start with that night she was raped. Everything seemed to have gone downhill from that point. Sighing, Deedee tried to shake the thought. It always made her depressed, but at other times she had been able to go on a wild shopping spree, which would offer temporary refuge. Not now. She walked to her room-sized closet and yawned. There were enough racks of designer clothing and shoes hanging in unopened boxes to clothe a tiny island of teen girls. It definitely wasn't a need for clothes that made Deedee yearn to shop. It was the escape from a painful reality that the whole process offered.

Acquiring new things seemed to have the effect of refreshing her. Not having that luxury worsened her feelings of depression. Deedee feigned a smile. Luckily her uncle had bought her the new car. But then the car made her think of the explosion at the Hamptons mansion, and of Reggie's death. Deedee tried to control the feeling of guilt tormenting her as she reminisced.

She was naked, curled up, quietly asleep and Reggie moved closer to her. The rising of her breasts from her quiet breathing turned him on. He bent over and kissed her. She stirred and locked her lips with Reggie's.

His hands wasted no time in searching her supple body. A smile suddenly spread across Reggie's face when his fingers made contact with her treasured spot. She was juicy with anticipation. Her legs wiggled free and he tried to enter her, but Deedee was ready and slipped her leg around his, blocking his entry.

"You've gotta use a condom. This time it's for real," Deedee firmly said.

"Babe, it's early I'll get it later," Reggie said, kissing her softly. "But I don't need a condom to do this," he continued and immediately flipped her over.

Before Deedee could protest she felt his tongue on her clit. Reggie sucked at her pussy lips, and Deedee's muscles relaxed. Her juices flowed.

"Oh no..." she moaned. Her sounds faded to unintelligibly uttering as Reggie's tongue penetrated deep inside her. "Uh... Oh ugh..."

She felt her legs kicking involuntarily and Deedee grabbed his head. She pulled at his hair and a scream gurgled in her throat.

"Oh please oh please stop...Oh no..."

Reggie kept munching and sucking. His fingers tickled the entrance to her asshole sending shivers all through Deedee's spine. Her body wiggled and she held on tightly to Reggie's head and exploded in his face.

"Ooh... Ooh... Ah... Ah... Oh yes!"

Deedee's naked body opened like a flower and Reggie hovered over her, kissing and sucking her nectar. He licked his lips heartily. A combination of his sweat mixing with her juices filled his palate. Reggie wanted more and tried to shove his hard dick into her, but again she moved her legs and blocked him.

"You did that shit last night, and that was on me. You're not gonna get anymore unless you get a condom."

"Your uncle don't got any stashed—"

"What? Reggie, go to the store and get a pack. Or you'll be going home without getting anymore. I swear!"

"A'ight cool, I'll do what you say. But babe, how am I gonna get to the store? I don't have a car, and you gave what's-her-name your ride."

"I gave Kim may car to get home. Also to take your shit-talking friend Tina outta my head," Deedee said and hopped out of the bed.

Reggie's eyes closely followed her nude body as she walked to the window, and back the bed, sliding into the sheets. Deedee smiled at him and said, "Uncle Eric's Jag's there. If you promise not to wreck it you can use it to go to the store."

"Do you have directions to one that's open this early?"

"It's seven in the morning. It's not that early. Just stay on this street and you won't miss a small shopping district with a service station."

"In a Jag that should be about five minutes," Reggie smiled, playfully.

"Boy don't you wreck my uncle's car."

"Where the keys...?"

Again Deedee got of the bed and walked outside. A few minutes later, she returned and said, "Check inside the car. Uncle E. More than likely left them there."

"Damn ain't he scared that someone steals it or sump'n...?"

"That's my uncle. He believes in playing it like that."

Reggie quickly stole a kiss and before walking out, turned back to ask, "You need anything...?"

Deedee smiled before responding. "You're thoughtful, huh?" she said with a grin. "Cool... Surprise me."

"I will do that," he smiled.

He kissed her again before walking out. This time he stared deep into Deedee's soft brown eyes and gently touched her lips with his. She pulled him close to her breasts and kissed him hungrily, moving her tongue against his. The ferocity of her passion consumed him causing Reggie to fall in a heap on top of her. He held her close, until his breath came in gasps. Mustering enough strength, Reggie managed to push away from Deedee's captivating presence.

"Hold onto that for now. I'll be back soon," he smiled.

"Be back soon," she smiled, blowing him a kiss.

He ran out of the room and headed down the stairs. Reggie saw that someone was in the mansion cleaning, and he kept it moving.

Pushing the door open, Reggie was off running down the long driveway to the garage on the far side.

Deedee chuckled from her window watching him run. He opened the door and gave her the thumbs up. She smiled that he had spotted her watching him. Deedee was about to walk away from the window when a loud explosion rocked the entire mansion.

The morning sky erupted into golden flames as soon as Reggie had turned on the ignition. Deedee eyes widened in surprise and her mouth dropped opened but no sound came. The car had exploded killing Reggie. She found herself pointing and staring at the fire as pieces of the luxury car blew off in the explosion. Fire raged and alarms went off, neighbors were running from their homes. Deedee lost control and started screaming.

It had been a couple of weeks now and the memory deepened her depression. She tried to stop the images from coming, but couldn't. She felt sadness surge through her being. The rush of emotion made her want to cry some more.

"I must think of all the goodness this situation can bring," she smiled, nodding.

She hastily did her morning stretches. After couple sets of push-ups and sit-ups Deedee walked back to her bedroom with a sense of relief. The fact that her uncle had finally put the mansion on the selling block brought some bittersweet relief. Deedee's father who was Eric's older brother had purchased the mansion in the Hamptons.

He had been shot to death in his car seven years ago. Since then Deedee had always shared the mansion with his brother, her uncle, Eric Ascot. Now she felt she could never return there, even though it was one of the last places her father had resided and held special memories. But those recollections were tarnished by Reggie Mills' untimely death. Deedee sensed her dark depression closing in. Seeking refuge, she hurriedly pulled out her cell phone and dialed Coco's number. After a few rings she heard the voice of her best friend.

"Hey Dee... So wassup yo...?"

"Hey Coco, how're you?"

"Chillin', but how you really doing, yo? How'd the test go? "

"I'll tell you in person..."

"Okay, bet."

"I'm coming to get you, Coco. Let's hang out."

"You mean you can't tell me on the phone, yo?"

"Girl, I'll come and get you I said. Just chill, I gotta get used to the idea too..."

"A'ight yo..."

"See you soon," Deedee said, glancing around her room ful of clothing.

From the Dolce and Gabbana section to the different Cavalli jeans and Donna Karan blouses, Deedee searched for something to ease the pain she felt. Even with Gucci heels, Christian Louboutin and Prada designer shoes all over the place, she couldn't find the right combination. Deedee wanted to feel special, but it was proving difficult. Wishing she could go shopping, she started dressing. Suddenly she held her stomach, broke down, and tears flowed again.

Eventually Deedee pulled her outfit and herself together. Then she strutted out of the apartment still managing to look fresh. She rode the elevator downstairs to the garage silently going through her cell phone. Deedee erased the messages from Rightchus without responding. Downstairs in her BMW, she sat in the driver's seat checking her reflection in the rearview mirror. Slipping on the oversized Gucci shades, Deedee put the car in gear and was on her way to meet with her best friend.

She pulled to a stop outside Coco's apartment building. Deedee dialed Coco from the cell phone.

"Coco, I'm downstairs..."

"Okay, yo. Give a second and I'll be down."

Deedee turned up the music on the radio. She was strumming her finger to the beat like her uncle used to do, when suddenly a nauseating feeling overtook her. Deedee felt tremors in her stomach and soon she felt a rush coming up her throat. Panic stricken, Deedee quickly let down the window in time. Then she spat outside.

Vomit stains swiveled from the saliva on her lips. Reaching for tissue from her glove compartment, Deedee wiped the residue left dribbling from the corners of her mouth. She spat again and again, attracting the attention of the small crowd in front of the building.

"Shut da front door, bitch! I bet you wouldn't guess who I just saw calling Earl...?" Tina said in urgent, hushed tones. In a building not far away from Coco's in a sixth-floor apartment, Kim was taking care of her son, Roshawn, and simultaneously carrying on a phone conversation with her childhood friend, Tina.

"You by my building...?"

"I'm not that far away," Tina said.

"How far is not that far away...?"

"I'm outside that show-off, wanna-be rapper's building. And guess who just pulled up vomiting all over the place?"

"Deedee...?"

"Bingo! That rapper bitch just came out her building now. They probably going to the abortion clinic now... Ha, ha. I told you..."

"Just c'mon upstairs and lemme drop off Roshawn by my mother."

"Chill out bitch. I'm watching what them two up to..."

"What they doing...?"

"They just hug and sitting in Deedee's car running their mouths. Deedee probably telling that gay bitch about her pregnancy...

And the gay bitch probably telling her that they should live together and let the baby have two mamis," Tina loudly laughed.

"Oh you're too much. C'mon up—I gotta go get my hair did and shyt," Kim said.

"I wish I was a fly. I'd just fly over there and hear what 'em bitches talkin' 'bout."

Tina stood a few feet out of sight, watching Coco and Deedee. The teens continued talking for a couple of beats. Then the BMW rolled away.

"What they doing now, fly...?"

"Deedee drove off. They outta here...and who you callin' fly, bitch...?"

"Look, you running up my Verizon bill. So just bring your ass upstairs so I can get off this call and take care of my baby boy..."

"A'ight, give me a minute. I'm a buy some cigarettes and shit and then I'm on my way up to see your stank black ass..." Tina chuckled.

"Whateva bitch...!" Kim answered and hung up.

She was dialing the number to her mother when she heard the downstairs bell buzzing. A few minutes later Kim hung up the call to her mother when Tina rang the doorbell.

"Easy chica—what, there's a fire or sump'n?"

"Let me in, Kim. Can't you tell I'm in a rush, bitch?" Tina asked, barging through as soon as the door was opened. "I wanna use your bathroom," she continued, running through the small hallway.

Kim shook her from side to side as she watched Tina race inside the bathroom. She closed the door and locked it while Kim was still looking at the bathroom door. Kim was waiting when Tina finally emerged from the bathroom.

"Every time you come here, you run straight to the bathroom. Your place is just around the corner. Don't you know you wanna piss or shit before you leave? Or is your system too weak to handle the journey?"

"It ain't like that. I was downstairs looking at—"

"You were downstairs being nosy, and forgot that you wanted to take a shyt, bitch?"

"Shut da front door. I only took a piss, ho. Next time—"

"Next time...? There shouldn't be a next time. Cause your ass got a—"

"Will you stop cutting me off? I was telling you that Reggie must've pushed something up in that bitch, Deedee—"

"Wait a minute don't be coming up in my place telling me what I can and cannot do. You hear?"

"A'ight already. Like I was saying before I was rudely interrupted. That bourgeois-ass bitch from downtown outside in da projects in the morning, vomiting like some ghetto girl..."

"Damn, she must be having morning sickness and all that shyt," Kim mused.

"Reggie did his J-O-B," Tina laughed.

"What's that shyt?"

"He done put a bun up in that oven, ho."

"Huh-uh!"

"I told you that young nigga had a big ass dick. And you know them young boys, they ready to fire off and impregnate your ass with da quickness."

"Yeah you should know, bitch," Kim said. "You laughing like you're the one pregnant."

"Shut your trap, ho. That nigga dead. He gone. He can't raise no kids or even get money to raise a child. She assed out if she keeps that baby."

"Yeah, you right, bitch. But she probably ain't gonna keep that baby. Her uncle full of money, I'm sure she's gonna get an abortion."

"An early abortion, huh? You probably right, ho. That's what she gonna do. I know her bourgie-ass ain't planning on having no fatherless child. Especially when the daddy dead," Tina said.

"You're such a fake-ass—"

"Oh please, lemme go see my new boo," Tina said with a chuckle.

Her cynical laugh echoed through the apartment. Both Roshawn and Kim stared at her as if she was a lunatic. Tina happily rushed over to the infant and he smiled when he saw her.

"Hey Roshawn," Tina said, lifting the infant in the air. "Wouldn't you have love to hear them two bitches discussing their BI? Next is that ho-ass-lesbo, Coco."

"A'ight Tina. Be very careful with my son," Kim said. "And don't bring him into any of your shenanigans, Miss Tina."

"Shut your face, bitch. I wouldn't do that. You think it's a boy or girl?"

"Shyt, it don't make me no difference."

"You might be right, ho. She ain't gonna keep it anyways."

"I don't think so. And please stop saying B's and H's around my son. When he goes to preschool he gonna be calling his teachers B's and ho's cuz that's all he hear coming outta your mouth."

"Damn ho, I'm real curious about that."

"What's there to be curious about, bitch? Roshawn will be three and a half next month. He can start preschool in the fall."

"Shut your face. I know 'bout that—I'm talking about Deedee and her baby."

"Tina, I think you're possessed by the devil himself. Okay...?"

"Whatever, ho—oops I'm sorry Roshawn."

"You're working on not getting invited back. And furthermore I think you just mad that it ain't your ass that's prego," Kim laughed.

"Shut da front door! Why would I even want some nappy-headed-nigga-who's-dead baby...? My son Angel is my little man and he got real nice hair. Speaking of which, bitch, ain't you gonna get your hair did?"

"For once you right. Roshawn stay with your crazy auntie while your sane mother get dressed. Okay baby boy...?" Kim said, smiling at her son.

She handed the infant a couple of his toys and started to walk away. Making sure Roshawn was safe, Kim turned and saw Tina dialing on the phone.

"You calling one of your johns?"

"Yes, it's all about that dollar, girlfriend," Tina said waiting for an answer. "I gotta make it to get up out this hood and live like the rich and famous."

"Please child, that's the song on every poor bird's lips," Kim said.

"Aw hell no! Them ghetto birds ain't doing what I'm doing 'bout it,"

"You're always conniving... Who you conspiring with now?"

"Don't you worry. Just hurry and wash your stink ass, ho. We gotta make a stop downtown."

"Didn't I just told you about cursing around my son? You are gonna let me go upside that wooden head of yours, Tina."

"I'll make it up. We can go shoe shopping later. It's on me, baby," Tina smiled.

"Balling! But don't you be dropping no more H-bombs and B-bombs around my child. No F-bombs either. Dammit! See now you got me cursing," Kim hastily said.

"Look just hurry the F-up and get ready, I got Roshawn, and I promise not to curse around him. We just gonna watch some videos."

"Watch cartoons instead. I don't like Roshawn watching them video ho's shaking their stink asses," Kim said.

"Kim stop hatin'," Tina said. "Go wash your stink A..." Tina laughed.

They strolled through Central Park on a warm sunny day. Coco and Deedee held hands and stopped several times to embrace. Both shared their problems and bared their souls to each other. Consoling each other when necessary, Coco and Deedee walked along the curving promenades of the park. The pair avoided midday bikers and runners out enjoying summer by staying on the long stretches of green grass. They wound up outside a small play area built for young children.

Then came the hypnotic chiming from the ice cream truck. Deedee watched several parents and children reacting in the same manner, running in the direction of the refreshment vehicle. Some kids had to drag their parents toward the truck while others walked along with their mothers.

"I know what you thinking, yo."

"What am I thinking, Coco?"

"You're thinking, 'My kid is not gonna be bossing me around. He's gonna be cool like me.' Sump'n like that..."

"Close, I was just wondering what it would be like if I keep it?"

"I thought you said it's a decision you've already made. It sounded like you already made up your mind and the only person you gotta tell is your uncle."

"I don't know Coco. I've been thinking about all possibilities, but I don't know. I mean I feel like I should keep it and then... I don't know."

"I guess it's hard to make up your mind at this point, yo. But you can't be waiting too long."

Deedee glanced at the throng of children at the ice cream truck. She heard their laughter and felt their innocent happiness. Hugging her belly, she turned her attention at Coco.

"What would you do if it was you, Coco?" Deedee asked.

Coco looked away. She pulled out two cigarettes and offered Deedee one. At first, Deedee declined then she took the cigarette. Coco lit both and they inhaled.

"I'd get rid of it," Coco exhaled.

Deedee stared at her as Coco's answer sank in. Cool and calculating, Deedee thought sizing up Coco. She inhaled then exhaled before continuing the conversation.

"Just like that? I mean, why?"

"For my own selfish reasons," Coco said.

"Such as..."

"With madukes condition and all the shit going on in my life, right now wouldn't be a good time for me or the baby that's all."

"But what if you can't live with yourself after you have that abortion, Coco?"

"I'm just saying, me, personally—I wouldn't be able to do it and I'd have to live with that."

"But why?"

"Why? I ain't got money like you Dee. I mean you could afford to do all that. But I can't, yo."

"Please, my uncle took away my car and I can't even shop."

"Damn, I hear you. But even when you can't wild out on shopping sprees, you're still way richer than me. My family income is at the bottom of the chart. In order for me to accomplish anything, I gotta downsize. I can't be having no kids and all that. My mother... We on welfare. That shit ain't fun, yo. Your uncle is a millionaire. Y'all are rich."

"Hmm, I don't feel that way right now."

"Me, I'd be a broke-ass bitch on welfare. And I really don't want to be that. Plus I won't have no time to do what I want to do if I had a kid. For real, yo."

"Yes, you're right. Having a baby takes a lot. I don't know Coco. I just started thinking seriously about it after I took the test this morning. I mean it hit me then. And I gotta make a decision."

"Well, I want you to know that whatever you decide, I'm gonna support you, Dee. I'll be by your side."

"I know, Coco."

"C'mon let's go get ice-cream cones," Deedee suggested.

"Nah, ma. I want a strawberry sundae, yo."

"Don't yo me. I'm not a yo-yo," Deedee said with a twinkle in her eyes.

Both girls laughed, hurrying toward the ice cream truck. The first throng of customers had been served and dissipated to enjoy their treats. Deedee ordered, then the girls walked away arm in arm, licking matching strawberry ice-cream cones.

"Now that you can't shop till you drop, what're you gonna do,

Deedee?"

"I'm gonna be your best friend again, Coco."

"Again...?"

"Yes, again. I think we had a little separation there for a minute, but we got a lot of time to make up for it," Deedee said.

She smiled and licked her ice cream cone while glancing at Coco. The sound of Deedee's soft lips smacking made Coco laugh. Pointing her finger at Deedee, she said,

"You're soo hood, yo."

"I can't be less than a ghetto girl, hanging with you Coco. You taught me well," Deedee laughed, countering.

"Whateva," Coco said, feigning disdain. "Anyway, I don't know if I'll finish recording my first album, yo."

"You were really looking forward to getting that done, huh?"

"Like hell yeah, yo. I mean this summer has been soo fucked up so far. Damn!"

"It over yet, Coco. Uncle E will get it together. He always rises above obstacles."

"I know he will, Dee. He better, yo. Or else..."

"He will, Coco."

The girls threw their bodies against each other in a tight embrace. Coco and Deedee hugged quietly, blending into a park of lovers and children playing under their parents watchful eyes. Their chests rose and fell in unison. Bated breaths escaped from the slight opening of their lips. The girls gazed into each other's eyes. Then their lips met. Deedee planted a deep kiss on Coco's quivering lips.

She was totally surprised by Deedee's open display of affection. It was an aggressive act, but Coco managed a shy smile. They were still in each other's embrace when staring into Deedee's soft brown eyes, Coco returned Deedee's kiss. They hugged for a few more pulsing heartbeats, before they smiled and started walking.

Coco's knees felt weak and she almost stumbled trying to

ease into her familiar bop. She held on tightly to Deedee's seemingly strong arm, trying to prevent the sudden rush of emotion she felt overwhelming her. Her face was flushed, and she was lightheaded. All she could think about was the kiss.

"Why'd you do that, yo? Coco finally asked.

"It must be the air. I mean the park, the weather, sometimes when I'm with you, Coco, everything just seems right."

"And I guess you felt like you had to kiss me...?"

"I was trying to show you love," Deedee answered.

They were still hand in hand walking silently in the park while chatting. Deedee looked at Coco, who was busy glancing at the birds in the trees. There was a slight wind blowing, And strands of Coco's afro flew around her face. Coco was trying to avoid eye contact, but Deedee recognized the gleam in her friend's eyes.

"Hope I didn't offend you, Coco," Deedee said, squeezing Coco's hands.

"No, it wasn't like that, yo." "It was just... Ah, you know kind a sudden, spontaneous," Coco continued with a faint smile.

"Spontaneity is good sometimes," Deedee said, returning Coco's attempt at a smile.

They walked smiling, hand in hand, through the park. Both girls had entered with different thoughts weighing on their minds. The same feeling, surging and charging their bodies, now united them.

Coco found her swagger and easily bounced in her bop by the time they reached the car. Deedee opened the door with a remote starter. They made plans to continue hanging together for the rest of the evening.

"Coco, let's go see that new Ice Cube movie."

"I can but you'd have to take me to see my mother first, yo."

"Okay cool. It's a deal. Maybe we can grab something to eat on the way to the movie."

Deedee started the car and hit the road, heading in the

direction of Harlem Hospital. They arrived there in a flash and Coco jumped out the car.

"I'll see you in a few, yo."

"No you won't. I'm parking and coming in with you."

"You don't really have to. I mean she might be awake, but she's not able to stay up for too long. So I'm—"

"I'm with you all the way, Coco. And that's all," Deedee said, waving her hand interrupting Coco.

Coco smiled and stood watching as Deedee quickly found parking. She joined Coco and together they strutted into the hospital.

"Furthermore, I've visited your mother when she was in the hospital before," Deedee said.

"I know, yo."

"You might be visiting me in the hospital soon," Deedee chuckled.

"Oh please, Dee. If she's up, do not mention anything about you being pregnant. That'd certainly cause her to check out yo."

"And we both know how much she'd love nothing but to do that."

"I'm talking really checking out, yo."

"You mean like... flat line...?"

"Yeah yo. I'm talking that."

"Okay, I won't forget," Deedee said in a serious tone. "And I won't talk about boys, hanging out..." she added with a wink. "I told you that I've been here visiting her before."

"Yeah, this hospital thing has been a regular revolving door thing with madukes, yo."

"Hey, Coco there are vending machines over there," Deedee said, making a beeline for the small snack area.

"Are you that hungry, yo?" Coco asked, following.

"You forgot? I'm eating for two now. Let's get couple hot chocolates, ring dings, yo-yo's... anything chocolate," Deedee smiled.

"You're trippin' right now, yo. Let's just get the hot chocolates. We can eat before we go to the flicks."

Hospital security waved Coco and Deedee on. Carrying hot cups of chocolate, the girls got on an elevator heading up. They got off and Deedee sipped quietly, trailing Coco. She saw patients as she passed open doors. Deedee imagined being cooped up in a hospital bed and a frown appeared on her face.

When they reached the room, Ms. Harvey was lying with her eyes closed. Heart monitors, a breathing apparatus and tubes were connected to every organ of her emaciated body. Deedee's jaw dropped in surprise and the cup of hot chocolate slipped out of her hands. It splashed on the white tiled floor. Coco jumped, staring at Deedee. She realized that this was the first time Deedee visited.

Coco quickly handed Deedee her cup of hot chocolate then attended to her mother. She found a small towel and moistened it with warm water. Coco wiped sweat from her ailing mother's perspiring face. A nurse happened to walk by, and looked in.

"Hi Coco," she spoke with familiarity. "How're you feeling?"

"Hey, Nurse Roberts. I'm good, how's my mom?" Coco responded.

"You are not here at your usual time, I see," the nurse said. "You're a few hours late. She was up briefly and has been in and out. She even managed to drink some fluid."

"You mean she woke up? Wow, that's good right, Nurse Roberts?"

"Yes it's always a good sign when the patient regains consciousness. In your mother's case, it proves that some of the drugs are working. And let's not forget all the talking you've been doing in here at all times of night and day. Every bit helps and goes a long way toward helping with her recovery. Keep it up, Coco. You've been in here like clockwork everyday for the past couple of weeks."

"That was my fault. I sort of took Coco out of her normal

routine," Deedee said.

"I had to meet up with my friend. I'm sorry, this is my friend, Deedee."

"Hello, Nurse Roberts. It's nice to meet you," Deedee said.

"Hi there, Deedee. Let me see how your mom is doing and get back to my rounds," nurse Roberts said.

The nurse checked Ms. Harvey, and after making adjustments to the machines and tubes, she fixed the bed.

"Well nice to see you Deedee and Coco," the nurse said, pulling the drapes on the window. "She may wake up for a few minutes. Try not to stay too long, Coco, and stop at the desk before you leave."

"A'ight, I will. Coco said

"Thanks for the good news," Deedee said.

"Okay, see you both," the nurse said, walking out the room.

Coco and Deedee sat staring at the frail woman lying in the bed. They remained silent, and could hear the all life-saving machines humming loudly throughout the hospital. Deedee walked to the window and glanced out at the rooftops of Harlem, while Coco, tears in her eyes, kept wiping at her mother's face.

Deedee could feel the sadness welling up inside her. She remembered the time that she found out that she had lost her mother. Deedee had never accepted the explanation. She wasn't even sure about her uncle's version. Her mother could be alive living somewhere, she didn't know for sure and no one seemed to care. Funny how someone so important could be gone with so little fanfare. Living or dead, Denise Ascot's disappearance remained a mystery that seemed to matter only to her daughter.

Deedee walked over to Coco and hugged her best friend. Coco saw tears rolling down Deedee's cheeks.

"Why are you crying, yo?"

"I'm feeling your pain, Coco," Deedee said bravely.

Coco squeezed her arms tightly around Deedee's neck.

Deedee reached forward and placed a tender kiss on Coco's soft lips. They were crying in each other's embrace only to be startled by the sound of someone clearing their throat. Coco and Deedee were still in each other's arms, when they heard a distinct voice.

"What's goin' on here?"

"Ah... I'm here with Coco and..."

"Oh my gosh!" Coco jumped back in surprise.

It was the first time this had happened and Coco both embarrassed and surprised. Deedee stared wide-eyed at Ms. Harvey's ghostlike figure rose up and bent forward to look at them.

"So, y'all gots to hug and carry on like y'all need a room or sump'n...?"

The teen girls stared at each other then back at the person in the hospital bed who now seemed to have fallen back asleep. Coco thought of calling the nurse but was stopped dead in her tracks by her mother's menacing tone.

"Don't bother callin' that heffa," she snapped from her prone position. "Her ass probably too busy eating a damn ham sandwich, and drinking her coffee to even bother with me. That bitch hyper like she wound up when she come up in this room. Makes me scared. The white nurse, she mean and all, but she's calm and look like she knows what she's doin'. This one she act like she drunk or hung over and have to drink coffee all night. I tell you speakin' of drinkin'... Coco, come closer girl lemme holla in your ears..."

Coco timidly moved in the direction of her mother's bed. The woman was unmoving but her mouth was moving like her mother's. Because of Ms. Harvey's inability to eat, the doctors had prescribed intravenous nutrition. The voice was familiar, but Coco found it difficult to recognize the woman lying in the hospital bed.

She saw bony, sticklike fingers twitching and beckoning her on. Coco floated like she was wrapped in a cloud, gently moving in the direction of her mother's bed. Coco's mind seemed to fail in the surreal situation; it was difficult to grasp what was happening. Then she heard her mother's voce again.

"Coco, you moving like you nine months pregnant! I ain't got much time," Ms. Harvey said.

Her mother's tone propelled Coco forward. She tried to spring toward the person who had raised her. But Coco felt hazy, and hesitated. She saw Deedee reaching forward to hug her mother. When Ms. Harvey shouted, Coco realized it wasn't a dream. Everything was real.

"Okay, take it easy now, what's your name. Um Danielle, or Josephine? Y'all the same," Ms. Harvey said in a strained whisper to

Deedee.

"I'm Deedee, Miss Harvey," Deedee said loudly.

"Dee, I don't care. Just don't lead my daughter astray. Come closer child lemme talk to you a minute. Don't be hangin' too much with the likes of that one."

Coco blinked a couple times confused by her own mother. She thought that medications her mother was taking had caused her to be delusional. Coco was hesitant until she heard her mother's hoarse whisper.

"Come closer, girl."

Coco got right up in her mother's face. She could see the strain the illness had caused. Coco couldn't hide the pain she felt inside. Suddenly her tears flowed.

"Stop cryin', so much, girl. I know you got enough street smart to know that that girl is a dyke..."

"Ma...? Ma, c'mon. You're embarrassing me."

"You don't hear me complainin' about you," Rachel Harvey whispered in her confused daughter's ears.

"What're you talking 'bout, Ma?"

"Don't 'Ma' me, Coco. I'm your mother you're not pulling any wool over my eyes, even though they're half way closed. I still see things, Coco."

Coco stared in amazement at what her mother was saying then she glanced back at Deedee, who was now sitting quietly on the window sill. She too was wearing an expression of bewilderment. Deedee raised both hands in a gesture bordering complete hopelessness.

"Coco, you don't have to ask anyone else. Just sneak a taste up in here for your mother, girl. That's all your mother needs to help her out," Ms. Harvey whispered.

"Mom, mother all you're getting is water. You cannot mix alcohol and—"

"You're in the apartment dirtying it up or you been hanging

with your queen? I personally don't care—"

"Mother! I've been in the apartment and I've cleaned it up real good. Trust me on that. I want to paint—"

"Paint what? Girl, don't even waste your time. How's it going in the record world. One of the nurses told me you all over the news. That's my daughter all over the damn news but can't even bring her mother a lil' sip of sump'n..."

Ms. Harvey's voice trailed, and Coco stared at her. Her sick mother's request left Coco speechless. The woman closed her eyes and Coco jumped forward, holding her mother's weak frame. Rachel Harvey was unresponsive. Coco spotted it, and immediately signaled to Deedee.

"Dee, get the nurse, yo!" Coco shouted.

The panic in her tone hit Deedee. She sprang up from the windowsill and shot out of the room like a speeding bullet, heading for the nurse's station.

"Use the buzzer, yo!" Coco shouted.

Deedee was already down the hallway. She gently laid her mother down on the hospital bed. Coco tried to tune out the humming noise of the life saving machines. She felt trapped in a strange dream where nothing was working. Ms Harvey had deteriorated to a mindless shell. She was no longer able to control bodily function.

Her emotions got the best of her and Coco started to sob. She was heaving with sadness when she felt a hand gently on her shoulders. Nurse Roberts seemed to be part of what wasn't working right. A distraught Coco glanced up with big round eyes at the woman dressed hospital blues. The nurse had to pry Coco from her mother, and immediately went to work, checking a stilled Ms. Harvey. After doing quick examination, the nurse glanced at the anguished face of the Coco for a beat.

"I'm gonna have to ask you both to wait outside," she said, sweating profusely.

"Is she...?"

The question hung while the nurse reached into her pockets and resumed attending to the Ms. Harvey. Deedee rushed to Coco's rescue, tugging on her best friend's arm.

"Let's go outside, Coco," Deedee said.

"Nurse Roberts! Is she...?"

"We have to leave the room and let the nurse do her job, Coco," Deedee said.

Coco's stared back with a trance-like expression and Deedee helped her toward the door. They were exiting the room when two doctors rushed past them, closed the door, and pulled the shades. Coco's lithe body shook from the slamming sound the door made.

Coco paced up and down the hallway. She paused only to do it again. Under the sympathetic gaze of Deedee's watching eyes, she continued at it for the next half hour. Coco couldn't stop and Deedee tried to halt the anxiety.

"You're gonna wear a groove in this hallway," Deedee said, catching up to Coco.

"Dee, I wanna leave but I have to hear what's up with madukes first," Coco said. "You can go if you wanna. We'll hook up another time, yo."

"I'm staying with you, Coco," Deedee said, joining Coco.

They both paced the hallway, Coco and Deedee walking with their arms interlocked. Deedee in a show of support for her best friend, smiled at Coco. The distraught teen leaned her head against Deedee's shoulder and tears rolled tenderly from both their eyes.

The girls were in the midstep when they saw the doctors emerging from the room. They hurried and met Nurse Roberts as she exited the room.

"She's resting stable. But I'm afraid you'll have to visit tomorrow," the nurse said.

"Okay, thank you very much," Deedee said. "Good Night."

Coco mustered only a nod accompanied by a pained expression on her face. Her mother's health crisis had sapped all her reserves. She felt the gentle tug on her arm and turned to see Deedee. A loud sigh escaped her soft lips, and Coco held onto her friend. In silence, Coco and Deedee slowly walked to the elevator.

Exiting the lobby, to the cool midsummer evening, the girls quietly walked to the parked car. As Deedee deactivated the security system, without saying anything, both girls got inside. Coco stared silently at the road ahead as Deedee pulled in to traffic. She drove a few minutes before Coco spoke.

"I've stayed later at the hospital. Something must be wrong, yo."

"Coco, maybe and maybe not. The nurse said she was resting. They'll do all they can for her."

"I hear you, Dee. But that waiting is killing me, yo. I don't if she's gonna make it or not."

"I know what you mean, Coco. But there's always tomorrow. And besides you have to take care that you don't worry yourself to death," Deedee warned.

Coco glanced at her and saw compassion written on Deedee's face. There was also a certain confidence that framed the contours of Deedee's face. Coco stared at her until Deedee spoke.

"I know you love your mother, but you have to love yourself too. For instance, besides the ice cream we had in the park, what else have you eaten all day, Coco?"

"That's it, yo," Coco said after several beats too long.

"There it is, " Deedee said, pulling up alongside a restaurant.

"I get the point, yo."

It was after nine in the evening that Coco and Deedee walked inside Amy Ruth's restaurant. They were seated, and in a few minutes, they ordered their meals. The girls dove into fried chicken, ox tail with mashed potatoes, sweet yams, and corn bread. Deedee watched Coco digging in and filling up. They were washing it down with lemonades when Coco spoke.

"Oh wow, that really hit the spot, yo."

"Yes you can say that again. You look sleepy. Are you tired?" Deedee asked.

"It's just all that shit with Madukes, yo," Coco said, wiping her mouth with a napkin. "I mean that shit be buggin' me out."

"Don't let it get the best of you, Coco."

"You know it's the dumb shit that does. Like every time she's awake, she always asking for liquor. Madukes be fiendin' for that liquor, yo," Coco exclaimed.

"Damn that bad...?"

"I be hatin' going up in there, yo."

"Don't hate it. Just bring her some damn liquor or a bottle or sump'n. Don't let it bother you, girl. It'll get the best of you."

"I ain't gonna let it get the best of me, yo. I'll handle madukes and her problem. Thanks for looking out, Dee."

With the check taken care of, Coco and Deedee walked to the car. Deedee lit a cigarette and offered one to Coco. She declined and sat listening to the music from the car system. Deedee wrapped her lips around the cigarette and sucked.

"I think I'll have one now, yo."

Deedee glanced at Coco and smiled then said, "What made you change your mind? I respect the fact that you trying to quit. Too much going on for you to quit, huh, Coco?"

"Nah, I don't think it's that. I think that you make smoking look soo cool, yo."

"Coco, I swear you're the zaniest—"

"Let's go catch that flick, yo."

The car pulled away, joining the flow of traffic heading downtown. Deedee guided the car while Coco lit the cigarette and bobbed her head to the music of Beenie Siegal.

I still close my eyes, I still see visions
Still hear that voice in the back of my mind
So what I do? I still take heed, I still listen
I still paint that perfect picture,
I still shine bright like a prism

Eric Ascot sat eating dinner with his attorney, Max Roose in a crowded midtown restaurant. He took his time chewing on the facts that Roose, a slick-talking attorney was providing regarding the upcoming trial. Eric wanted to rid himself of this inconvenience and the attorney assured him that it was possible.

"It's gonna be an expensive stunt, but it can be done," Max Roose said, fingering his groomed mustache. "We'll have to wait and see what type of concrete evidence the state can come up with. They'll have someone who will testify that you planned these murders with Busta. Anyone you might know?"

"No, I mean only this crack-head who lives uptown—"

"Do you know this crack-head's name?"

"Yes, I don't know his real name, but he goes by something like Rightchus—"

"Do you know how we can reach him?"

"No, but I'll find out and let you know," Eric said, pausing.

He resumed eating his steak while Max Roose pulled out a pad, jotted down a few quick notes, and returned to his barbecue chicken.

"That information may prove to be vital. Also do you remember talking to anyone while you incarcerated?"

"No, I wasn't a very social person. Why?"

"Well it seems that besides your former fiancée, there's someone else out there whose testimony the state is relying on heavily."

"I don't know any such person. Everyone who seemed to be connected to this case has been killed. This is crazy 'cause despite that, someone is still making attempts on my life and endangering the lives of people around me," Eric said.

His frustrations echoed in his tone. He seemed on the verge of yelling, but Eric remained calm. Instead he swallowed a glass of red wine and followed quickly with another. Max Roose continued to eat, watching his client.

"Man, they shut down my studio, and if it wasn't for you they'd have put a freeze on my bank accounts. I'd have no way to get any money after they took away shit."

Eric Ascot downed another glass of red wine and raised his hand. The waiter arrived and he ordered another bottle.

"You stick with me and we'll have everything cleared up. But you've gotta take it easy, Eric."

"Max, you try taking it easy when the government is making it impossible for you to get anything done. Man, I want all this bullshit to end!"

"It'll end soon enough. In a couple of weeks, the case will be in front of the judge. We'll see what they got then. You can bank on that."

"I'm sure it'll cost me a pretty price," Eric said and continued to nibble at his food.

"I wouldn't worry too much about that. Have been in touch with your ex-fiancée?"

"Yes, why?"

"Please be cautious about the fact that she's one of their main witnesses against you."

"I don't have too much to say to her," Eric seethed beneath his breath.

"You shouldn't hold too much against her. Sophia's hands are tied, and she's been forced to play their game. How much she actually knows, and what exactly can be ruled as hearsay is all that's important to us."

"How do we find out exactly what she knows or is willing to talk about?"

"We simply must talk to Sophia."

"You mean I have to talk to her?"

"Well since you've been lovers, yes. I think that's the right call," the lawyer said with a wink.

"I can tell you that that's not happening," Eric said, wagging his index finger.

"Why not?"

"It simply isn't," Eric said, sitting back.

He may have been drinking wine but that wasn't enough to blind him to the reality of his situation with Sophia. She had betrayed his trust by cooperating with DA's investigation of him. Eric glanced around the eatery and saw all the couples seemingly having a good time eating. They appeared to be enjoying themselves and he remembered when he too did the same with Sophia. She was with him from the beginning and knew everything, Eric thought reminiscing.

Sophia rejoined Eric downstairs. He had downed two more beers and was working fast on the third.

"Hey, big guy, don't drink yourself silly—save me some," Sophia said.

"That silliness is not a bad idea. As for the beer, there's plenty in the fridge," Eric answered flatly.

"Thanks. Please don't kill me with kindness," Sophia said.

"Listen, my niece was..." his voice trailed.

"I know honey. What happened to her is a terrible thing. We've got to be supportive of each other and try to get something positive—"

"Something positive out of a young girl being raped?" Eric demanded.

"Out of this evil try to find the good. Maybe you can overwhelm her with good—and goods."

"Like?"

"Like a shopping spree, getting clothes. Like sending her flowers. And more shopping. Try to help her to forget. I have friends who can provide counseling and other kinds of support too. In time, this horrible experience can move to the back of her mind."

"Is that possible?" Eric asked, his eyes searching.

"Yes. You won't be able to take it all away. But, you have to try," Sophia said between sips of the newly opened brew.

"Sophia, that shit really hurts me. I don't know..."

"Yeah, I understand. What did the police—"

"Later for them assholes. They've never helped me. Never."

Sophia saw anger in Eric. The furrow in his brow became pronounced as he stared at a picture of him and, Dennis, his older brother. She knew where it all stemmed from. Eric's brother had been murdered not long before Sophia met Eric, so she was with him when he learned the truth about his brother's death. Something in Eric changed after that, and

Sophia knew not to press the issue with him.

Men wearing hoods had tried to mug his older brother, he was told. Dennis fired at them with his .38 Smith and Wesson, but one attacker got behind him and shot him dead. Eric knew Dennis had gone to an address given to him by Xtrigaphan, the hot rap group Dennis wanted to sign. Dennis had taken $10,000 in cash with him to lure the group to sign. Eric knew his brother dabbled in cocaine, but also knew Dennis wasn't dealing. He knew that the cash was a signing bonus. The police weren't interested in Eric's version of his brother's murder, since then his hatred for the police bordered on obsession. Sophia decided to try another approach.

"Well, have you spoken to Deedee, to find out what happened?"

"No."

"Do you know what happened?"

"Not entirely, except that she was raped and the car was stolen."

"By whom? Where?" Sophia queried.

"Look, the cops told me what happened. They called me and told me they found her badly beaten. Told me that she had been sexually assaulted."

"So you haven't spoken to Deedee about any of this?"

"I told you. No," Eric said.

He was annoyed now. Sophia Lawrence, with her lawyer's mind, he thought. She suspended the questioning when she saw Eric's resentment. Tilting the beer upwards, she looked at his reflection through the beer bottle. His face appeared contorted, and he looked fat with anger. Eric Ascot turned his back. He was rehashing his brother's death.

"I didn't want to include the cops," he said, turning to face her. "Not after the way they treated my brother. Like he was some unknown, drug-dealing nigga. Now I'm gonna handle this shit the way it should be handled."

Eric turned away. Then he stopped. The pain showed on his face when he said, "Soph, whatever it takes to make her better. Please don't *spare the cost. Get her the best. That's my niece laid up there."*

Sophia stared at his pain-stricken face and nodded. He sighed in relief, knowing his fiancée would do all she could to help him.

Sitting inside the eatery with his attorney, Eric Ascot pondered what Sophia shared with the district attorney's office. Sophia had told him that she would have to cooperate, but he worried how much she had revealed. She was with him from the beginning of it all. Eric's mind kept going and he downed another glass of wine in a vain attempt to slow the thought process.

"Hey Eric, cheer up some for heaven's sake. You still have a small studio inside that apartment of yours," Max Roose said, requesting the check. "I tell you, stick with me and it'll all work out. You can trust Max."

Eric Ascot said nothing. After paying the tab and walking outside with Max Roose at his side, Eric was still drudging through a funk. There was a dark cloud over his head. He knew he had to clear it up before going to trial. He had to see Sophia one more time.

"Hey Eric, remember to get that contact info on Rightchus and please try to talk to Sophia. It's business, Eric—your freedom. Good night," Max said and slipped into his waiting car.

"Yes, good night," Eric replied, getting into his chauffeur-driven ride.

"Where to sir?" The armed chauffeur requested.

"Just drive around for a minute I've gotta make this call first," Eric said, pulling out his cell phone.

He scanned the directory of his contacts. Finally Eric came to a name, and his fingers stopped scrolling. As he stared at the information, his face slowly twisted in anger and he clenched his teeth.

"Take me to my place," Eric said.

"Which one?"

"My apartment," Eric said. "It's the only one I got right now."

"Gotcha," the chauffeur said.

The limousine raced across town with Eric Ascot still glancing at the information on his cellphone screen. Sophia Lawrence was her given name, but sometimes she went by Sophia Sullivan, the person Eric remembered putting through law school. A beautiful young woman, he had been dating her since his brother's best friend, Busta, had introduced them.

Sophia and Eric were engaged not long after Deedee came to live with him. He thought getting hitched was a good idea when he found out that he would be the legal guardian to his niece. Sophia and Deedee hit it off like they were meant to be. Smart, worldly and working toward a degree in corporate law, Sophia had been the type of woman Eric wanted in his niece's life. He paid the way to help her through law school.

They were almost like a real family and Eric was planning to marry Sophia. But after Deedee was raped and the legal fiasco erupted, his world had changed. He needed security for his niece and himself. The engagement was off and Sophia was cooperating with the people who were trying to take him down. Eric sighed when the car pulled to a stop.

"Good night," he said, jumping out and walking to the building.

He took the elevator up, and it opened to his foyer. Eric heard his niece's voice as soon as he opened the apartment door.

"I can't do that. Are you kidding me?" Deedee said loudly.

"I think you should, yo."

"My uncle would go ape-shit over that," Deedee said.

Coco and Deedee voices' dropped when Eric walked in on them in the kitchen. The girls were at the table finishing off a bottle of wine.

"Ape-shit over what?" Eric asked, walking to refrigerator and getting a bottle of beer.

The girls looked at each other in surprise then back at Eric without saying anything. He opened the beer, threw it to his head, and swallowed.

"If you're talking about all the illegal contact you've had with Sophia, then don't respond to anymore of her requests. Okay? Also do you still have Rightchus' contact info? I'm gonna need that for the attorney."

Deedee paused taking in his words. "Okay, Uncle. I'll write down Rightchus' number. It's somewhere in my cellphone."

Eric downed his beer in a couple of gulps and was about to walk away. He turned back and stared at Coco.

"And by the way Coco, you'll be in the studio first thing tomorrow morning," he said.

"You mean the studio has been reopened, Uncle E?" Deedee excitedly asked.

"Not exactly, but I've got some of the best recording equipment here. So why not operate from home base for now?"

"Sounds, like a plan to me, yo. I'll be here in the morning."

"Okay, I'll see you then about ten... Good night ladies," Eric said.

Deedee gave him a hug and so did Coco. Eric walked away and went straight to his room. Coco waited until the door shut before continuing.

"Now was a good time to tell him, yo."

"He started talking about Sophia. I mean he must've had her on his mind. Obviously he must've wanted to mention that. I still think Uncle E loves her."

"He just told you to stay away from her so I don't know how much he's feeling her, yo."

"Yeah, I wonder why? I mean, my uncle and I already had that discussion," Deedee mused.

"Maybe he hollered at her and she told him something about that, yo."

"Or maybe his attorney told him something. Because now he wants Rightchus' number. He never asked for that before. He knew I had spoken to Rightchus and all he told me was—"

"Stay out of grown folks' biz," Coco joined in.

"Exactly," Deedee chuckled.

Coco and Deedee laughed together loudly. Raising her eyebrows, Coco pointed in the direction of Eric's room.

"Oh please girl, a bomb could go off and you wouldn't hear shit in there. Haven't you seen how huge this place is...?"

"I know it's huge, but damn what if he had his ears to the door, yo?"

"Coco, my uncle doesn't do anything like that."

Eric Ascot eased his ear away from the door, and went to bed with a cigarette dangling from his lips. The girls kept chatting through the night and eventually parted ways. Coco bunked in the guest room and Deedee fell asleep in a good mood.

The next morning, true to his words, Eric Ascot was up in the studio loading beats and compiling songs for Coco's music catalog. In his lab, he sampled different sounds from R&B to funk, calypso and reggae. Eric mixed down the sounds in an attempt to produce a classic sound he knew audiences would love to hear. Working diligently, he hardly noticed that Coco had walked in.

"I'm ready, Uncle E," she said.

"Let's go to work," he replied without raising his head.

Eric saw Deedee walk into the small makeshift studio. She paused, waiting for him to acknowledge her.

"Close the door," he said. "Once that door is shut this place will be airtight."

Deedee closed the door and Eric pumped the beat up. It

sounded like rock and Coco nodded her head to it. She smiled and started humming a tune.

"I got sump'n for this, yo," she said smiling.

"Alright, let's hear it, Coco. If you ain't claustrophobic, get inside that booth. You can go rap away to your heart's content."

Coco stepped into the booth and picked up the headset. She slipped the headphones on and picked up the microphone. Then she launched into a verbal flow that pasted a smile on her listeners' faces. Eric and Deedee nodded their heads while Coco laced the track with her vocals.

> I'm alone cornered in a room
> It ain't paranoia just thoughts
> Start poppin' off like hammers
> I'm ready to go bananas
> beatin' on my chest
> Feelin' I'm ready to go off
> 2 techs verbal grammar
> Problems hangin' from my neck
> extra clips My mind ain't playin tricks
> I ain't goin' skitzo Nobody slip me a mick
> oh just voices from past in my head
> Coco go loco they said hurt 'em 'fore they do you
> Even the ones who swear they know you
> Others comin' at you just to know you
> Whatever you do know who you're puffin' after
> Just play your cards right against all odds
> You'll succeed superseding all expectations
> Shoot for the moon missing will only make you a star

Her head was steady nodding in rhythm as the teen paused her incredible flow to catch her breath. Both Eric and Deedee broke out in a long applause.

"Thank you," Coco smiled. "I gotta get some water for my throat, yo."

"All those verses need is a nasty hook and we got ourselves something we can work with. What you think, Dee?"

"I'm still caught up how easy she makes it look," Deedee said, smiling. "Coco is a superstar."

"Alright take a water break. Let me mix this vocal in and I think we have it done on one take. Come back from your water break with a good hook, Coco."

"Yes sir, I'll be thinking about it."

"Uncle E, here's Rightchus' info," Deedee said, handing Eric a piece of paper.

She walked out of the recording studio with Coco. They entered the kitchen together.

"I feel *so* lucky to be working with your uncle one-on-one like this. You can't imagine what it means to an up-and-coming artist like me, yo," Coco gushed.

"Me personally, I feel kinda famished," Deedee said. "I puked again this morning."

"Morning sickness again...? Dee, when are you gonna see a doctor?"

"Oh I don't know, Coco. That's gonna involve my uncle, don't you think?"

"Not necessarily, and you're talking about me not taking care of myself, yo?"

"I've been soo busy taking care of you that I've totally forgotten about taking care of me," Deedee said.

"Very funny, yo. You've gotta make a doctor's appointment."

"I will, once I know exactly what I want to do."

"I thought you did... Oh, I got it—today you changed your mind, huh? Time's running out, yo..."

"I hear you, Coco."

Eric Ascot walked in beaming. He was clearly happy with what he had heard and his anticipation rushed to the surface when he spoke.

"Oh we're gonna kill 'em dead with that joint, Coco. It's a winner. I mixed it down some and I hope you're talking about the hook."

"Yeah, I'm on it, yo."

"Let's try to wrap up after breakfast. You guys are gonna stay in? I'm gonna go down to that French café. You guys care to join me?"

"Yes," Coco said.

"No," Deedee said. "I already started making breakfast here, Uncle, thanks."

"See you when I get back. Be ready to go, Coco," Eric said and walked out the apartment.

"Why didn't you wanna go, yo?"

"You remember you said you know how to deal with your mother?"

"Yes."

"Well I know how to deal with my uncle. Let him go eat his French breakfast, flirt with the waitresses and read his newspaper. He was just being nice. And if you'd gone—oh, he would have talked our heads off about music. You don't know my uncle like I do. He'd rather be alone."

"You know him better, yo."

Dressed in Armani slacks and shirt, Eric Ascot was escorted by his bodyguard downstairs. His cell phone went off the moment the summer air hit his unshaven face. It was Max Roose.

"Max..."

"Hey good morning, Eric."

"Morning, Max, do you have spies on me?"

"Why?"

"Don't worry. What's the reason for this call, Max? How much is it gonna cost me?"

"Not much this time. Do you have that info for me?"

"Oh damn. My niece gave it to me while I was excited about this beat I was working on."

"So you took my advice and set that studio in your apartment to good use, huh?"

"Yes... Coco has to come back and finish her first song from my home-base studio. I was feelin' that and totally forgot the info. Let me two-way a call and get his number."

"Okay that's fine. I'll hold the line," Max Roose said.

Eric put his lawyer on hold and called his niece. Deedee read Rightchus' phone number to her uncle who relayed it to his attorney.

"And Eric, please don't forget to speak to your ex-fiancée."

"Okay, I got you. Bye, Max."

"Take it easy, Eric."

He hung the call and stopped to pick up the *Times*. Eric and his bodyguard walked leisurely to the French café. Eric sat thumbing through the newspaper. In the local section, he found an article about his upcoming trial. He read it with a smirk on his face and started feeling pressured to call Sophia.

Momentarily the pretty waitress in a miniskirt disrupted Eric's thoughts. She smiled, working her hips rapidly toward his table. The bodyguard greeted her with a smile while she filled his cup with coffee, then she did the same for Eric. He nodded politely.

"Where's Mona?" Eric asked sounding disappointed.

"She called in sick. I guess I'll have to do today, Mr. Ascot."

"You're not Mona, but you'll do."

"Do you both know what y'all want?"

"Yes," Eric said.

Having taken their orders, the waitress was off to another table. Eric picked up his cell phone and scrolled through his contacts. Again he stopped and stared at the name on his screen, deep in thought. He had to make the call to Sophia, but somehow did not feel like doing it. Eric sat wondering what to do. As his conflicted mind spun, he reminisced about his former lover.

+

"Sophia, I didn't see you. I'm sorry. Uncle E home also?" Deedee asked.

When she bumped into Sophia in the kitchen at the Long Island mansion. It had been a couple of days since the incident and Deedee was trying to make it through another day.

"Yes. He's upstairs, I think. He was about to make breakfast, but I guess I'll have to do it."

"You're not a bad cook, Sophia," Deedee teased. "But I'm not really hungry."

"Okay, how about getting downtown to do some shopping, you know?" Sophia asked with a wink.

"Aren't you supposed to be working today?" Deedee was a little excited at the new suggestion.

"No, I'm off today, honey. I have time," Sophia smiled.

"You'll be needing money for shopping," Eric said, announcing his presence. He had been standing, unnoticed. Deedee looked rested, he thought. "How much?"

"Well, ten thousand dollars would be nice, wouldn't you say, Dee?" Sophia smiled.

Deedee turned and looked at both of them. They looked as if they were waiting for the punch line. Oh what the hell, I'll play along, she decided. Deedee shook her head from side to side and snapped her fingers.

"You know, I could handle that very well." The words tumbled out. They were meant to be spontaneous, but the pause lasted longer than she intended. It was like a bad joke. She felt her timing was off. "So, who's gonna do breakfast between y'all?" Deedee asked as she seized the moment to patch things up.

"Ah, Eric had promised to do that earlier," Sophia said with a smile.

"Oh no, it ain't going down like that," Eric smiled. He widened his eyes as he turned to look at Sophia. "Sophia," he said with a big grin, "You *owe me."*

"Alright, you got it," Sophia sighed. "But this will be all the cooking I'm doing today," she said with a wry smile.

"Okay," Deedee said. "Why don't we all eat out?"

"Hmm... Sounds good to me," Eric said.

"Sophia?" Both niece and uncle asked at the same time.

"Sure, sure, double-team me," Sophia said with a mock stern tone.

"Alright, you guys go ahead. I'll see you on the outside," Deedee said.

"Uh-huh, we're not going for that," her uncle said, smiling. "We know you're gonna lock yourself in the room. Oh no. You're coming right now."

"No, I won't be long. I promise Uncle E. I'm just gonna get a coat. I promise."

"It's pretty warm outside, honey," Eric said.

He reached out to hold her, but she resisted, twisting her arms free of his hands. She was about to walk away and Sophia called after her.

"Dee, get your coat, girl," Sophia said, walking toward Deedee. "Maybe I should get one while we're downtown. Yeah! And I saw this nice Versace the other day. Mmm hmm."

Deedee smiled and ran upstairs. It was as if what Sophia said had ignited her. Sophia and Eric went outside.

"Let her be," Sophia whispered to Eric.

It was quite warm. The humidity was slowly working its way up the scale. The sun's brightness made the morning glow with life. Eric, with the press of a switch, disarmed the car alarm and unlocked the doors to the Range Rover. They got in and waited for Deedee, listening to the radio.

"How much are we getting?" Sophia chuckled.

"We?" Eric asked.

"Eric, stop being such a cheapo."

"A cheapo?"

"Yes. Need I repeat myself? Stop being a cheapo. Tell me how much we're getting."

"Alright, alright. I'll give you the figures after breakfast," he said.

"Game..." Sophia said, her voice trailing.

They waited in the car, listening to the radio, teasing and laughing at each other. Deedee emerged from the front door. She locked it and turned on the alarm. As she walked toward the car, they both noticed that instead of her usual fitted jeans and ribbed blouse, she was wearing a pink, baggy, cotton warm-up suit and a maroon spring coat. They looked at each other.

"Let her be, Eric," Sophia said then she shouted out the window. "C'mon girl, hurry. I'm starved."

Deedee quickened her step. The flashes of her plain white tennis shoes with matching socks emphasized her pace. She slid through the open door and the vehicle seemed cramped and crowded to her. She lowered the window.

"I'm ready," she announced with a sigh of relief.

"For food? Where?" Eric asked.

"Let's go to the pancake house on Lex," Deedee suggested.

"That sounds delicious," Sophia said.

"Done deal," Eric said.

The vehicle rolled toward Main Street. Eric made a right and hit the expressway heading into the city.

"I brought these for the trip," Deedee said handing out breakfast bars to Eric and Sophia.

Sophia and Deedee closed their eyelids immediately after downing their breakfast bars. Forty-five minutes later they awoke to found themselves on Lexington Avenue. Eric was pulling easily into a parking spot. Sophia awoke, blinked and watched as Deedee alighted from the Range.

She put her hands in her coat pockets. She completed her disguise by donning a white Colorado Rockies baseball cap worn backwards.

While Deedee and Sophia were seated in the buzzing waffle house, Eric remained outside, conversing on his cell phone.

"Good morning. You ladies ready to order?" A smiling waiter greeted. "Something to drink maybe?"

"Well—"

"I'll have hot chocolate with whipped cream," Deedee chirped.

"And two regular coffees. Thanks," Sophia added. "Let me go get that guy. 'Cause if we let him, he'll talk right through breakfast. Music business is so demanding," Sophia said as she left the table. She returned a few lonely minutes later with Eric.

"Hey, don't you like the hot chocolate? You're looking sad, girl," Eric said.

He had been standing next to Deedee for a while, her unaware of his presence. She was buried too deep into her thoughts to have noticed.

"No, it's alright. I was just thinking."

Sophia had been, at times, like a mother to her. Now she treated her as a friend. The reason was clear. Deedee felt compelled to verbalize her feelings but knew she could not. She tried not to think too much about things.

"Well, think of how you're gonna be spending five thousand dollars, baby," Sophia said and then winked.

"Five thousand dollars?" Eric repeated incredulously. "Where you gonna get all that dough from?"

"Well, how much then?" Sophia asked with mock annoyance. "I thought you said..."

"Okay," Eric said.

"We settled on..."

Sophia pouted. Deedee stared. Eric fumbled for a number. Then, finally, he turned to Deedee.

"Dee, what do you think? Five G's, or not?"

It made Deedee smile, just knowing she would have five thousand dollars to spend. Wow, she thought, I could shop for days, nonstop.

"Ah, five sounds all right, but I was looking forward to the ten grand," she joked.

Her joke made her uncle smile. He was happy that Sophia had concocted this little scheme, and that it had brought a smile to his niece's face. Deedee reflected. The humor was sick, but a five-thousand-dollar shopping spree sounded good. It probably would bring a smile to anyone's face. But she knew not even ten thousand dollars would erase the bitter and ugly experience, and her memories of the cruelest people she'd ever met.

"What are you having, Dee?" Eric asked attentively.

The waiter and Sophia also looked concerned. What are they staring at, she wondered? Deedee kept the smirk on her face while speaking.

"Oh, I'll have two German pancakes, and eggs. Sunny-side up."

"Anything to drink?" The well-mannered waiter asked.

"Yeah. We'll all have apple juice," Eric said.

His cell phone rang, and he sprang out of his chair. He left the table and headed outside, away from the other patrons.

"Yeah, Eric, this is Busta. How're you?" the caller asked.

"I'm fine. I need a major hit. We gotta talk."

"E, let's meet at Geez at about seven. Eric, I've got these crazy nice girls you gotta hear. And as a matter of fact, they're all dimes."

"That's fine," Eric said. "See you then."

He folded the black instrument and shoved it into a front pocket of his jeans. Eric headed back to his seat at the table.

"Alright," he announced. "It's on."

"What did she want?" Sophia teased.

"It wasn't her," Eric smiled. "It was Busta. Got to meet with him later. But first we're gonna eat, and then spend some money."

The meal arrived and they all settled into breakfast. Deedee was afraid she wouldn't be able to stomach the food, but German pancakes were her favorite. After one bite, she succumbed to the pleasures of the meal.

After a hearty breakfast, Deedee and Sophia took Eric on a shopping extravaganza that cost him over ten thousand dollars. He also had to carry nearly all of the shopping bags. When the clothes became too much to carry, they returned to the parking lot and stowed the bags in the Range Rover.

"Thank you, Uncle," Deedee said, and planted a kiss on Eric's sweating cheek.

"You are more than welcome," he said, returning the kiss.

"And thanks, Sophia. I love your style."

"You're welcome, sweetheart." She opened her arms. Deedee lunged forward for the hug. "Movie, anyone?" Sophia asked as Eric started the engine.

"How about later we have dinner and a movie?" Deedee said.

"Ah..." Eric looked at his watch. "Why don't both of you go ahead and I'll catch up to you later?"

"You tired of us already?" Sophia asked. A smug expression belied her feelings.

"No, no," Eric answered taking the bait. "I've got to meet with Busta."

"Uncle E, you know we're not gonna make it to the movies if we wait around for you and your business," Deedee said, sounding disappointed.

"Alright, here's my phone." Eric gave Sophia the cell phone. "Let's synchronize our watches. It's 6:40 p.m. At exactly 8:30 p.m., I'll call you, and we'll catch the 9:00 p.m. movie."

"Okay. Sounds good to me," Deedee said.

"Yeah, because if you get into a meeting or on this phone," Sophia said, pointing to the black instrument, "it's all over."

They all laughed and Eric eased the car out of the parking lot. He headed uptown to Cozy Geez, a nighttime hangout for the famous and infamous.

"Be careful, babes," Sophia said. Eric kissed her soft, moist lips.

"See you later, over dinner. You guys decide what movie y'all wanna see."

"Don't forget to call us, Uncle E," Deedee said as he gently clasped her hand in his.

"I will, sugar. Eight-thirty, right?"

"No shady deals," Sophia laughed.

"That's right," Deedee called.

They watched Eric cross the street, dodging traffic. He walked by the dark-suited bouncers and through the brown wooden doors. There was no need for a search. Eric Ascot was familiar to most as one of the city's hottest music producers.

Things had been difficult after his brother's death, but Dennis had left him with good connections. Eric had produced one of the year's best rhythm-and-blues albums. This raised him from ordinary contender to being in the running for Music Producer of the Year.

Eric strolled to a table for two in the rear. The waiter brought him his usual, straight Hennessy with a twist of lemon.

"Good evening, sir," the waiter said.

That call and meeting with Busta had changed his life. Eric sat at his table in the French café and thought about Sophia. She had been a major part of his daily existence, and her presence was invaluable in the life of his niece.

Sophia was there when Deedee was raped, and her assistance in his niece's recovery couldn't be overlooked. Yet, Sophia was privy to a lot of information that could send him to jail. She was no longer with him, but he wasn't sure if the love he felt was gone. Eric was still debating himself over whether to call her when he heard a voice.

"Do you want something else to drink?" the waitress in the miniskirt asked.

She watched Eric for a beat. After staring at his plate of toast and jelly, he finally raised up his head. He looked her up and down like it was the first time he had seen her. She was very pretty, as pretty as Sophia.

"Yes, a glass of apple juice, please," he said with a smile.

Eric's eyes followed her shapely ass until it disappeared behind the counter. It had been a year since Sophia had broken off their engagement. He couldn't blame her for that, but he felt sick thinking about how she had cooperated with the investigation against him. He felt Sophia should've stayed in his corner and the thought kept circling in his mind, when the waitress returned with the apple juice. He thought this young woman could be a college student.

Sophia was working as a waitress and dancer in Busta's nightclub when Eric first met her. She was supporting herself through college. Busta introduced Eric to her and he started dating her. When his brother was killed and Deedee came to live with him, Sophia became more than his girlfriend.

He spent money on her tuition, and helped her through college. She forged a great relationship with his niece and was always with him when she wasn't in classes. Then she went to law school and Eric made sure she had the best. The bond grew stronger between his niece and Sophia. Eric made it official by getting an engagement ring for Sophia. With his career on its way and his plans to marry Sophia settled, Eric focused and climbed to the top of his craft.

"Will there be anything else?" The waitress asked and interrupted his ruminations.

Eric glanced at her then at his bodyguard. Eric pulled out a hundred dollar bill and shoved it at her and said,

"This should cover the damage. Thanks."

"Change...?" she asked.

"No," he said. "Just tell me this—are you in college?"

"Yes," she answered.

"Good luck," he said.

"Thank you," the waitress said, staring incredulously at Eric exiting the restaurant.

He walked down the block with a smile on his face. Eric Ascot was faced with the possibility of going to prison based on evidence provided by Sophia. Busta was killed and several attempts had been made on his life. Eric did not know who was behind it, but had realized he was being framed for crimes he had not committed.

It had started with one phone call. He held the cell phone to his ear and was about to press send, but changed his mind. Eric Ascot returned the cell phone to his pocket and walked inside the building. The security took up position downstairs and waited by the elevator. Indecision seemed to cloud his mind. Eric again walked out of the building and dialed.

"Hello," he said, after the phone rang couple times.

"Sophia, how you...?

"Can we talk...?"

"You better hurry and get that hook right, before Uncle E gets here. You know, that's gonna be the first thing he'll be harping on, Coco."

"Your uncle is a beast, yo."

"Mmm hmm. He goes in. When he starts a project, he gets it done. No ifs, ands, or buts."

"Don't worry. I'll have sump'n for him, yo. I'm a make him love it."

Coco and Deedee had finished eating omelets for breakfast. They sat at the long table after loading the dishwasher and smiled. The girls had prepared breakfast together and were enjoying hot chocolates with their chitchat."Yeah, let me hear what you got," Deedee smiled. "I'll tell you if he's going to love it."

"A'ight it gonna be somewhat like this...Huh..."

"'Huh...'?" Deedee repeated. You gotta come better than some

'Huh,'" Deedee said, laughing.

"Wait a minute, yo. I was just getting ready," Coco said humming.

Huh... Can you feel my pain...?
Can you feel my pain I have no one to blame...?
Can you feel me I ain't scared I'm here to stay?
I can still hear voices singing I have no one to blame.
Can you feel my pain? I can feel your pain..."

"Hmm... Sounds like poetry. It's good I think he'll like it. But do you think it's a little too—too long?" Deedee mused.

"I don't know. It might be, yo. But I'm sure your uncle will fix whatever needs fixing."

The cell phone rang in her pocket, and Coco immediately took the call. She held the cell phone to her ear, closed her eyes and nervously listened to the voice on the line.

"I gotta get to the hospital right away. Madukes just got up and was asking for me, yo," Coco said, putting down her cup.

"Okay, I'll take you," Deedee said.

They were walking out when Eric was coming in. He seemed excited about finishing the song.

"We could do it in one take again, Coco. I know you got that phat hook to go with the joint. I was thinking about playing up the rock guitar to your lyrics. You know, have a guitarist play it live then remix it as if you're actually live. You feeling me on that?" Eric said, greeting Coco.

It was clear that he had planned on working with her to complete the project, just like Deedee had said he would. Coco should have been excited but her body language told the story. Eric reached out and hugged the teen.

"What's wrong? Everything's good?" he asked.

"Her mother... I'm taking her to hospital in Harlem," Deedee said.

"Oh, I'm really sorry to hear that. What can I do to help? How's the hospital treatment? You know hospitals ain't no fun. What's wrong with her, Coco? She's been in for a minute now?"

"My mother goes in for her heart. She's constantly in and out—seems to make an annual visit."

"Her heart is bad, and she has to get treatment?"

"Kind-a. But try this. Her heart is bad, and she keeps abusing crack. When madukes went in this time for her heart condition, she wasn't reacting to the medication. So the doctors did some tests, including HIV. And she came up positive, Mr. Ascot."

"Coco, I'm really sorry to hear that. How are you holding up?"

"I'm dealing, yo," Coco said.

Eric Ascot saw her tears and embraced the anguished teen. Coco sobbed loudly on his chest. Deedee cried too and joined in hugging both Coco and her uncle. He stood there with both teen girls on his shoulders weeping their hearts out. Eric let their tears subside then he spoke.

"You're not in any condition to drive, Dee. I'll get the chauffeur to take you and wait." "I'll be alright," Deedee said. " I was just caught up in the moment."

"Coco let me know what way I can help. You hear? How's everyone else in your family taking this?"

"Coco has no one else, Uncle E. There's just her and her mother..." Deedee said.

"Is that right? What about your father? I'm sure—"

"I don't know my father. I mean I never met him or anything, yo."

Coco's answer jolted Eric. He felt the negative charge racing through his body and depleting his mind of his creative excitement. Stunned, he stared at Deedee then back at Coco.

"You know what? I'll go to the hospital with you," he said.

They went down and were escorted to the waiting limousine.

The chauffeur stood by and watched as Coco, Deedee, and Eric entered the car.

"Mr. Ascot, I need to ask you a favor."

"Sure Coco go ahead," Ascot replied.

"Can we stop at a liquor store?"

"Why? I thought—"

"It's for my mother. She's been asking me—"

"Imploring you..."

"Telling me, begging me to bring her a sniff of liquor," Coco said. "And maybe you can get her a bottle of grape brandy, and I'll do the rest."

"What're you gonna do, sneak it into the hospital room?"

"No, I'll do a switcheroo..."

"A switcheroo, huh?"

"Yeah, I have a cranberry and grape juice that'll do the trick," Coco laughed.

They stopped at the liquor store and Eric Ascot bought a pint of peach brandy. Coco emptied the flask. Then carefully, she poured grape and cranberry juice together into the flask, shook it around, and smiled.

"Where'd you think— do you think it's gonna work?"

"Yes. It worked when Dee did it. It'll work again," Coco said confidently.

"I did my switcheroo with fake clothing, and real labels," Deedee said, recalling how she'd outsmarted a pushy, young woman eager for name brand fashion. "This is entirely new to me. But it might work," Deedee said.

"Just the smell of the bottle will get her, yo."

"Okay, let's go," Eric said, taking a whiff of Coco's mix. "She'll be right. I'm feeling drunk already," Eric joked.

They all laughed as the chauffeur drove them uptown to Harlem hospital. In a jiffy, he was slowing down in front of the hospital and parking.

"I really appreciate this Mr. Ascot," Coco said, hiding her bottle of fake liquor in her knapsack.

"You're welcome. Now stop calling me Mr. Ascot. It's Uncle E."

"Good looking out, Uncle E."

"I shouldn't be long," Eric said to the chauffeur.

"No problem, sir. Just call when you're ready to go."

Coco managed a smile as they entered the hospital. She was grateful to Deedee and Eric. They didn't have to be here with her, but they were. Coco rushed past security but they stopped Eric and Deedee.

"They're with me, yo," Coco said.

"Okay, but they have to sign in over there by the desk, and be given a pass," the hospital security said.

Eric and Deedee walked over to the security desk. The woman behind the desk gave them both passes after they wrote their names and the name of the patient they were visiting. Then she looked at the names carefully and recognized Eric.

"You're a famous music producer," she smiled.

"Yes, you got me. That's me in the flesh," Eric said, jokingly.

"I knew you from way back when you were working with Silky Black and them," she said in an excited tone.

Coco anxiously paced by the elevator waiting for them. Eric waved and moved on. He bought a bouquet of flowers, then joined Coco and Deedee. All three boarded the next elevator going up, and quietly got off. They walked abreast with Coco, and she quickly found the room. Inside the room was Ms. Harvey, laying still in the bed. The television was on, and there was Red Foxx was in his usual rage, playing Fred Sanford in the sitcom, *Sanford and Son*. Coco was unsure if her mother was asleep or awake. She was quiet until she heard the voice.

"Coco, is that you?" Ms. Harvey said.

"Yes, mother. And I brought some friends—"

"You've gotta stop smoking," Ms. Harvey said, interrupting Coco. "You smell just like a chimney."

"I brought some friends—"

"Your friends are all dead. Coco nobody's gonna be your friend—"

"Ma, will you listen to me. Mr. Eric Ascot, and his niece are here with me, yo."

"Don't give me any of your street attitude. If Mr. Eric what's-his-face is here, why didn't you just say so. Deedee is his wife?"

"No, ma. Deedee is his niece."

"Okay I see... Who's Deedee?"

"Hi, Ms. Harvey. How are you feeling?"

"I maybe sick, but I'm not deaf. So you don't have to count your words when you getting ready to conversate with me."

"Hey, Ms. Harvey, how're you doing?" Eric greeted. "I bought you some flowers. I'll put the vase over here."

"Hey Eric, you're getting fat. From the last time I saw you 'til now you must've put on at least sixty pounds. Damn, you get any bigger you're gonna wind up inside here with me," Ms. Harvey said.

"Uh-huh, Ma, I see you're at your usual self—"

"Coco, I'm just speaking my mind. I gotta set my conscience free. I don't have much time here on this earth. The Lord is gonna get me in his rapture and I'll be gone."

"Ma please, stop it. You're being over-dramatic. And you know I don't like when you talk like that. So stop!"

"Well dammit, you talk the way you feel. All the yo's and ho's and all that street lingo. Do you even hear me when I speak to you? Can you understand normal English is what I'm asking you!"

"I'm a'ight."

"There you go again. I'm a'ight, yo this, and then it's yo that. Coco when are you gonna learn to speak like you decent and not a ghetto girl? I mean, just because you from the hood, don't mean you gotta act like you from da hood."

"Okay ma. I see you've got a lot of energy," Coco said with a smile. "That's a good sign."

"Good sign for me. Bad sign for you. I seen you showing your ass off on television, bopping up and down with handcuffs like you're a criminal. You think I went anywhere, huh? I'm still here. Coco, I'm tellin' you what you do in the dark will come to light. These are some nice flowers, Mr. Ah... Come closer, Coco. Did you bring that bottle like I asked you," Ms. Harvey whispered.

"Really, Ma? You cannot be serious," Coco retorted. "How many ways can I say N-O?"

"But Coco, they got me cooped up in here going crazy. The white nurse with alcohol on her breath and the black one with her stank ass. I gotta have a lil' nip of sump'n. It bothers me to know the girl I raised turned out to be a damn criminal on prime-time news on national TV. Next time, what program you gonna be on, *America's Most Wanted*?"

"Ma, Eric and I—"

"Don't tell me he marrying you too. Cuz I'll not allow. No, no, no... That's not happening—"

"Ma, that's not what I'm saying."

"Then why don't you tell me what're you're saying. Cuz you probably lying like a damn broccoli—that's why you can't talk. You gotta speak in codes. Yo, ho."

"Ma, we're working on the musical album together."

"We're doing a couple of songs, and they're going great," Eric said.

"Coco, why didn't you tell me that?" Ms. Harvey asked.

"That's what I was saying, yo."

"I tell you about all the yo's and ho's. Do not use them around me. That's why when you talk, nobody understand you, Coco. So how's it goin?"

"The process was slowed down for a few days, but we're back on track," Eric said, smiling.

"Oh! So you're the man Coco was arrested with. I thought you looked kind a familiar. But you're someone famous, aren't you?"

"Ma, I told you he's Deedee's uncle and—"

"I don't care. He's the man who was arrested with you on the television. Don't you get my daughter in no more trouble, Mr. Ascot. Trouble must follow you. It's that black cloud over your head. You must step into the light... Marry that girl. Make her legal. Things will be better."

"Ma, that's Eric Ascot's niece, Deedee. She was here with me at the hospital. It was only yesterday. Gosh don't you remember, yo?"

"I remember you came with a lesbian-looking chick. You mean she switched up overnight? You know back in the days that kind a shit wouldn't go down. The only thing that remains the same is how the government still give out drugs, guns and disease to the poor."

"That's true in a sense," Deedee said.

"Dee, please don't get her going again, yo."

"Let her have her say," Eric said.

"Yes, Coco, please fall back as you like to say. They should call their damn agencies 'Go-Kill-Yourselves,' cuz that's what they do. Every single one of 'em... I'm in the last one, a medical experiment. A drug addict, with an incurable disease and a daughter gettin' arrested with guns."

"Ma, it wasn't guns—"

"Everything now is about guns, guns, guns, drugs and guns, sex and guns, guns that makes you sexy. Back in the days we did it with our fists," Ms. Harvey said. Pointing her bony finger, she said, "You're old enough to remember all this stuff," Ms. Harvey addressed Eric Ascot.

"I remember—"

"Tell these kids out there to respect knowledge. Knowledge is power. Remember back in the days the government did the Tuskegee experiment...? Nowadays they got AIDS. They arrest all the teenagers, and run 'em through their system... I'm at the last of their system. Medical. I got the monster they can't cure. But I still have no gun charges on my daughter. Please God don't let that happen to her."

"Mother, I told you it was for assaulting an officer. And they already dropped the charges. So please stop harping on it already."

"And I guess that makes it better, Coco? When I'm dead, girl, who's gonna look after you. I mean this man has a nice heart, I can tell. But he's getting arrested day in and day out. Then what are you left with? Deedee, she just like having sex and hanging out. Wasn't she the one who was raped?"

"I think we should leave right now," Eric said.

"Sorry, I have to be very real with my daughter."

"Well, it was good visiting with you. Hope you get well soon, okay," Eric said.

"You know a lot of people ain't real with their children. I let Coco know how things is. I mean back in the days it would be the whole neighborhood raising the child. Nowadays it's just the mother and the TV."

"That's good. Well, anyway I gotta get back to doing some work. Coco will let me know how I can help," Eric said.

"I know you need a few more minutes with your daughter, so I'll see you again Ms. Harvey," Deedee said, extending her hand.

Ms. Harvey appeared confused as if she didn't know what Deedee was doing. Until Coco said, "Ma, Deedee is trying to shake hands."

"Okay Deedee, thank you and your uncle for coming and seeing me. And thanks for the flowers Mr. Ah..."

"Ascot," Eric said. You're welcome Ms. Harvey. Take care."

"Coco hit me up when you're through," Deedee said, walking

out with her uncle.

"A'ight. Thanks for coming through and all, yo."

Coco waited until Deedee and Eric were outside, then she unveiled the bottle. Ms. Harvey's face lit up. She had wanted the bottle so badly she took it immediately. She attempted to open it but wasn't strong enough.

"Here Ma, let me help you."

"Yes Coco. Pop the cork for me. I want a taste."

Coco stood and watched her mother licking her lips. The anticipation for liquor was a great suffering Coco thought, pouring the mixed juices in a small cup.

"Here, smell that, Ma," Coco said, waving the bottle across Ms. Harvey's nostril.

"Why you had to get this, Coco?"

"Ma, you forgot? I'm under age. This is all I could get."

The woman took the cup and mumbled before drinking it down. She sighed and smiled, looking at Coco. Then she took a swig and swallowed.

"Ah.. They don't make nothing like they used to. Back in the days you could get good liquor. Nowadays it's all water-down."

"Are you complaining?"

"I'm just sayin'."

"Well you said too much. Cuz this ain't back in the days," Coco said.

"You can say that again. This certainly ain't back in the days."

Ms. Harvey finished her cup and smiled at Coco. She was completely satisfied and laid her head against the pillow.

"Thanks Coco. I needed that," she said, licking her lips.

"I'm glad you did. Now you can stop harassing me about a drink."

"That did it, girl. I don't want anymore for now. I can't have my breath smelling like that white nurse. She always come in reeking of liquor and looking like she hung over. I don't know how she can deal with the patients when she's drunk. Shush, always with the alcohol on her breath. God bless you, Coco. Just leave the bottle and don't you bother sitting here all night like a damn watchman. I know what I'm doing."

"I'm afraid of that. But if you insist, I'll leave the bottle but you can't drink it all at once, Ma."

"Don't Ma me, I'm your damn mother."

"Okay mother, I hear you, mother. I'm gonna leave the bottle with you. But please, please do not drink anymore today."

"I feel so tired now. It's that cheap liquor making me go to sleep.

"You used up a lot of energy, mother. Go to sleep. I'll stay here for a while."

"You will...?"

Coco went to the bathroom, and by the time she returned her mother had fallen asleep. The woman seemed so peaceful. Coco had to check to make sure she was breathing. She sat at the bedside watching her mother sleep. No matter what, Coco knew she would miss her. Coco reached over and kissed the frail woman's hollowed cheek. Then she walked out of the hospital room.

"Hey Coco, just a minute," a voice said.

Coco was about to ease into her bop, but paused and turned to see Nurse Roberts. She walked back to the woman in white uniform.

"Please remember to tell all your mother's boyfriends—the ones you know of course. Tell them to come in and get themselves checked."

Coco stared at the woman and bit her lips listening attentively. She wanted to give her a response like "I don't even know who my father is." Instead Coco nodded and silently turned away.

Easing into her bop she walked to the elevator and went downstairs to the lobby. The nurse's request was still on her mind when the hospital security looked lecherously at her and winked. Smirking, She thought about telling Nurse Roberts about the bottle, but somehow forgot and Coco walked out of the hospital.

It was a cool summer's evening. The wind was picking up, and rain seemed imminent. Coco walked home under a dark cloud, rummaging through her mind, searching for clues about her father. She had often dismissed it, but her mother's life hung tenuously by inches. Even though she had seen improvements, her mother was bound to mess up again. Coco thought about what Nurse Roberts had requested and that triggered renewed interest in who her father was. Over the years, her mother had resisted giving any information about him. Coco tired to evade it all by putting her headphones on, and turning up the music.

Bopping toward her building while listening to her music, Coco saw the usual gathering of hustlers in the front. Coco noticed that more people than usual seemed to be moving in and out. The

Friday evening had drawn more hustlers, buyers, and sellers. She decided to chill for a minute, observing what was going down.

When you stand in front of the building, people do take notice. Coco received all the greetings of a superstar. She was a top rapper and singer working with Eric Ascot—a winning combination. Her notoriety drew attention and before long, people, fans, friends and haters alike surrounded her with their questions.

"Yo Coco, whaddup, girl?" a member of the crowd greeted.

"Hey yo, Coco wanna cop sump'n?'

"Nah, I'm good, yo."

"What's good, Coco? How's the flow?" another member of the crowd shouted.

"It's goin' down, yo."

"How's your Madukes, Coco?"

"She's doing better. I just came from seeing her, yo."

"That's peace. Tell her the block's praying for her when you see her again, Coco."

"A'ight, I'll do that, yo."

"What's gonna be your new joint. You smashin' 'em on the streets with that *Tougher Than Dice,* shit!"

"Word up, you slayin' all that other shit out there."

"When you dropping sump'n new, Coco?"

Coco stared at the crowd gathering around her. They stared at her, clinging to her answers like students taking notes. Class was in session, she thought for a moment. They seemed to be under the impression that she was about offer something. Coco delivered.

Sometimes when I feel I'm losing my mind /
I call out your names... I hear y'all listening
Things don't always work the way we plan 'em/
Your voices live through me just the same/
Be my number one fan and I will succeed
I'll be felt the champion title I will claim

I'm making a stand feeling hard to defeat
We taking over just the way we planned/
From the start doing it from our hearts...
Sisters always dreaming us on top forever /
Reigning hopes never die you'll always remain
So fly.../Jo, Dani, Bebop living for you /
Missing Miss Katie's voice y'all got her/
Listening made me nicer music game sicker/
Lyrics lock tighter feeling invincible Truth is
Her wisdom helped me survive all my fights
Made me stronger now I'm tougher than dice..."
I-I-I'm tougher than dice...tough...tougher than dice
My name's Coco and I'm tougher than dice...

Coco came out of her zone and found the crowd had grown to a much larger size. They were excited jumping around and dancing to her impromptu acappella performance. Those who knew the hook were still reciting it long after she was finished. Coco clapped her hands to the chanting of the crowd.

"Lyrics lock tighter feeling invincible Truth is her wisdom helped me survive all my fights Made me stronger now I'm tougher than dice...I-I-I'm tougher than dice...tough...tougher than dice the name's Coco and I'm tougher than dice..."

She laughed at the excitement that her music had created. The crowd was buzzing when someone turned on a boom box and pumped up the volume. The crowd gathered in front of her building was rocking and jumping to her song, *Tougher Than Dice.*

It was a Friday evening to remember. Coco smiled when she realized that this wasn't a drug. It was her God-given talent drawing the hustlers, buyers, and sellers. She decided chilling out front for a minute wasn't such a bad idea.

"Shyt, Coco, these peeps really feelin' you, huh?"

Coco turned to see Kim. She was holding her son, trying to keep him from getting crushed by the crowd.

"Hey Kim," Coco said. "Wow your son gown up, yo."

"I was taking Roshawn to the babysitter on the first floor and I was thinking, 'The Bloods and Crips started a riot?' Then a cop on the corner said it was a chick rapping. And I had a feeling it was you, girl. What da deal? You takin' it live?"

"Five-Oh—five-oh!" someone shouted.

"Oh that was just some—shit!

The sirens closed in and the crowd began running in all directions. Those who were the dirtiest were running the fastest. Kim held Roshawn against her chest to prevent him being trampled. She was standing next to Coco, and could feel to the crush.

"Turn that music off and everyone go home. If you're caught out here loitering, you'll be arrested," one of the officers shouted.

"It's TGIF, and there's no pity in the naked city. Time for me and Roshawn to get inside before they start ackin' da fool out here, Coco."

"Yes, you right, yo. These po-po out here don't even need a reason, yo."

"You got your keys, right? Cuz this damn sitter must be deaf at times. Shyt, it seems like I gotta ring her bell five and six times for her to let me inside."

"Yeah, I have my keys, yo," Coco laughed and turned to open the door.

They walked inside and Kim walked to the babysitter's apartment on the first floor. Coco continued upstairs to the third floor. She walked to her apartment and went to the window. Shaking her head, she saw the officers searching and frisking a group of teen boys. They were lined up against a fence with their backs to the officers. Police searched each of them, releasing some while handcuffing others, and placing those in a waiting paddy wagon. Coco was smirking when she heard the doorbell.

"Who dat?"

"It's Kim," the voice outside the door said.

"Whaddup, yo?" Coco greeted, opening the door.

Kim walked inside and Coco looked at her strangely. Wondering if Kim had lost something, Coco waited while the unexpected visitor glanced around. Then she spoke.

"I've never been here before."

"I don't think you were ever invited, yo."

"Oh, I knew your mother, Coco. When my baby-father used to sell crack, she was a real customer."

"Yes, you right, Déjà was a dealer, wasn't he?"

"Yes, he was. God bless his soul, Déjà was good to your mother. He would let her have jumbo after jumbo and she didn't have to leave her welfare card. May his soul rest in peace. He was mad cool," Kim said solemnly.

Coco stared at her in disbelief without saying anything. This must be a joke. She wanted to laugh but refrained, and instead tried to welcome Kim's annoying visit.

"You wanna chill for a minute or you in a hurry somewhere, yo?"

"Shyt, I got time. Me and Tina going downtown to get our shopping on," Kim said walking to the sofa. "I see you dressing like a pretty girl now, Coco. We all gotta move on."

"That's all Deedee. She likes the stores, yo."

"I hear that. I'm a clothes ho' myself. But I gotta save money for my son's school gonna cost money. I want the best schooling for him so he can be a doctor. I don't know why, but I feel that's what he's born to do. He's really smart. Roshawn's only three and he already knows his ABC's... And he can count up to ten and say 'Mommy,' all the time and he's—"

"Do you want a drink of water or—?"

"Do you wanna smoke a blunt?" Kim asked, pulling out a bag.

"Damn, you walking round with all that weed, yo?"

"This just sump'n for me and Tina. We can't be goin' 'round coppin' on da streets. That shit's dangerous," Kim warned. "So my babysitter cops ounces for me, and I pay her. I'll break you off a lil' sump'n if you don't wanna smoke right now."

Coco watched curiously while Kim set about removing some of the weed from the large ounce sack. She walked to the kitchen and opened the refrigerator.

"That looks like some good sticky type right there, yo.

"It's da shyt, Coco," Kim smiled.

"We can spark sump'n in here, yo."

Coco broke the Dutch Master down, and Kim rolled up some weed. Coco lit it and they were soon puffing. She started coughing and Coco poured two cups of fruit punch. The weed was strong and Coco puffed her problems away. She stopped thinking about her mother and more about her impromptu performance. She passed the smoldering weed to Kim. Kim puffed and stared coughing.

"This shyt is real chronic, Coco," she said.

"This ain't for no light-head, yo."

"We were at this party last night and smoked couple of this shyt. The whole party was *soo* lit up the whole night. Everyone was copping from Tina and me, they were like we must get some o' that shyt, Kim. So me and Tina—well Tina actually—went and re-up. But it's for the two of us. That shyt was crazy," Kim smiled while recounting the happenings.

"You had mad fun, huh?"

"What...? We were dancing the whole night. That shyt was rocking. I'm tellin' you Coco, you gotta come hang with me and Tina just once. You'd love..." Kim said and her voice trailed. "I guess you still have feelings about back in the days how we used to pick on you, huh?" Kim said, puffing the weed.

"I don't hold nothing against you or, ah, Tina, yo. I'm good on all that back in days beefs."

"I know we had our run-ins but you were always real, Coco. And you're skinny but you never back down," Kim said, passing the blunt.

"There was nowhere to back down to," Coco said, puffing. "I mean I had to come home from school and you and Tina were always out there on the Ave. Ain't shit I could do but fight my way home. I'm through with all that BS now, yo."

"Shyt that's how I feel too," Kim said high-fiving Coco. "I'm on my grown-woman shyt. And I definitely see you on some music shyt."

"I'm taking this music game more serious, yo. And working with Eric Ascot is a blessing. I'm learning a lot."

"Eric Ascot, hmm-hmm—that's one fine-ass nigga. Lord whew!" Kim said, waving her hands like fan blades. "He could get this shyt," she laughed, waving at her ass. "Coco, you look at me as if I'm buggin' out."

"I know peeps bug on him. He's good-looking but he's a real talent. A great man, yo."

"No doubt," Kim joined in. "I love the way he walks, hmm."

"I don't be getting all the way deep like that, yo. Doing this music thing is what it's all about, yo."

"That's good, Coco. Cuz you can sing, dance, rap and you're pretty. I used to think you were a butch, but I see how you move. You're very quiet. You like Prince—you're just androgynous. But when it comes time for the music shyt—you go all the way indeed."

"I'm androgynous...? That's the first time I heard that one, yo."

"Shyt we, you know, me and Tina sorta thinking that maybe you and Deedee were into a relationship. But then after Reggie started dating her, well that was it. Too bad about Reggie, huh? It gets me sick when I think about it."

"Yeah, that was fucked up, yo."

"Yeah, you know as quiet as it was kept, he was dating Tina

first, and then wham! He saw Deedee's sexy ass, and shyt. That was a wrap."

"I hear you," Coco said, puffing on the blunt.

"Deedee was lucky she didn't get in that car with Reggie. She would've been history. God was on her side. Shyt, you know she's probably here to do something great. That's why she never got in the car."

"I hear you," Coco said, passing the blunt.

"She was probably devastated, huh? I mean they slept together. At least he was screwing Tina for sure. I know cuz she likes to show out about her pussy power. Tina was sayin' that nigga was just tryin' a get a woman pregos. You think Deedee prego by him, Coco? You don't know what they were doing—you weren't there. Why?" Kim said.

"I was recording late and went to visit madukes in the hospital, yo."

"How's she doing?"

"She was up two days in row, yo."

"Is that good?"

"I mean, I've been to the hospital, and before that she didnn't even open her eyes, yo."

"Shyt, that must make you feel sad by all that shyt, huh?"

"She's trying. Madukes' all I have, yo."

"Shyt, don't you have other relatives I mean...?"

"Madukes never talk about anyone, yo," Coco said, puffing and thinking for a beat. "I never met anyone. From the moment I was born I've been with this woman with a deadly drug problem. All I know is her. She's my only family."

"Shyt girl! What about your father?"

"She used to talk about him."

"You don't know who your father is, Coco?" Kim asked.

"She said he was some type of a musician who be traveling around a lot. And that's why we never seen him, yo."

"Coco, let me put you down on the score, girl. You know Rightchus? That's your father, girl," Kim said.

There was a pause as Coco's mind slowly wrapped itself around this explosive piece of information. Coco stared incredulously at Kim. Her tongue was known for gossiping and licking dicks. Coco's mind did laps and slowed.

"So you're telling me that Rightchus is my father? You're saying that lil' 'itty bit con artist is my father? Unbelievable, yo."

"Shyt, Coco, my mother has live around these projects for a minute. She was the one who told me that Rightchus and your mother were lovers back in the days. They even went to the same church as she did. My mother still go to the Abyssinian Baptist Church, Coco. Your mother used to be in the choir and then she became pregnant. Rightchus got into crack and they broke up. By the time you were born your mother was on drugs. I ain't lying. You can come and meet my mother. She knows you; she used to babysit you."

"Are you fuckin' kiddin' me, yo? Get da fuck outta here! Rightchus? My father, yo? I gotta get used to the idea. Where's your mother?"

"She's home, two buildings over. She used to babysit you, Coco. Shyt, you come with me right now, she'll still remember you," Kim said.

"No bullshit? Alright, I'm ready—let's go!"

"Here, let me pack this weed up and we can go and verify all that info. This is for you. Put it away," Kim said, handing Coco a few buds. "My mother have no reason to lie," she continued.

"Good looking out," Coco said, taking the weed and wrapping it up.

She checked the kitchen found a place to stash the weed in a cupboard. Then she walked out the door with Kim.

"The elevator doesn't work?"

"The elevator never works, yo."

"You ever notice that in some of these buildings the elevators never working or they always getting repaired."

"I'm telling you, this is one of those buildings, yo. The elevator has never worked. It's constantly getting repaired."

They raced down the stairs and passed the people in front of the building. Coco's lips remained pursed as she went past them. She nodded and kept it moving. They were still reliving the performance she gave earlier.

"She was rocking out crazy sump'n…"

"That's nice that they love you, Coco," Kim said.

"Yes it's cool. I want the whole world to love me, yo."

Coco and Kim quickly walked the short distance. Kim was soon ringing the doorbell. Her mother buzzed her in, and Kim led Coco to the elevator.

"This shyt always workin'," she said, pushing the button.

When they got inside the elevator, Kim pressed the button for the eighth floor. Coco brooded over the possibility of Rightchus being her father. Kim fussed with her designer gear, while Coco fidgeted with her thoughts.

"You've gotta speak a little loud for her to hear you. She's kinda losing her hearing," Kim said. "She getting' ancient and shyt. Gotta tell her shyt three or four times. That's why I gotta take Roshawn to that sitter by you. Shyt, my son could be right next to her choking to death, God forbid—Mommy would be just thinking he laughing and shyt."

Coco nodded in silence and before long they were standing in front of the door. Coco's thoughts weighed heavy on her mind causing small beads of sweat to form on her forehead. She felt like she was being led to the court of public opinion. Coco remained calm while waiting in front of the apartment door. An older woman opened the door and stood smiling like a teacher on the first day of school, greeting her new pupil, Coco. Kim walked ahead and entered the well-kept apartment with plastic covering the living room set. The place smelled of baked cookies.

"Mommy, you always baking cookies. Roshawn can't eat too much of that. His teeth will get rotten," Kim said.

"Oh you so crazy, Kimberly," the older woman said, chuckling. "I can bake for my grandson anytime. How's he doing?"

"Roshawn is fine with his bad self. I brought you an old friend," Kim announced. "Remember Coco?"

"Of course I 'member Coco. It's only my ears going bad. Hi Coco. You don't remember me, huh Coco? I'm Kimberly's mother, Mrs. Jones," the woman announced.

Coco stared at her with a dumbfounded expression all over her face. The woman had a stark resemblance to Kim, but was older. Her face appeared to be kind. Coco wondered how Kim became the person she did, after living with this seemingly nice person.

"Your mother used to bring you right here, and I babysat for her when you were first born. After that Katie Patterson, may she rest in peace, took over. So see, you don't remember cuz you were a newborn then. Now look at you all grown up and pretty as ever," Mrs. Jones said, gushing like an artist at work.

"Thank you," Coco said.

The older woman was caressing the outline of Coco's face, touching her cheeks and brushing her eyebrow. Coco took the time to look at the woman carefully. She had a pretty face dotted by a black mark on her nose.

"You mother was such a beautiful woman..." Mrs. Jones let her voice trail. Her tone was harsh when she asked, "How's she doing?"

Coco was in the process of opening her mouth to answer Mrs. Jones, when she heard the woman speaking.

"You don't have to tell me. That damn drug destroyed her," she scoffed. "I hate that damn drug with a passion. I've see it destroy too many, too many lives. Too many, dear Lord," Mrs. Jones said in a pleading tone. "Once she took up with crack, her life was over and I know it's that man Rightchus who turned her on to it. Before that she was happily going to church and working as a stenographer. He and his damn drug kept going after her and you know once she started doing it, I never saw her again," Mrs. Jones continued.

"Uh-huh," Kim said.

"You ain't heard it from me. I ain't the one to spread gossip and all. But I know for a fact that your mother used to hide when she used to see me coming. Then she started going out late in the night cuz she didn't wanna bump into me. I ain't the one to spread gossip. I'm just sayin' I ain't seen her for months now..."

"My mother's been in the hospital..."

"What...? Kimberly, why you never told me that?" the older woman said with hands akimbo.

"I not too long ago found out, Mommy," Kim said. "Coco was outside rapping and I saw her and that's when we started talking. Shit if I knew— you'd know. You should know, I'm not into people's biz like that, Mommy."

"Which hospital is she in, Coco?"

"Harlem," Coco said.

"When I get a chance, I have to go visit her then," Mrs. Jones said. "My prayers are constantly gon' be with your mother. Coco you want some delicious oatmeal cookies?"

Questions were hot and stirring in her mind. Coco wanted to clear her head. So much was happening, she didn't know exactly where to begin. Mrs. Jones walked into the kitchen and took the tray of cookies out of the oven. She separated morsels of the cookie and placed them on a napkin.

"Here, taste," she said, shoving the morsels into Coco's mouth. "The same shy girl, huh, Coco?"

"Just give her a beat and all that shyness will be zapped from her," Kim said with a smile. "She'll transform into Coco, the rapper, slash singer, slash dancer. Coco's a monster—she's very talented, Mommy."

"Really, that's good. Ever since she was a baby she was always quiet and snapping her fingers to any sound. Her daddy was a talented man. He used to go on tours with a lot of bands and sing in nightclubs. Then the crack got the best of him, and he just fell off like the archangel," Mrs. Jones said.

"You mean he went to heaven?" Kim asked.

"Heaven, hmm. More like he in hell with that crack. But you know he was dibbing and dabbing in drugs like all them artists and singers do, but it was the crack, the crack. Oh Lord. Where's Rightchus now?"

"I heard he got shot and left the city. Some people said he's dead," Kim said.

"You never know with that man. He's always in bad company. He was the one who turned your mother on to crack. She was such a sweet girl. The two o' them started dating and her personality started changing. By the time you were born—they had already split up."

"Told you, Coco. I told you," Kim said.

"Yes, Kimberly should know. She's six years older than you. She's my last and I used to keep both you and her close by. She used to watch you and smile at you all the time, even when you were crying. Your mother never brought you back after Rightchus ran off."

Coco was speechless at the revelation. She was curious, but her mouth was filled with morsels of cookie. Coco wanted to spit it all out. She wanted it all taken back. Rightchus was her father. Her thoughts were still churning when the voice of Mrs. Jones crept back into her mind.

"The old folks who are still alive remember. But many people done passed away since then. Katie would remember, but she's dead. Only God knows why he ran off with the teenage, Spanish girl. He went to jail for a couple years cuz she was a minor. They said he kidnapped her, and held her against her will. Your mother was embarrassed. She stopped talking to everyone and took refuge in drinking and drugs. They were gonna get married, but only God knows why that didn't happen," Mrs. Jones said.

"Shyt, I told you... What I said, Coco...? Same thing," Kim said.

"Kim, please. Stop cursing. Yes, you know cuz you older than she and you're not gonna remember all that when you are an infant. Unless someone tells you. Your mother begged Miss Katie not to tell you. I know that for sure. Katie was loyal, God bless her soul. She never talked about your mother's business to anyone. All she did was prayed for her."

"That's probably why she never did bring you back here, Coco. Cuz my mother would've told you everything a long time ago," Kim said.

Coco chewed on the morsels of cookie Mrs. Jones had shoved in her mouth, and felt nauseous. The black mark on the woman's nose appeared to have grown into a blob. Coco wanted to vomit, but hugged herself, trying to hold onto her wits. Her mind was speeding and couldn't slow down. She could feel her heart pounding beneath her shirt. Coco's vision became momentarily blurred. She remembered smoking the weed, and maybe the buzz was catching up to her.

Her body swayed, Coco could see both Kim and Mrs. Jones looks of concern. She attempted to walk to the bathroom. Her legs felt like lead and she felt the room spinning just before she blacked out.

"Bring her some water!" Mrs. Jones shouted.

Kim ran to refrigerator and returned carrying a glass of water. Coco awoke with cold sweat on her face and neck. She was on the sofa, her mind caught in a web of confusion. She felt the cold liquid against her lips and shook her head.

"It's okay, Coco. You just take deep breaths. I worked in a doctor's office for twenty-five years. I seen many a people faint," Mrs. Jones said. "Breathe girl, breathe..."

The sound of her cellphone went off, and Kim answered it.

"I'm at my mother's apartment," she said. "Tina sez hi, Mommy."

"Say hello to that Tina for me too," Mrs. Jones said, waving her arm in disgust.

Her attention was focused on Coco. The teen managed to sit up and started coughing. Mrs. Jones gave her the rest of the water.

"Drink all of this, Coco," she said.

Coco took the glass and drank the rest of the water. Mrs. Jones went to the bathroom, and returned carrying a bottle of Robitussin.

"You're still very sensitive, ain't you Coco?" she asked. "Just like when you were a baby. I had to spend a lot of time with you. Remember Kim? You never liked that, huh?"

"I ah, huh—" Coco began.

"I lost the call. Let me call Tina back," Kim said, interrupting the confused teen. "What up, Tina...? Why don't you get a better carrier? You're always dropping calls," Kim said.

Coco was watching Kim walking away and talking on the phone. Coco was trying to make sense of why she suddenly was feeling faint, when she heard her cell phone ringing.

"It's Grand Central up in here now. These darn cell phones sure ring loud!" Mrs. Jones said.

Coco was peering around like she had forgotten where she was. She saw Kim still smiling, and chatting on her cell phone. Mrs. Jones's hands were busy applying ointment on her back. Coco got up, and tried to steady herself. The room appeared foggy, and she felt like her head was swimming in a cloud. Her legs buckled, and she sat back down. Coco's eyes were blinking rapidly, and Mrs. Jones held her down when she tried to stand up again.

"You're stubborn like your mother. Coco, you can't jump up too quickly," Mrs. Jones said, holding the teen. "I think your cell phone ringing too, Coco."

Feeling dazed, and a little wobbled, Coco checked her jeans pocket for her cell phone. She shoved the instrument to her ear and waited.

"Don't let what I say about your father get you discombobulated, girl. One thing for sure, you're as pretty as your mommy was before all that drinkin' and druggin'," Mrs. Jones said.

"Coco, you a'ight, girl?" Kim asked. "You want me to get the call for you," she continued when the cell phone rang again.

"I got this, yo," Coco said, realizing she had not pressed the answer button. "Hello Dee... A'ight, I'll see you out front in a few."

"You good enough? Maybe you should have her meet you in here," Kim said. "Mommy won't mind. Will you, Mommy?"

"I don't mind at all. Like I said before, I used to care for you like you were one of my own when you were a baby girl, Coco," Mrs. Jones said with a chuckle. "And Kim," she continued, pointing at her daughter. "She'd always be complain, 'Why you takin' care of her so much? You love Coco more than you love me!' Remember, Kim? Back in the days you never did like Coco. Always complainin' 'bout, 'Coco cry too much,'" Mrs. Jones chuckled.

"That was back in the days. I done moved on from all that. Now I got my own baby," Kim said. "My own worries..."

"Don't you call my grandson 'worries,' girl. When you had him—"

"You can have him, Mommy," Kim said, her tone becoming serious.

"Girl, you know if you bring my grandson to me, I will always take him. Never will I turn him away. And you only gonna come running back begging after a day or so."

"I need the break. I might make it a month or so," Kim said.

"You'd never do that. You're all talk, and talk as far as I'm concerned, is still cheap," Mrs. Jones said.

Coco quietly listened to the chatter going back and forth

between mother and daughter. She sighed then stood up. Her gait was unsteady at first, but Coco was determined to leave.

"I better get going, yo. Thanks for all your ah..."

"Not a problem," Kim said. "Give me a second, and I'll walk down with you, Coco. You sure you wanna leave? I mean Deedee could meet you here," Kim offered, hurrying inside the bathroom.

"Nah, I think I'm good, yo."

"I won't be long, just gotta freshen my makeup."

"The fresh air might do you some good, Coco. I hope you continue in school. If it's one thing your mother did was brag about you and your school. I heard it through the grapevine that you got a scholarship or something like that...?"

"Yes, I got accepted to Harvard. They offered me a scholarship. I'm also completing my first album."

"What kind of album?"

"Music, hip hop, and R&B mixes. I sing and rap."

"Oh, so you did get your some of your father's talent. Back in the days, Rightchus sang back up for all 'em big Motown acts."

"I don't know if he's even my father. But I'll definitely ask my mother when I see her."

"Hey Coco, you ready? I am."

"Well, Mrs. Jones, nice meeting you again," Coco said, extending her hand.

Passing up Coco's attempt at a handshake, Mrs. Jones gave her a tight embrace. Crushed to the woman's chest, Coco smiled.

"You're still shy, and quiet, huh Coco? And you're soo humble. I don't know who you got that trait from. Maybe me," Mrs. Jones laughed. "It was soo good to see you and talk to you after all this time, Coco. I gotta go see your mother soon," Mrs. Jones said, still hugging the teen. "Kim told you she can sing too?"

"I heard her—"

"I wish somebody would help her out cause she running with

that Tina, and don't have time for nothing else," Mrs. Jones scoffed.

"Alright Mommy, I'll see you later," Kim said. "Coco, I'm ready to go now."

As they walked out of the door, the smell of baked cookies wafted into the hallway. Mrs. Jones stood at the door for a few beats and watched Coco and Kim getting in the elevator.

"I hope she don't become a damn drug addict like her mother," she said under her breath then closed the door.

The summer night air wasn't enough. Coco needed assistance and Kim held her arm, supporting the groggy-teen. They were outside the building and Coco was trying her best not to look conspicuous.

"I think that's Deedee over there," Kim said, pointing to the BMW.

"Where yo," Coco asked gazing in the wrong direction.

"Over there, Coco," Kim said.

Coco peered through her dazed view and was unable to see where Deedee was parked. Then she heard the familiar sound of her best friend's voice, and her burden felt lighter.

"Hey Coco," Deedee greeted.

"Dee, whassup, yo?"

"Hey Kim," Deedee said, waving.

"Hi Deedee, I'm glad you came when you did. Coco don't feel

too good. We were hanging at my mom's place and she fainted. So be careful, she might—"

"I'm a'ight. For real, I'm good, yo," Coco said, shaking free of Kim's arm.

The action caused her to lose balance and sent her tumbling forward. Coco spun around and danced out of falling down. Deedee stared wide-eyed above the rim of her sunglasses. Kim's jaw dropped in complete amazement. They watched as Coco suddenly jumped and flipped in the air with cat-like precision.

"Oh shyt! Kim shouted excitedly. "I thought you were about to bust your ass against the asphalt. You are fuckin car-razy, girl."

"You'd be very surprised by the things Coco can do, yo," Deedee said, mimicking Coco.

Coco smiled at both of them then they all burst out in laughter. Coco waved at Kim and walked away with Deedee.

"Bye, Kim," Deedee said, walking away.

"See y'all," Kim shouted, shaking her head, and walking away.

She met Tina who was impatiently waiting at the corner. Tina was smoking and impatiently hurled the cigarette away when Kim got close.

"When you say in a couple minutes, you mean like a half hour later. You know how long I been standing on this corner? All these nasty-ass men trying to pick me up and shit..."

"Tina, I thought you liked all the attention, bitch," Kim laughed.

"I'm not in the mood for your BS. What was you doing for the past half hour, ho? You should've just let me know—"

"Shyt, bitch! I told you I was with Coco and the bitch passed out at my mother's apartment," Kim said.

"Oh really ho...? That was half hour ago."

"Yes, and we had to wait for Deedee to come. I didn't wanna leave her out there by herself."

"Shut da front door! When did you get so sympathetic to her?"

"Coco's cool peeps. We went to my mother's cuz she ain't know that Rightchus' her daddy. Her mother never told her."

"She needs to wake up and smell the coffee," Tina laughed. "And that's what made her sick?"

"Shyt the weed I gave her, and it was like she could hardly see—"

"Shut da fuck up! Tell me you didn't give her all my weed, trying to be her friend and sucking up to that ghetto girl," Tina said.

"I left her a pinch of the shyt, and we smoked a blunt. What bitch?"

"Did you find out if Deedee got a baby bump or not...?"

"Baby bump?"

"Yes, is she pregnant?"

"No, not a thing. Coco is real. She don't say shyt about shyt!"

"Coco is real, she don't say shyt about shyt," Tina said, mimicking Kim. She chuckled and said, "Soo, you went through all that—even sharing my weed and all. And you found out nada, ho?"

"Yes bitch. I never knew I was supposed to be spying for your ass!"

"I said find out what you could—"

"And I was supposed to give her some type of truth serum and then she gonna start spitting shyt out of her ass...?" Kim said.

Her neck was moving with every syllable. Tina stared at her for couple beats then she laughed.

"Shut da front door. Ho, you know what? I really don't have time for you. I gotta go downtown and pick up this money. You ready?"

"You said money, bitch...? Lead the way."

"Let's catch a cab."

She raised her arm and three cabbies responded simultaneously. Tina smiled at all the attention she received. The driver kept his eyes on them as Kim and Tina entered the cab.

"Where are you headed, ladies?" he asked.

"Downtown," Tina said. "And turn up the music please," she added.

Chit chatting in the back, Kim and Tina laughed and drew the attention of the driver. Tina caught him occasionally looking at them. She didn't mind and moved her legs when he adjusted his rearview.

"I can't believe you, bitch. You were with her all-evening, and didn't find out nothing? And you left her weed...? Oh my gosh!"

Kim pulled out the ounce of marijuana and held it up. Shaking the bag at Tina, she said, "I can't believe your ass is still complaining 'bout da shyt! Look! See, you can't even tell that shyt was taken out, huh?"

"Why don't you just announce it on the radio, ho? Put that shit down, bitch!" Tina said, looking at the driver.

He was staring at her and saw the bag of weed. Tina opened her legs wider and his eyes followed her hand all the way up to the crack. His eyes were riveted directly on the spot she wanted him to look.

"You'd like to rub my pussy, wouldn't you?" Tina asked him.

"Huh...? No I wouldn't!" Kim said.

"I ain't talking to you, ho. I'm talking to the driver."

"Oh you dirty, nasty, lil' bitch!"

"Shut your face! Please put the bag away before you lose it. I wanted to know if the sucio driving us wanted to rub my pussy. He's welcome. But he better keep his eyes on the road 'fore we crash!"

"Oh my God! You over here teasing the poor man... Nasty bitch, of course he gon' crash, you have your legs wide open. Shyt, he could look all the way up to your throat."

"Shut your face, bitch! He ain't complainin'."

"I'm riding in the cab too and I have a son who I wanna see through college. And your dumbass in the back seat rubbing your pussy."

"Shut your mouth."

"You are fuckin' crazy, bitch! I just saw Coco do some wild shit but you beat her by a mile with your crazy ass! Close your legs!"

"Really, I don't mind," the driver said.

"You don't mind cuz your ass ain't had no pussy in a long ass time, my man!" Kim said.

"I have pussy every night. I'm a married man!"

"Then why are you all up her asshole like that?"

"I look—I see road, rearview, and road!" he shouted, pointing at traffic.

"Your eyes should be on the road," Kim countered.

"Pull over here for me, thanks. How much?" Tina asked.

"Ten dollars," the driver said. "Pay me."

"Shyt, we got you, your freaky ass. Damn perv!" Kim said.

"You made this habib mad as hell," Tina laughed. "All you had to do was shut your pie-hole, and we could've had a free ride!"

"There are no free rides, ho. Somebody has to pay," Kim said, getting out of the back seat.

Together they walked to the building that housed several law offices. Tina and Kim were familiar with the place. They walked up to a secretary.

"Hi. Mr. Roose is expecting me," she said.

"Yes, go on in," the secretary said.

"Wait here for me, ho," Tina said and walked away. "And don't piss all over the furniture."

"Just hurry, bitch. I'd like to walk down Fifth Ave., and have time to do some window shopping," Kim said, picking up a magazine, and slowly leafing through it.

Her hips swaying with extra intensity, Tina disappeared into the office and into the waiting arms of Max Roose.

"Here's my girl," he laughed. "Just in time for lunch," Roose said, pushing her head down to his crotch.

"I've got a bag of money for you. Twenty-five thousand. It's yours. All you have to do is one little thing for me," he said.

Max Roose sat back and watched Tina going to work. Undoing his fly, she pulled out his dick and wiped the lipstick from her soft lips. Then she opened her mouth, and her lips engulfed his head.

Sucking and licking until his dick was pointing toward the ceiling, Tina smiled. She massaged and moistened the head until it was shiny. Then she eased him back and sent waves through his body flicking her tongue all over his balls.

"Ah yeah..." Max Roose moaned softly, biting his lips.

Rubbing her hands over his hardened shaft, she felt him pulsing and knew the time was at hand. Max Roose would pop off soon.

"Oh ugh ah..." he moaned. "Suck it bitch! Lick it all up!"

Tina opened her mouth, and Max Roose squirted a load of sperm into her mouth. She swallowed it all, and jerked him off while his body shuddered. His legs shook and she knew it was over. Rising from her knees, Tina walked to the small bathroom.

Later, she walked out smiling.

"Good evening, Ms. Martinez," the secretary said.

Kim was sitting, chatting on her cell phone with the magazine in her lap. She looked at Tina and spoke.

"I guess that was a quickie, huh, nasty bitch?" Kim asked.

"I knew exactly what he wanted and I gave it to him," Tina said.

"He must be a two-minute man," Kim said.

"Poor people are the ones who spend time just fucking," Tina said. "Rich people, they ain't got time for all that. They busy making paper all day long, bitch. So shut your face and learn that," Tina said.

"Where your paper?"

"Here, lemme show you sump'n," Tina said, opening the bag and raising it to Kim's face. "Peep this, bitch."

"Damn, girl. That's a lot of fucking paper right there. What did you have to do for it? Lay somebody out?"

They walked out to the lobby, and Tina turned to the surprised

Kim. She stared at her for a beat. Kim opened her mouth then seemingly she changed her mind. She paused as if she was thinking before she started to speak.

"Shut your face. You ain't gonna ever get rich sitting on your big ass," Tina said."

"Shyt, you can say that again," Kim said.

"You want your son to go to good schools, then that's gonna take money, lots of it. There's lots of money out there. Poor people scared to go get it, and they get mad at the rich peeps for staying on their job. Making money is gonna be my full-time job. All day every day."

"Go on bitch, do your thang. I ain't gon' hate on ya ass," Kim said.

"Good, cuz Kim, I ain't never going back to being poor. Never again."

"There's just one thing I wanna know. What you gotta do to do get all that money? It's gotta be thousands in that bag."

"Twenty thousand, two stacks," Tina lied. "And I'm gonna give you half. Ten G's, bitch," she continued.

"And what do I have to give up or do for this money?"

"Shut your damn mouth, and do nothing. You can consider it a donation toward to Roshawn's education fund," Tina said. "Now let's go do some shopping on Fifth Ave., bitch."

"Well alright. Say no more, bitch. I'm definitely with that."

The evening came soon and the stores had begun closing their shutters along the fashionable walk. Pedestrians and shoppers were still combing the opened stores looking for bargains. Kim and Tina were amongst them, rubbing elbows with the super wealthy and the not so rich. They went inside the Gucci store.

"Ain't those the shoes Coco had on. I thought you never liked those shoes," Kim said.

"I didn't like how they looked on her. So I'm gonna get 'em in black. Just to have 'em. You never know," Tina said.

"Excuse me, y'all. There's a hater in the house," Kim said.

"Shut your face! I ain't no hater, you ho!"

"You better not, bitch. I'd like two of these shoes in size six," Tina said to a salesgirl. "There needs to be more cute guys up in this piece here, and I ain't talking 'bout the gay ones either."

"Why's that, bitch?" Kim asked.

"Guys be willing to give you a break with these high-ass prices," Tina said. "I'm trying to pop tags—I ain't tryin' a go broke doing it!"

"Oh you feel if niggas are here you could show 'em your pussy and...?"

"Some o' these bitches will jump on it way before a nigga will. These bitches dyke as hell," Tina laughed and Kim joined her.

The salesgirl returned with the two pairs of shoes. Kim and Tina tried the shoes on. They were a perfect fit, and Tina paid for the two pairs. Smiles all around, Kim and Tina walked out of the store carrying many shopping bags.

"Remember to open a bank account with that lil' dough, Kim. You can save up some money for you and Roshawn."

"Tina, you don't have to tell me what to do, bitch. I'll definitely do the right thing. This 'lil' dough' like you put it—that shyt is big money to me, bitch."

"I hear you, ho. Mami, I'm just saying," Tina started but Kim cut her off.

"Shyt say no more, bitch. I got this."

"Cool, then let's catch a cab and get uptown so we can get fresh. It's T-G-I-F—let's live it loud!"

"Shyt!" Kim screamed. "We gonna live it up, girl!"

They high-fived and cabbies raced to their position. The driver got out and assisted the girls with their bags. From the moment he came close to Tina she was feeling on him. Accidently bumping into his crotch, Tina copped a quick feel. The driver smiled and slapped her ass. Kim was shaking her head, and got in behind Tina.

The excited cabbie stared lecherously at Kim's round ass. He was about to touch her round ass, but Kim gave him a mean look and changed his mind. Backing off, and showing both his hands, the man got in the car.

"Where are you going, ladies?"

"Uptown, East One-Twelfth and Lex."

Tina then sat back and spread her legs so he could see all the way to her split. Smiling like he was hypnotized, the driver adjusted his rearview mirror. He drove off still looking at Tina's exposed crotch and almost hit a pedestrian.

"Keep your eyes on the road or we we'll crash," Tina smiled, licking her lips.

She kept stroking her pussy. Exposing her hidden mound so that the driver could see that it was shaved. The driver could hardly keep his eyes on the road and twice almost ran into the back of the same car.

"Oh you're trying to kill me, huh?" Tina asked closing her legs.

"No, no, no, I'm soo sorry. Please, I take you there for free. Please show me that pussy again," he pleadingly apologized.

Tina opened her legs again and the smile returned on the driver's face. Kim stared on in mock bewilderment. Then she high-fived Tina when the driver turned up the music and started singing.

"Beautiful, amore. I love that pussy," he sang, smiling.

He joyfully drove Kim and Tina uptown to their desired destination. Once they arrived, the cabbie not only helped them with their shopping bags, but even smoked a cigarette with them.

"Just one more thing," he said.

"What's that?" Tina asked.

"Can I touch the pussy?"

"Aw hell no!" Tina protested. "Then you gonna wanna feel and poke your fingers inside me."

"No, I promise not to. I will not," he said.

"Okay just one touch," Tina said.

The cabbie reached up under her mini skirt and felt her hairless mound. He smiled broadly when Tina let him rub her hot spot. The same smile occupied his face and his expression remained the same as he waved and drove away.

"You and that man are perverted, bitch," Kim said, shaking her head. "Whatever country he's from he's gonna be writing back telling them how he touched crazy American-girl pussy."

"Shut your face and stop hatin', ho!" Tina said. "Tonight is party night. Let's go try on our new dresses."

"I'm wearing my new jeans," Kim said.

They ran inside the building toting shopping bags filled with new gear. Kim was feeling elated at the prospect of opening a bank account and saving money for her son's education. In the elevator, she reached over and kissed Tina on the lips.

"What's that for, ho?" Tina protested.

"I just wanted to say thank you for what you did. You're such a nice person when you wanna be," Kim smiled.

"Shut da front door. You look like you gonna cry or sump'n, ho."

"I really do feel like crying, bitch. That's a good thing you did, ma. Déjà was the only other person to ever give me a stack like that, you know on the strength..."

"Shut your face. It's all good. You're gonna make me cry too, ho."

"You could cry in front of me. We've been friends for life..."

"And that's what real friends do. If I have money—we have money."

"I hear you. But talk's cheap and when you find someone who about action then that's sump'n else... "

"Okay, already, ho, just shut your face about it and stop bawling now. You making me trickle..." Tina's voice trailed and she dabbed at her eyes.

"That still good looking out, bitch," Kim whispered as they hugged.

They got out of the elevator of Tina's building and hugged, walking in to Tina's two-bedroom apartment.

"A'ight let's get ready to go party like there's no tomorrow!" Tina shouted.

"There's always a tomorrow as long as Roshawn here with me."

"Shut your face, bitch. Roshawn is with you so let's party anyway."

"I gotta put away my ten G's first. Damn! I got that money now." Kim said, jumping around.

Tina in the meantime was already coming out of her clothes. When Kim saw her undressing, she whirled and ran toward her. Kim draped herself all over the half naked Tina, smiling she said, "Come here sexy," Kim growled... "Let me get at you..."

"Shut da front door! Get off me bitch, lemme put on my new Gucci!"

They laughed and chatted then dressed, admiring each other's new outfits until they found the right ones for the evening.

"I couldn't believe all that BS they were kickin'. I just kept thinking, what the fuck, yo? Rightchus of all the fucking people... You mean madukes couldn't come up with anyone else, yo."

The summer breeze rushed in from Jersey Shore. Where Coco and Deedee sat at an outdoor café, sipping frozen strawberry lemonade. Deedee listened attentively while Coco related her experiences with Kim and her mother, Mrs. Jones.

"Wow, that's crazy, Coco. So do you believe this woman you never met before? You said she gossips a lot like her daughter," Deedee said.

"Yeah, except she attends church, and has the biggest wart on her nose," Coco said, sipping her drink.

"Do you remember how you first met Rightchus? I mean like

when?" Deedee asked, chuckling and pulling out a pack of cigarettes.

"I don't even know, yo."

Lighting two, Deedee became serious as she handed a cigarette to Coco. They smoked in eerie silence while Coco's mind traveled back to Rightchus. Coco's reflective tone broke into the sound of the rushing waves.

"He was always coming around me and the girls. I mean I used to see him around the way back in the days all the time. But I ain't really talk to him. Not more than a nod or 'Hi.' Then one day, I was in the park and he was playing basketball—or trying to, cuz he short as hell, yo," Coco laughed.

It was a nervous laugh and Deedee watched as her best friend went silent for a beat. Then Coco took a sip and started talking about her rumored father again.

"I'm telling you, Deedee. I had no idea, yo. He was just this man who wanted to be around us all the time... Rightchus always showed up and helped me out in his own weird way... Like Deja, Kim's baby father. I knew he liked me he was always tryin' a throw signals, making suggestions. One evening, I was bummed out doing laundry and here's Deja trying to get me fucked up on some shit, cuz I know that nigga be puffin' woola..."

"Woola...?" Deedee echoed.

"Weed and coke, yo," Coco said.

"Okay..."

"That was Deja's shit. His girl, used to be my best friend, and she told me all about how he put coke in the weed and they'd get fucked up and get busy. So Deja came 'round and Rightchus appeared outta nowhere to my rescue, yo."

"Damn girl, where you goin' in such a hurry?"

"To do my laundry," Coco answered.

"That's a lotta shit right there," Deja said.

Coco turned around and saw that it was Deja. He had been visiting his son and his son's mother who lived in the building.

"What's up, Deja? What ya doing 'round these parts, yo?" Coco asked.

"Doin' ma thang. Ya know me," Deja said, smiling.

He grabbed the front of the cart and guided the wheels down the steps. Finally they reached the bottom.

"Good looking out, Deja," Coco said, genuinely grateful. "It would've been hell."

"That's a'ight. Wanna burn some weed, Coco?"

Coco thought about the high and was tempted. Then she smirked and gave Deja a disappointing answer.

"I'm a pass, yo," Coco said almost shocking her own self.

"You sure, now?" Deja asked, a little surprised at Coco's answer. She had always smoked with him. "Coco, I'm telling you, this some good shit you turning down."

He held the blunt to her face. Its brown paper wrap was moist from the licking his tongue had given it.

Coco smirked and said, "Nah, I ain't fucking wid that, yo. I got things to do," she said.

But her mind wandered. Why don't I just hit it a couple of times? One or two drags then chill. Just say no. I don't know what's wrapped up in it. It might not even be just chronic. Guided by her judgments, Coco made good on her escape.

"That's never stopped your ass before," Deja yelled as he went up the stairs, leaving out of the building.

That bitch was acting nervous, he reflected. Edgy fucking bitches. One day they on one side of da edge, next they on da other muthafuckin' side.

"That's why the land gave man da herb's blessing," he said aloud.

Once he was out of the building, Deja placed the brown homemade cigar between his lips.

"Peace, God," he said and squeezed a blue-tinted lighter.

The silver tip sparked and Deja inhaled deeply, pulling the flame up to the tip of the blunt. He held the smoke in his lungs, and then exhaled, extinguishing the flame's dance on the cigar tip. Another smoker, Rightchus, moved out of the shadows and came toward Déjà.

"What's up, Rightchus," Deja said.

He clasped Rightchus' hand with his right hand. They bumped shoulders and held each other's hand in a tight-fisted embrace. They released each other's hands, fists clashing.

"Good to see ya, Rightchus," Deja laughed. He choked on the smoke of the weed. "So whazzup? Want some?"

He passed the blunt to Rightchus. He had never been known to turn down weed or anything else he could smoke. They smoked and talked.

"Wow, man, this shit got some power to it," Rightchus announced. "You know about the cosmic," he continued.

"Cos-what?" Deja asked.

"Rightchus later saw me, and told me the cigar Deja was smoking was filled with coke, yo. From then on, I've been like, don't pass me nothing already rolled."

"Rightchus was there at random moments helping you out, Coco. Maybe—"

"Maybe nothing. I gotta hear it from my mother's own mouth before I believe, yo. I can't wait to see her tomorrow and ask her. I wanna hear what she have to say, yo."

"I'm sure you do, Coco. I remember him *so* well. But I had no idea that he was..."

Deedee let her voice trail. She and Coco stared at each other thinking the implausible. Then Deedee recounted the first time meeting Rightchus.

"I think I was chilling with you and the girls..." she started to say, but paused as if in deep thoughts.

"I don't know. But what I know is whenever sump'n was about to jump off, Rightchus was always around, yo. Like that evening when Danielle was acting all crazy like she run things. He was there."

"I don't remember," Deedee said.

"She felt that I had too much lead time singing and all that. So she sort of made the rehearsal into a challenge. I remember we were at school—me, Danielle, her boyfriend and Jo... Back in the days we used to rehearse in the auditorium."

The group headed for the school auditorium. This was not going to be an ordinary rehearsal. A showdown had been shaping up ever since Danielle had confronted the girls. Threatened or not, Coco had been put on her guard. Josephine played peacemaker. She was happy that the rehearsal would be recorded and critiqued. Da Crew knew they were ready. They exchanged wary smiles, except for Coco.

On stage, Danielle moved enticingly. The camera rolled. Coco moved back and forth, heels and toes tapping street sounds to the beat. Josephine circled, moving faster and faster, as if on ice. They balanced one another.

It was like the first day, when they met at the audition for the video shoot. All three danced with different groups and each girl was chosen from these groups. It had been that easy for them. They had competed for the dance video, and when Coco learned that the other two girls were recent transfers at her school, they started hanging out. The girls became a trio. But now, a little competition didn't hurt.

The dance movements were complex, but the girls made them look easy. Coco, at the lead, performed a combination of hip-hop jazz steps, moving out against the girls. A simple tap and a few rolls to the floor brought Danielle's kicks to the changes in the beat. It was high-tempo. The girls were getting warm. The pace was furious. Coco slid to floor in the background on two knees.

Then it was Danielle's turn. She seductively jumped and pranced for the camera and the man. She ended on beat with a split, a la James Brown. The place was wildly funky. Josephine perpetuated the beat by skipping, taking flight and, vaulting over Danielle's cat-like, crouched figure. Josephine bounded with acrobatic skill and landed in a graceful ballerina's pose. She rolled up into hip-hop contortions. Coco prowled and leaped, flipping her body into the middle of the hoopla. The three danced easily together, moving in time to rehearsed steps. Cory recorded it all, and the camera intensified the mood.

It was Coco's turn again, or was it? She relinquished the lead. Josephine moved to the forefront with a split and quickly put down the break moves. She slid easily into a snail's crawl, freezing herself en vogue. Coco came through like a butterfly, landing softly on petals, wings beating a seductive rhythm. For one moment, time froze as the camera caught Coco in flight. Her gestures, her steps, said she was a dancer. When she was sure that they had enough, she quickly tumbled and rolled up on her stomach. She showed complete mastery of her muscles and limbs. It shook the other girls. The cameraman turned his head and held the camera in place. He watched Coco dance an unbelievable groove to up-tempo sounds. Josephine refused to follow.

"Yo, hold up, hold up. I think we've all flexed enough. Let's not lose focus, alright? The winner is Coco," Josephine shouted and clapped sarcastically. "Let's take a break."

Cory stopped filming and applauded. The girls had danced for nearly an hour and their clothes were soaked in sweat.

"That was no rehearsal. That shit was for-real dance warfare," Josephine said between sips of water. Coco turned and looked at her. She lit a cigarette without answering. Danielle walked over to her boyfriend Cory, a few feet away. They huddled for a minute.

"I'm saying you were the best out there, baby. But Coco is bad."

"What do you mean?" Danielle asked. It was clear that she was annoyed. "Did you get it all?"

"Think so," Cory said.

"We're gonna do voices next, and that'll be it. So take five." She kissed him on the cheek, twitched her hips, and rejoined Coco and Josephine.

"Did he get us?" Josephine asked. Her emphasis on "he" made Coco look up from her smoke break.

"Yep he did," Danielle answered. "Okay, instead of singing one or two numbers as a group, how about each of us solo on a song of our own choice?"

Coco and Josephine looked at each other in mock horror, then they all laughed and high-fived.

"Oh, the contest is still on?" Josephine asked.

"Who says it's a contest?" Danielle retorted.

"A'ight, stop bitching at each other. Let's do it, yo," Coco said as she put out her cigarette.

"Josephine, you'll be first up. Or, do you want me to go?" Danielle asked.

She was eager to show her vocal range. She had taken voice lessons with a trainer and she claimed the trainer had coached a couple of famous singers. She felt that put her in another class.

The equipment and the cameraman were ready. Danielle took the *microphone and belted out "Neither One of Us," Gladys Knight–style. Even without the Pips help, Danielle did an excellent job. She received applause from a new member of the audience.*

"Don't worry. I'm not the heat. I'm just gonna sit here and check y'all nice, talented people out," the man shouted while still clapping.

Josephine was next. She chose a difficult number by Whitney Houston. Her enthusiasm kept her going and when she was done, it was Coco's turn. Sitting at the edge of the auditorium stage, Coco lit another cigarette. My turn came quickly, she thought, inhaling. Well, I could try 'Diana the Boss'. But there were no Supremes.

Coco dragged on the cigarette, and the microphone amplified its hiss. She held the cigarette and microphone in her right hand. With her left hand, she removed her sweat-laden baseball cap, and tousled her hair. She was searching her mind for something. Then she found it. It was her mother's favorite. Coco raised the microphone and the cigarette, and sang Billie Holiday's, 'My Man'.

The newcomer was clapping from the beginning of the first stanza. He shouted, "Yeah!" Each time Coco paused. She held the other girls captive with her nonchalance. She was good. They thought of Diana and the Supremes, but when the Supremes sat down, Coco became Ms. Holiday. Then it was over. The newcomer raced down the aisle to the front of the stage. He got down on his knees, begging Coco to continue.

"Do some more for me. I'm Rightchus your new number-one fan," he shouted. Coco beamed and jumped off the stage.

"Y'all are some talented people," Rightchus said. "I watched and listened to you, and you," he said, pointing to each of the girls in turn. Then, he turned to Cory. "And you look like you have talent too, being the bodyguard and the cameraman." Rightchus laughed, amused by his own joke.

"Thanks," the girls said.

They walked toward the exit. Cory joined them, and so did Rightchus.

"You did that song, girl," Josephine said. "I didn't know you feelin' Billie Holiday like that?"

"She's maduke's favorite," Coco said.

She was visibly overcome by the admission. Danielle locked the door as they left and ran off to return the key to the maintenance staff. She had chosen that role ever since the girls got permission to use the small auditorium when it was idle.

"So, we'll be seeing you, yo," Coco said to Rightchus.

"Oh, yo. If I didn't say it, forgive me. My name is Rightchus. When I do my thing, folks call me da Shorty-Wop-It Man. Hey, y'all can call me Shorty-Wop, cuz I seen y'all's performance, n' y'all are there. Bad! Nah mean?"

He raised his arms, barely four feet, ten inches tall. Coco, five ten in her boots, towered over him. He was decked out in an inside-out Free Mike Tyson T-shirt, rolled-up blue jeans, and sandals.

"Yeah, I could sing, too. I could do my thing. Can I get a cigarette?" Rightchus asked.

They gathered around the car. The girls relaxed, as all the pre-rehearsal tension was gone. Coco gave Rightchus a cigarette and a light. Josephine and Danielle shared a joint.

"Anyone want a Bud?" Rightchus asked. He produced a brown-paper sack.

"But y'all probably don't want this light stuff. Y'all probably want da gasoline stuff, da crooked-eye stuff." He winked.

A big smile appeared on Rightchus's face. Cory moved closer and took two cans from the package. He gave Danielle a can. Rightchus moved over to Coco, offering her a can. She hesitated then took one. He looked at Josephine, and she looked at Danielle.

"I'm not sharing, yo. Take a beer," Coco said as she sipped on the now-open can.

"Yeah, I can tell you're good peoples. See, I know. When you've spent your whole day talking to people who are constantly trying to beat you outta shit, then you know good peoples," Rightchus said. The group nodded and guzzled their beers.

"You from around here?" Josephine asked.

"What do you care?" Coco asked.

"Nah, nah," Rightchus answered. "This guy I met at a job interview told me whenever I was in da hood, jus' stop by. He's large in da hood. I stopped by and da muthafucka had nothing," he grinned and Cory laughed, encouraging Rightchus. "He was begging me. I had to give him a dollar bill," continued Rightchus. "Is she your girl?" Rightchus asked, pointing at Josephine, and speaking to Cory.

"No," Cory said. He pointed to Danielle. "She's my girl."

"No disrespect. I know you love her, but I'm telling you, don't get married. When you marry, you stop growing. Two people can't grow together. One has to stop growing and let the other, or they will wind up butting heads. I'm telling you."

"People make it," Josephine said. "I mean there are a lot of successful married people out there."

"Yeah," Rightchus agreed. "But they have the minds of eight-year-olds. They'll be forty years old, acting like eight-year-olds. They've got the minds of children."

The group of teens broke out laughing. Clearly taken in by the stranger, Cory clapped his hands and pumped his fist. Rightchus was harmless.

"See, I knew y'all were nice people. So far, nobody tried to beat me outta shit. That's what it's all about. You have to enjoy life. Like me, I got crazy, Bobby-Brown style. Whenever y'all ready. My name's Rightchus, but you can call me Shorty-Wop. An' when I do ma thing, I'll be blowing up da spot. Peace. Y'all take care. I've got to be out before da police escorts me into da cell. Y'all know how they love to fuck wid da black man cuz he's da true an' living god."

Rightchus hobbled down the street, tugging at the brim of his cap. He vanished as quickly as he had appeared, leaving the group with *beer on their lips and smiles on their faces.*

"I'm out, yo," Coco said.

"We'll give you a lift. Let's do something, hang out for a minute," Danielle said.

"I'm down," Josephine said.

"A'ight, yo. Sounds good to me too," Coco said.

She was feeling the beer. Coco and Josephine got in the backseat. Cory and Danielle sat up front. As Cory started the car, he looked back. Coco gazed out the window, and Josephine smiled at him, approvingly.

"Where to?" Cory asked.

"Downtown," Josephine suggested.

Soon they were on the way. They passed Déjà on Tenth Ave., hustling drugs, and whatever else came his way.

"Down for some smokes?" Danielle asked.

"Sure. Here's two dollars," Josephine said, "And a dollar from y'all."

"Hold this, yo," Coco said, giving Danielle a dollar.

"Get it from Déjà, yo. His shit is always best," Coco whispered.

"He would just always show up on some random visits, yo."

"Josephine and Danielle knew him too, huh?"

"Yes they did. He always tried to come see us perform and all, yo."

"He was like the number-one fan of Da Crew, huh? He knew your mom too?"

"I guess. I mean, I heard things about him and my mother before, but it was just crack-head talk. You know they all stick together tight in the building, yo. Although, I did have to step to him once for showing his ass, yo."

"Word...? Tell me about it," Deedee said.

"It was just me being over-protective of Madukes cuz I know he was cracking, so I just tried to keep my mother away from him and vice versa. And one night he just was ringing my doorbell. I mean I broke on his ass..."

"Who da fuck is ringing my damn doorbell? Let a nigga get some rest." Coco saw Rightchus emerging from the shadows. "Rightchus what da fuck is so important?"

"Why don't you ask your mother? She's da one paging me 9-1-1."

"She's asleep alright. So get da fuck on, muthafucka!" Coco slammed the window. She stared at her mother grumbling something inaudible. Coco brought a blanket and placed it over her mother's outstretched figure. She fell asleep on the new sofa listening to her mother's relentless heavy snoring.

"I remember seeing you almost punch his lights out once, remember, Coco?"

"Oh yes, I do—on the block and you had just drop me off or sump'n."

"I think you were going to visit someone in the hospital—"

"Yes, I was gonna visit Ms. Katie, God bless her soul. You pulled up and Rightchus came around to go upstairs and I wanted him to stay away from my mother, yo."

"I remembered that all of sudden you just took off after him..."

Coco was about to get inside the car then abruptly changed her direction and quickly walked to the other side of the street. Deedee's eyes curiously followed Coco who was talking with Rightchus. Deedee let the window down in order to hear the conversation.

"Don't be selling her that shit. You hear me bum-ass nigga, don't be seeing her. Or I'm a come see you and fuck your shit up..."

"Cuz you see me in da street doin' ma thing, don't mean you know me, a'ight, Coco?"

"Rightchus, I'm telling you. You ain't shit but a crack-head."

"And I'm tellin' you just cuz you see shit this way don't necessarily mean they that way. I'm tellin' you if your mother wasn't a crack-head you wouldn't be calling me one. I remember when your mother used to wake up crack-head crabby, looking for me. She was so skinny you could see her brain stems coming out da back of her head."

"Just remember nigga, I will come looking for your lil' ol' ugly ass..."

"Yo, I do you a favor—I'll tell you where them bitches, Kim and her girl Tina, hang out. Them is who you got beef wit' Coco, not me. I ain't busting no gun at you."

Coco shook her head and walked back to the car.

"Is everything alright, Coco?" Deedee asked.

"Yeah, yeah, it's all good. I just had to straighten out some shit wit that Shorty-Wop. Can I get a ride over to the hospital, yo?"

"I should've knocked his lil' ass out that day. Ooh, he pissed me off!"

"He was like you said, a crack-head. And I mean, I don't even know if you can let someone like that piss you off. I thought he was just funny and a know-it-all. I remember when he showed up to warn us about Lil' Long. I hope that nigga rot in hell... Oh Rightchus was really high that night," Deedee said.

"Yeah, I remember..."

It was seven in the evening. The girls heard ranting from behind them. They turned and saw Rightchus approaching the door of the parked Range. The bodyguards stepped to the front. Rightchus pulled out a long knife.

"Coco, Deedee. My, my, what are you two beautiful beings doing here? Who's that? Don't tell me, Josephine, what's goin' on y'all? I ain't seen you in a minute."

"Hi," Josephine said.

"Sorry to burst your bubble, but we gotta go, Mr. Rightchus," Deedee said.

"I gotta get da fuck up, yo?" Coco exclaimed.

"Everyone is in a hurry. I'm in a hurry, too. If I didn't have the Maruichi brothers coming after me, I'd be cool. I didn't know the shit wasn't real. It ain't my damn fault. It's them cheap-ass drug dealers dancing up an' down on da product."

"Yo, what da fuck you yapping' bout nigga? We ain't got time to

yap about no coke, Wop. I gotta be gone like yesterday."

"Yeah, I feel you," Rightchus said putting away the chopper. "I mean, shoot, we need to conversate on lots of subjects. I'm a person with all kinds of knowledge. Great minds think alike—feel me, Coco? But I'm saying, what is da real science, girl?"

"Rightchus don't start with that bullshit..."

"A'ight, a'ight, I hear you, I hear you, girl. Well, in reference to that, I wanna say, I don't wanna start fucking with y'all young girls anyways, cuz I always gets fucked around, see? I'm not having my shit screwed up on y'all's account. Every time I get around y'all young chickens, shit happens. Bullets start flying, people dropping. I don't get down like that. Speaking of dropping, I've seen the walking dead..."

"You and everybody else living in these parts, yo," Coco said, interrupting Rightchus.

"Then you know what I'm dealing with, Coco?"

"'The Walking Dead'—isn't that a scary movie?" Deedee asked, cutting off Rightchus's explanation.

"I could tell y'all ain't serious. Peeps all the time wanna run up on a nigga, ya know. Reason why I'm here is cuz me an some fuckin' peeps at war, ya know. Can't go home an' all. But I'm build me a MTV crib with bullet-proof everything, all in time, still..." Rightchus said.

"All right Mr. Rightchus we gotta be moving on..." The bodyguard pushed Rightchus as he spoke.

"Nah, don't do that. A muthafucka can't be takin' aim over here. I can see y'all just right. What y'all should be more interested in is the muthafucka I be seein'. Saw him. Yesterday... last night...Hmm, things get fuzzy. Old age."

"Negative. Too much drugs, Wop. Your brain is fried. Gone out to lunch, yo."

"Coco, you can keep spitting all that BS. But I'm telling you girl, you need to put me down. Me da Shorty-Wop, cuz I've seen him. I've seen da nigga," Rightchus said.

"Seen who, yo?" Coco asked. She threw her hands in the air, perplexed.

"I've seen him," repeated Rightchus. He took a couple steps back and noticed the security team moving in front of the girls.

Coco and Deedee stood close to the security team, Josephine stood next to the Range. Rightchus was in his flow. "I'm saying, I've seen him. I've seen that nigga, Lil' Long."

Silence descended like an eagle, swallowing the atmosphere and leaving each girl with cold feet. There was a power to ruthlessness on the street. It was visible when the mention of a name conjured fear. The girls slowly acknowledged Rightchus's urgency. The mention of Lil' Long's name was a reminder of a brutal period in the girls' experiences. He had preyed on many victims and was responsible for the deaths of Coco's friends. He and his friend Vulcha had savagely raped and assaulted Deedee.

"I thought he was dead. Wasn't he killed at Deedee's uncle's place? I was there. And he was spitting up lead and all that, yo,"

"Yeah, I know, I know. I thought he was dead," Deedee said.

"Yeah, you and everybody else, right? But un'nerstan', I'm sayin' I seen da nigga. He doubled up like he got a hunchback or sump'n. I'm sayin' I seen him—I seen da muthafucka. You know? He be wearing dark shades covering his eyes, limpin'. I'm tellin' da truth. Coco, he knows, he knows. He limped away and broke out as soon as I was getting ready to step to him. Feel me? I'm Rightchus Allah. I'm da mu'fuckin' Shorty-Wopper. And y'all know that wopping ain't even easy. Peeps be acting cheesy, and all. But you know what?"

"What?" Coco and Deedee asked simultaneously.

"When I hit you, I hit you with da raw truths. No lies or tales follow my word, cuz my word is bond."

"Rightchus, Rightchus, listen. We're not sweating Lil' Long. We gotta be out, so hear me out. If Lil' Long wanna jump, he'll catch the worst beat-down of his life. And it's for ignorant people like him that we've got bodyguards. Know what I mean, yo?" Coco said.

"Matter o' fact, word on da streets is that his man Nesto is getting out of Elmira soon. And Coco, you know; that's Lil' Long's man. Let me get down with y'all. I'll supervise them big boys for you. I'll keep it on the down low. Them dumb bodyguards ain't got a thing on da Shorty-Wop. I'll wop a mu'fucka so fast his family be hurting," Rightchus said, shuffling his feet as if he was shadow-boxing.

"Rightchus, please stop. Just stop it, alright. Chill before something really does go down, yo," Coco said.

"Please, before you hurt yourself," Deedee added.

A gunshot fired close by and Rightchus took off running down the street. The bodyguards checked to make sure all was okay.

"We're all good? What happened to Shorty?" One of the bodyguards asked.

"I don't know, yo. Homey said he had beef with Maruichi peoples. I don't know, yo," Coco said.

"He was a nutcase, but some things he said were so on point. I mean when that incident went down, hmm... You're right—he was just there."

"Like the time he told me 'bout Lil' Long and Vulcha, yo."

"Oh, please don't mention them," Deedee said.

"He was the first one to bring that to my attention and I still had trouble believing what he was saying, yo."

"Why...?"

"Cuz he smoked mad crills. He was a full-time crack-head, yo. I had just come from visiting madukes, who was at the rehab program, and I saw him."

Outside, Coco eased into her bop as she made her way down the darkened streets. Danielle stayed on her mind, her death recorded in snapshots. Coco searched for answers. Coco halted as she recognized Rightchus.

"Whuddup?" Coco asked. The greeting came like a demand, but she couldn't take it back. "You following me around or what?"

"Nah, it's nothing like that," Rightchus said.

"Then what?"

"Chill, Coco, I ain't trying to put a rush on you or nothing. I'm just chilling. You know wha' I'm saying?"

"Yeah, yeah. Sure it's a free country. You weren't trying to rush me, huh, yo?"

"Nah, Coco, that ain't my style. Coco, I'm saying, I saw you, and so I'm stepping to you like a brother to a sister. You know wha' I'm saying?"

"A brother, huh? A brother? Then brother, you better start cleaning up your shit. You feel me?"

"I'm a righteous black man," Rightchus yelled, placing the palm of his right hand on his chest.

"Save it, yo. I ain't got time for da BS," Coco said, extending her arm and using her palm to block Rightchus's mug.

"Why you wanna play me like that?"

"Because you're a crack-head. Isn't that reason enough, yo?" Coco asked as she made a move to leave. "I ain't got time for front'n-ass niggas like you. I'm bouncing."

"Coco, before you step, I got sump'n to say. Hear me out," Rightchus pleaded.

Coco hesitated. She saw the plea in Rigtchus' eyes and she waited.

"A'ight yo, kick da shit. Then step da fuck off."

"A'ight, remember da shooting a week or so ago?"

"What shooting? Everyday people getting popped, yo."

"Yeah, but I'm saying da shooting wid Déjà and da honey from your building."

"You mean Bebop?"

"Honey wuz in da wrong place at da wrong time. See, 'em mu'fuckas were out to smoke Déjà."

"Whoa! Hold up. Who's them muthafuckas, yo?"

"Cool, I'm a tell ya soon enough. Someone put out a contract for a hit on Deja. Some shit that he raped a girl an' jacked her ride and shit. You wuz supposed to be involved and all."

"Wait up, yo. Deja was killed because he raped a girl?"

"Yeah, her uncle is, um, what's his name, uh..."

"You talkin' 'bout Eric Ascot, yo?"

"Word, that's da one."

"Wait up. You ain't nothing but a crack-head. Why da fuck should I believe your ass, huh?"

For a minute Coco thought he could be right. Maybe Deja's killing was a hit. Coco stared at Rightchus and thought about what he had told her.

"I'm saying, if you don't believe me, check da stats. Check da stats, baby. Someone set up Déjà to be killed. You and I know he ain't rape the girl. Them wuz two niggas sent by the devil."

"The Devil? You bugging out or what?"

"I'm saying."

"I'm saying you da crack-head. Why you wanna stress?"

"Stress? Coco, da muthafucka killed my man, my nigga, my ace boom."

"Yeah, yeah, and all that. So what? What did you do? Smoke some crack, yo?"

"I'm saying, them niggas... Them's da one responsible for your friend's death. And you know they hit that Spanish girl and da big dude she was wid. Them's Lil' Long and Vulcha. Coco, it's gonna take a nation to hold them muthafuckas back."

"You're saying that Lil' Long wid da 'fro, and that guy wid da trunk-of-funk Navigator, always partying, they been shooting up da town like that, yo? Why don't you go to the cops, then?"

"C'mon! And sell da brothers out like that? Be real, Coco. I'd rather see shit stay da same. Gotta stay real, you feel me?"

"So why you choose to stop me and try to feed all this bullshit to my ass, huh?"

"Yo, Coco, listen up. I ain't trying a run a game on you or nothing, but them niggas get picked up by the cops and come back wid bags of muthafucking dough. I'm talking G's and triple G's. Now, is them niggas working for da police, or what? I'm serious!" Rightchus yelled. Coco doubled over in laughter.

"You're saying—ha, ha, ha—Lil' Long and Vulcha, them false hoods, they working for da police? How deep is their cover?" Coco howled.

Rightchus stared, amazed at Coco's reaction. She seemed to choke with laughter.

"I know you think I'm only a crack-head, but I'm a street person who has knowledge of what's going down an' so on. When you check da stats you'll see. Boom! Rightchus was right. You gonna say, 'Yo,' Coco, 'boom.' Can I get five dollars? Yo, help a brother out. You a top celebrity an' all that."

"Muthafucka, now you clocking my papers, too? How you living? Here's a buck to start the scramble."

Coco handed Rightchus a dollar bill. He clasped it in both hands. Rightchus was gone as quickly as he had come. Coco continued her walk home. When she reached the building, Coco stopped and opened the door to her mother's place. She paused and turned on the lights. One bedroom reeked with a putrid scent. She went to the window and gazed out. Coco saw the street people, once more, scrambling around like rats.

She wondered if any of them bothered to clean their apartments, *or if they even had places to live. She cleaned the dirty kitchen first, and finished in the livingroom in the wee hours of the morning. Exhausted, Coco took a shower and passed out in front of the television.*

"That's soo crazy. He knew so many things that other peeps didn't even know about, yo."

"You're right Coco. Like he was he was random and all, but he knew everything that was going on. I remember so well now. You came over, and we were in the studio, and then you told us about what Rightchus said. Oh my God. I was like how did he know that? You remember right, Coco?"

"Remember that day, you were giving me a tour of your uncle home studio and we started talking about weed..." Coco said and her voice trailed.

"Yes, I surely do. We were smoking weed, and checking out the recording equipment for the first time and then you started telling me what Rightchus had told you."

"True, you brought the Harvey's and I had that blunt, yo...I was fucked up! And your ass kept me drinking."

"I remember that was my way of getting you to talk, Coco. I kept telling you to drink more," Deedee laughed.

"C'mon, Coco, you can't front. You know you could handle this,"

Deedee said, passing the blunt to Coco.

Coco was trying to stop, but yielded to temptation as Deedee had hoped. When the weed and liquor kicked in Coco would be more talkative. She would lose control.

"I know certain things that I'm checking before I even act on. You know that Rightchus?"

"Ah," Deedee struggled to link a face with the name. "Rightchus?" she repeated.

"Yeah, yeah. Rightchus, that real black, short con man who be hanging out by da clubs. He be out by da school late in da evenings. Always begging for money and cigarettes, yo."

Deedee's jaunt through her memory bank, cloudy from weed smoke and alcohol, yielded nothing but confusion.

"The name sounds familiar, I mean but I can't place the face..."

"He was at da club da night that shit went down, yo. That nigga pointing his fingers at Lil' Long and Vulcha."

"Word...? You don't say?" Deedee queried.

"Word up. He be knowing some shit, yo."

"Them niggas," muttered Deedee under her breath. "Coco," Deedee spoke in a louder tone. "You're saying that, that this guy, ah, Rightchus is saying they—Lil' Long and Vulcha—raped me?"

Deedee rose from the soft chair where she'd been sitting. Coco glanced around at the mass of recording equipment. Then she heard fury coming through in Deedee's voice.

"Them muthafuckas!" she yelled. "They deserve to fucking die."

"If they are really da ones, yo. They asses should be dead. Over, yo."

"But, but let me get it right. I think I'm sure. I mean, you're saying Rightchus is front'n?" Deedee paced from one side of the room to the other.

"I'm not sure, cuz Rightchus, he be cracking. He always front'n like he's got knowledge of self, but he smokes da rock. That shit just don't make sense. I just don't know..."

"Is there anyone else? Someone whose word is really bond? Then again, maybe it should just die, go away," Deedee said.

"You and I know it will never leave, yo. It's like luggage you have to carry forever to the grave," Coco said, turning and looking at Deedee. She temporarily halted her nervous walk. Then Coco's words proved to be the catalyst of dreaded thoughts. Deedee began her slow gait.

"We should go to the cops."

"Da tin badges? Are you for real?"

"I mean they'd investigate. I mean..."

"Da cops never look out for people like us, yo," Coco said. She rubbed her soft brown cheek. "Plus, if Rightchus is telling da truth, then them niggas must be well connected."

"Why so?"

"Cause every time they get picked up by da police, they be coming right back looking paid. Word, that's what Rightchus said, yo."

"They get paid by the cops?"

"I'm saying I'm not da one making da shit up. Don't be looking at me like I'm crazy. I'm just repeating sump'n I heard from a fucking crack-head. I mean, da shit might not mean nothing."

"So, how are we gonna find out if it's the truth or not?"

"I'm gonna approach them niggas, yo. I'm gonna be like, what. I don't give a fuck. Them niggas killed ma girl Bebop when they shot up Déjà's place, and they responsible for Danielle's death. You know wha' I'm saying, Deedee? Them niggas are the ones who raped you. Da cops don't give a fuck. We got to take matters in our own hands. I'm saying, we got to take care of our business!"

"How are we gonna do this, Coco?"

"I really don't know."

"Listen, Coco, my uncle has guns hidden. He doesn't know that I know where they are."

"What kinda guns?"

"Forty-fives, Nines."

"We could do some damage. Forty-fives, yo?"

"I got *soo* tore up that night, I started talking reckless about running up and killing niggas and all that BS, yo."

"We did try to murder that Lil' Long. Remember Kamilla running around with Rightchus?"

"That's right—that's how she knew where we had gone. Damn how did he know, yo?"

"He must have some good connection. He's the ghetto Internet."

"Rightchus was trying to save me from trouble, yo. But at the end o' the day he was pretty much just a crack-head and he couldn't be trusted. I had seen him on the Ave, getting his payoff from Lil' Long, and he ain't seen me. I crept on him and smacked all that shit out of his hand so fast, his head was spinning."

"He must've been mad. What did he do, Coco?"

"Not a damn thing. He tried to con me, but I had seen him and Lil' Long. And he didn't know. I mean I seen the whole shit, yo."

Lil' Long reached into his pockets and pulled out about a dozen tiny redcap vials filled with cheap, yellow-stained, cocaine rocks. He poured them in Rightchus' out-stretched hands.

"Now, you remember who really feeds you, muthafucka. Go on and enjoy. It's on da house," Lil' Long said with a deadly smile.

Horns blared as Vulcha pulled the SUV abruptly into the traffic. They departed, leaving Rightchus standing on the corner. Coco ran over and slapped Rightchus' hands. The vials of crack littered the pavement.

"Bitch!" Rightchus yelled. "What da fuck you think you're doing,

girl?"

"Saving your muthafuckin', no good-ass life. Your ass best tell me da truth about this whole shit or you ain't smoking none of these goddamn rocks, yo."

Coco scrambled on the sidewalk, picking up as many of the small vials as she could. Rightchus couldn't keep up with her and soon she had collected most of the vials.

"Aw c'mon, Coco. What truth? What da fuck you talkin' 'bout?"

"You know what da fuck I'm talkin' 'bout, nigga. Hello, da real fucking truth. You better start yakking away or everyone in da 'hood will know you is nothing but a fucking crack-head."

"I don't give a fuck 'bout no muthafuckas from da 'hood knowin' who I am. Everybody got a nasty habit. Mine's crack. So what? What's yours? Drinking, smoking dust? Cuz that's why your Spanish friend died. Too much fucking dust and coke. So don't step to Rightchus wid that bullshit."

"Bullshit! You fucking crack-head."

"Your mother is a crack-head! Look Coco, you best keep your ass out of this and stay in school, a'ight. I'm telling you, if you keep following this shit up, yo' ass will be ended. Can't say I ain't warned your ass."

"Well, you give it to me straight and I'll let you have your rocks back. And I'll handle my fucking bidness, a'ight?"

"Can't you handle bidness without my fucking involvement?"

"No, yo."

"Why?"

"Cuz you started this whole shit. So now you've got to come straight, muthafucka."

"You seen their guns?"

"I ain't scared of no guns. I have guns, too, yo."

"Guns? Guns? Listen up. You gonna need more than just guns to do battle wid them niggas. Drug dealers and cops. Fucking po-po be scared, and you wanna do battle? Coco, you stick to singing and doing your thing on the dance tip. Get your swerve that way. Let da big boys handle that type shit."

"Nigga please stop pissing me off!"

"Coco, I told you 'bout da time I auditioned for Eric Ascot. He loves ma shit, ma shit. He love da way I put it down. See, I was standing there. He comes along in a limo, pulls up, and start checking me doing my thing. At the end, he was like, 'Oh shit, we need you in a da studio right away.' He told me I was all this an' that an' he would love to work wid my ass soon. Soon as ya'll shit drops, he gonna work wid ma shit. Ma shit be out there on your radio, in stere-ereo. Off the hook, baby... That's da way I be doin' my thing ya heard..." Rightchus sang, stomping his feet in rhythm.

Coco gazed at Rightchus with eyes already reddened from staying up too late. They glowed more crimson red with anger at Rightchus' comedic babblings. Under the wrath of Coco's stare, the stirring of Shorty-Wop, a.k.a. Rightchus, ceased. She opened her fists, exposing small red and white-topped vials with yellow rocks inside. He read her intentions and opened his lips to plead.

"No, Coco. No, Coco, don't."

"Nigga, please," Coco said.

She hurled the vials at Rightchus. He failed miserably to catch all the vials. Most of them scattered in the street. Rightchus scrambled to retrieve them.

"Bitch, you best stay outta that shit. Leave peoples bidness alone or you gonna get toe-tagged."

"Fuck you! You crack-head low-life bastard!"

Coco entered the park, ready to walk home. She turned back to see Rightchus being joined by a congregation of emaciated people in dirty clothes. They prepared to sacrifice their lives in worship of the contents of the vials.

"Crack-heads," Coco whispered. Her bop came off a little shaky.

"Stay out of it, Coco! You ain't much. Just a regular girl," Rightchus said.

Then he turned and addressed his crowd. "Y'all muthafuckas come *on and collect your poison. But it ain't free though, it's gonna cost three."*

Business was brisk. Rightchus now concentrated on his growing flock.

"I don't know why I was so mad at that lil' ass nigga, yo."

"I mean you had reasons. But he saved us a lot and he was always around you. I don't know, Coco. Maybe he's really your father or—""

"Please, Deedee! Bite your tongue. Slow your roll! I really hope not. But remember his ass was outside with the po-po at the shooting. How did he get out there?"

"Probably with Kamilla..."

"Word, she did come in a cab..."

"All I remember hearing was the fussing she was doing when she walked into the place," Deedee said.

"Work on getting yourself a shower, my brother," Kamilla said over her shoulder.

"Why you wanna diss a brother? See, it's women like you that'll cause a brother to commit murder. Bitch wit' a problem!"

Kamilla didn't hear or see any of Rightchus' gestures. She was in the diner, where she spotted Coco and Deedee.

"Hi, I'm Kamilla. May I join y'all?" Kamilla asked. "We have to go see Eric Ascot."

"That's my uncle. What is it about?" Deedee asked. She was startled and impatient. Coco stared at the intruder.

"I overheard Vulcha this morning. He was on the phone. Something about being set up and paying back the person who did it. He mentioned Busta and the music producer, Eric. I will not let them kill anybody else," Kamilla said.

"Why? You were there when they did Danielle, yo."

"When I last saw Danielle, she was alive. Vulcha said that Lil' Long gave her a suicide knob to slob."

"Bullshit. Them muthafuckas killed her. As far as I know, y'all were together, yo!" Coco said. Her shrill voice attracted the attention of the other patrons.

"Why are y'all staring like that?" Deedee asked. "Let's go. My uncle should be home. They acting like they ain't never seen people have a discussion before," Deedee said as they headed for the exit.

"Ladies, ladies, you haven't paid," a disturbed waiter called.

"We raced out of that restaurant without paying, remember?" Deedee asked, sipping her drink.

"I think Kamilla paid, yo. I mean I was right behind you, but when I looked back, she was arguing with the waiter."

"She paid with her life too," Deedee said.

"Rightchus was out there spittin' shit, yo."

"He was trying to help us..."

"Really, it seemed that way, right, yo?"

"It sure seems that way, Coco."

"How much? Will this cover it?" Kamilla slipped the waiter couple of twenty-dollar bills.

"Yes. Wait, I'll get you your change."

The trio caught a taxi and the car sped away. Rightchus ran toward it. He banged on the door.

"Stay out of it. It's bigger than y'all," he shouted. "Y'all not listening. All right then, fuck it. Y'all handle your BI, and I'll handle mine."

"But he's such a fucking con-artist, who's gonna believe his ass, yo?"

"In the end, he was right. We should've stayed out of it, and called the police and let them handle it," Deedee said, reflecting.

An unmarked police car pulled up and two officers jumped out. They immediately cautioned Rightchus who was following them into the building.

"You better stay here and not move," one of the officers said.

"I ain't going nowhere. Think I'm stupid wit' all 'em guns going off?"

The officers ran to the mansion then one of them returned to the car. He keyed the radio and spoke.

"Confirmed shooting of Michael Lowe, a.k.a. Lil' Long and killing of a young woman, first name Kamilla last name unknown at this time... Two girls with him and young woman. We have someone by the name of

Rightchus, claims he knows both girls. He tipped us off that they would be coming here. Over."

"Rightchus. Ah, he's a good informant. Take care of him. He has given us some very useful tips. We may still be able to use his services."

Rightchus gazed intensely at the police radio. Now he understood his role.

"He was just trying to help, I guess, but he was there."

"That nigga was there when the shooting went down. He was standing out outside with the police."

"Deedee you're so fucking right, yo!"

"I know you want to..." Deedee's voice trailed.

She paused and stirred her strawberry lemonade and looked at it like a work of art. Coco was watching her and waiting.

"I want to what, Dee?" Coco asked impatiently.

"Call him...?" Deedee said. "I mean I still have his number in my cell phone."

"I wanna ask my mother first. That nigga could wait until I talk to madukes, yo."

"Okay, if you say so," Deedee said with a knowing smile.

"The last time I saw that nigga is the last time I will be seeing that nigga, yo. Cuz that shit didn't go down too nicely."

"Oh really? What happened?"

"I was with Jo, God bless her soul, and I went upstairs and heard all this commotion. I wasn't ready for all that...I got to my door opened it and it was just off the hook crazy, yo. Everybody from the hood was there!"

"Surprise!"

A crowd of people had been waiting to greet Coco inside her apartment. The space became even tinier. Her neighbors packed the walls. Some were still emerging from behind closet doors and other hiding places. Coco smiled as she received hugs and kisses.

"You've got four letters from these colleges. Harvard wants you to come and visit, they offered you an academic scholarship," Rachel Harvey announced.

"Ma, you been snooping in my mail..."

"They right over there next to your cake and the postcards," Rachel Harvey pointed Coco toward the kitchen.

She rifled through letters from Harvard, Howard, Penn State and Rutgers. Coco paused to dream of her possibilities.

"Coco, your song is on the radio!" Someone shouted.

"Coco, that's you rapping on the radio?" someone yelled from the living room.

"Turn that up!" another shouted.

Hooting and hollering, her neighbors began partying.

"I must say congrats are in order. Coco, you made the whole community proud. Number one song in the land. Top high-school graduate in the country... Highest scores in the SAT... smoking on da corners... You such a fucking lady, da American dream," Rightchus said.

"A'ight, a'ight you said your piece, now git da fuck outta here," Coco responded.

"Yo, Coco, I've been always in your corner down wit' cha. You can't say I ain't been rootin' all the time for your success. And this da way you treat me as soon as you start becoming successful. Girl, don't you get above your raisins. Remember where you from..."

"Why were you so mad at him?"

"Cuz I could tell he'd been in my house smokin' crack with madukes and doin' whatever, yo."

"I hear you. And that was the last time you saw him?" Deedee asked.

"That was the last time I saw his black ass," Coco said with a smirk.

She picked up her drink and slurped. They were sitting outside the café listening to the waves crashing against the shores. Deedee pulled out her phone and scanned through her calls.

"Are you sure you don't wanna talk to him?"

"I'm sure, Dee. You can call him, but I don't wanna talk to him right now. I gotta talk to madukes about this Rightchus bullshit first, yo."

"You ready to go?"

"Let's bounce, yo."

Coco felt Deedee's arm around her. She was still reeling from an emotional rollercoaster when she tried to stand and Deedee helped her to the car.

12

His body was bound tight in a chair. They gagged him and beat him brutally. Then gasoline was poured all over Rightchus. In the still of the summer's night, the sound of a match being struck was heard. Rightchus vainly twisted to and fro, but his life had run its course.

He screamed a gurgling, animalistic cry for help, but there was no assistance. In this wooded, quiet place way off from the main road, Rightchus seemed to have an appointment with death. Tied to a chair the flame quickly overtook the small room. There was no way he could miss his rendezvous.

The fire was spreading from his burning body and his blood-curdling scream came loud, but to no avail. No one came to his rescue even when fire shot up through the roof. The guys who had started it walked away to their waiting cars. A safe distance away, the men watched the flame. They smoked cigarettes waiting, while Rightchus' flesh burned crispy.

Rightchus had been holed up in a sleazy, run-down old shack of a motel in a rural part of South Carolina, called Rendezvous. Located on a dirt-covered path it was the only place he could hide out. This was not a road Rightchus planned to be on. The flea-bag motel provided only comfort of a bed. Rightchus wanted to take a shower, get out of his dirty rags, and rest up for his journey. He was on the run and had no other place to go.

It was early in the morning, and after taking a shower, Rightchus paused to smoke a cigarette. He had wanted to go straight, and was given a chance to do just that. But he had ended up backtracking into his old self and started stealing from the church.

Rightchus had been working at an old Baptist church in a rural part of South Carolina. Attempting to rid himself of the demons that haunted him in the big city, he had started attending the church. Rightchus proved to be a favorite of the elders because of his temperament. He was always quick with a joke—a quip here and laughter there. Rightchus held onto a deep secret, and never revealed it to anyone in the three months he worked at the church. He was a con artist and a thief who was spurred on by a rabid drug habit.

Somehow Rightchus worked his way into collecting the offering. Then he was delivering the offering and counting the money with the deacons. Dealing with money presented opportunities and tested his faith. One day, Rightchus couldn't pass up the occasion to help himself to take some of the offering. After more such lapses, he just started taking the money. Eventually the stolen money started adding up. The missing money became noticeable, and the minister gave Rightchus the third degree. He was forced to give back the money or leave.

Rightchus was now hiding from members of the church in a seedy motel. Like old times, he was still making moves, trying to get out of town with the quickness.

"Fuck, now she ain't gonna take my damn call..." he muttered, waiting for the outgoing message to end.

"This Rightchus. Hit me back. I ain't get da money you send me. I told y'all that already. Calling me would get me in trouble. Now I'm in a jam and you don't wanna pick up my call...?"

He put the cell phone down after leaving a message. He turned on the television, channel surfing, and mumbling.

"Fuck this I gotta get out of here... I'm a tell that girl."

As he muttered to himself, he became interested in an episode of *Maury*. Rightchus sipped from his bottle, and laughed pointing jokingly at the screen.

Rightchus was on the cell phone scrolling looking at numbers. He saw Deedee's number and started to dial. Then he was distracted by movements and noise coming from outside his room. His cell phone rang and he heard an unfamiliar voice.

"We know where you are. We got you now, Rightchus!"

"Maruichi...?" he said and quickly hung up the call.

He glanced at the cell phone like it was a foreign object. Rightchus examined and pulled it apart. Removing the SIM card, he ran to the bathroom and flushed it. He knew what time it was, and slowly walked backwards to the bed. He thought about how he had become involved in this whole setup.

. He had been down on his luck when the police approached him with an offer. Detective Kowalski from Manhattan South Task Force met him uptown.

"Let's go see your man Rightchus, then we'll drop in and see our shooter, Tina Torres. She called to give us insight as to what had happened," Kowalski said.

Sitting in a seedy place like this, running for his life, Rightchus kept trying not to think of why he had made the call and become involved. It was drugs and money.

Rightchus made a call for Kowalski and Hall who were doing paperwork at their desks. He mentioned that something major was going down in the hood. Kowalski was the first to jump at the informant's tip.

With the keys to his simple abode in his sweating hand, Rightchus hurried back to his apartment. He pushed against the lock and the door fell flat inside the apartment. He gasped for breath and looked around, his eyes widened.

"What da fuck!" he yelled and stared with a perplexed look at the set of keys in his hand. "Oh man, oh shit, those crazy Maruichi. Now the fucking landlord is gonna have ma muthafucking ass. No, he already has ma ass. He's gonna have my damn life."

Rightchus looked around shaking his head at his scattered wares. "I've got to get da fuck up out of here before that jerk, shit-head super finds me here."

He knew he was in over his head and found out everything he wanted to know. He knew it was time to leave, but that it was already too late.

Rightchus hustled about the place hastily retrieving the few belongings that mattered. He verbally checked each item.

"Now I gotta have my Beat Box with my demo tapes, and the pictures of my seeds. Now, now where are those damn pictures of my precious children?"

He examined them one by one while reflecting on the possibility of visiting his family. Rightchus quickly hit the block. He had his prized possessions and the scheme he hoped would put him back into the grace of the mainstream. He would take the offer from the cops and at the same time, this would keep Maruichi off his back. His steps quickened, and then slowed as he neared the bus stop. He stood there and nodded as people went by.

He remembered the setup with the police and mob. It was then he realized that the police and mob were fighting each other, but the same puppet master controlled them. Rightchus had a deal with Lil' Long to make his death happen in front of witnesses.

"I want those damn cops, Kowalski and Hall dead. I want them dead now." Maruichi yelled. His sons dialed rapidly on their cell phones.

"It's a done deal, Dad. Those bastards are good as dead." Eddie said, getting his father's undivided attention. "I just put a huge sum on both their heads. They'll be cold in another twenty-four hours."

Both sons were preoccupied with pleasing their dad. Neither saw when the riders approached the group. With guns drawn, the Caló death squad easily snatched all three and took them home. There they made Frankie get on the phone and call his lawyer.

The puppet master set it up perfectly, but Rightchus had figured it all out and remained one step ahead of their actions. He knew too much, it could blow the lid off a lot of plans. Rightchus had to leave town in secrecy and faked his own death.

The execution duo known as Caló had killed Nesto and all his cronies but still no ice had been recovered. They scouted the neighborhood searching for Lil' Long. He was next on the hit list. Rightchus saw the pair riding motorcycles, and stopped to flirt a little.

"That's such a cool thing to do—ride and just chill. Maybe I can help y'all ladies," he said, and limped directly to where they were sitting. "You're looking for Lil' Long, but I know he sold the diamonds to Maruichi and—" Rightchus said, and one of them pulled out a gun.

"Hold up, easy now, put that cannon away. I ain't tryin' a start no fight with y'all. If I did, I'd come with my kung-fu shit, see you don't know me. I'm a master at this."

"Is there something you're trying to tell us?" one of them asked.

"I'm saying, is there a reward or not in this for me. I ain't goin' 'gainst Lil' Long with no compensations."

"You will be rewarded for your information."

"A'ight, then let's talk, p.c." Rightchus said. "Yeah, I did my homework." He added when they gave him a strange look.

After the conversation with Rightchus, the Calió called for permission to hit the mob. The request was granted and they went after Maruichi. The family, Eddie, Jimmy and father sat in the back of the pizza parlor.

"I want those damn cops, Kowalski and Hall dead. I want them dead now." Maruichi yelled.

"Yeah, you gotta bring that thing here right now." Frankie Maruichi ordered. Within minutes, the attorney brought the diamonds and was surprised to see who the buyers were. Once they had procured the loot, the Calió fired shots at each of the Maruichi's heads killing them. They set the lawyer free.

Later that night they met with Rightchus and gave him a thousand dollars. Ecstatic, he tried to kiss both.

"Oh shit, oh shit. This all me? This all me?" he jumped jubilantly and yelled until his legs hurt. "Did you get Lil' Long yet?" Rightchus asked nervously. They rode away without saying a word. "I'm a buy me some fly gears, get me a nice girl—oh it's on now, muthafuckas."

Not long after they had ridden off, Lil' Long appeared and saw Rightchus limping on crutches and singing heartily.

"Yeah, I got that dough now, see in da stores now, buying all 'em fly gears. That Sean Jean and Akademiks shit now..."

"What da fuck you so happy 'bout?" Lil' Long asked. "Didn't I tell you not to let me catch your black ass out here on these streets?"

"Yea-yeah, I only came to cop ci-ci-cigarette," Rightchus said. Lil' Long stared at him for a fluttering heartbeat. Rightchus was nervous and *his voice shook when he saw Lil' Long unveiled both his guns. "You already shot me wi-wi-with both yo-yo-your guns..." Rightchus said.*

"Nigga you trying to mock me, huh. Here hold this then." Lil' Long aimed both guns at Rightchus. "In order for me to be immortal all y'all weak muthafuckas, bitches and snitches must die..." Lil' Long shouted then squeezed the trigger.

"No-o-o..." Rightchus bloodcurdling scream filled the air along with the explosion echoed loud into the night's air then dissipated. Rightchus bloodied mess fell silent. Lil' Long walked slowly away whispering.

"Snitch-ass nigga, yeah, you had that coming. Now I gotta go see them muthafuckin' rappin' ass bitches and that music producer." He said and waved for a taxi. A few minutes later, one pulled up.

"Where to, mister?" The driver asked. Lil' Long took a look and smiled. "I like you already," he said to the Asian female driving. "I'm goin' to see this rap show at club Deep." He said.

"Can do..." the driver said and drove off. There was a motorcycle right behind them.

"Y'all Chinese peeps have y'all hands in everything in da hood, huh?"

"Can do," the driver smiled. Lil' Long relaxed and enjoyed the ride.

So caught up in remembering and in his own fear, Rightchus totally forgot where he was. He puffed on the pipe inhaling the smoke of his past. Suddenly the door came crashing in, and Rightchus knew what time it was. He ran to bathroom and tried to jump out, but to no avail. A squad of cars awaited him.

"Maruichi... You got peoples everywhere?"

"That's why they call us da fuckin' mob! Been looking for

you for a while now, Rightchus," a voice said. "Faking your death and leaving the city—smart idea. But stealing money from the church was a dumb idea, Rightchus. Running from us—a very dumb idea!"

"I-I-I was planning to give it all back—"

"Shut da fuck up! You pissed a lot of people off with your bullshit, Rightchus. Tie him up. We're about to set your black ass on fire for causing the death of my brothers and my sister!"

Rightchus remained speechless, and fear enveloped his body. His past had caught up to him. The cell phone was going off in his hand. Someone reached out and took it from him.

"How long do you think you were gonna fool us?"

"I-I-I swear I had nothing to do with your brother's death," Rightchus shouted.

That would be last statement he would make before they bound and gagged him, cutting off his squeals for help. After gasoline was poured over his body, Rightchus was set afire.

"Are you sure you wanna spend the night alone, Coco?" Deedee asked while keeping her eyes on traffic.

"Yeah, ah... I mean, I'll be good, yo."

"You already know you're welcome to stay with me," Deedee said.

It was four-thirty in the morning, and Deedee was driving Coco uptown. They were stopped at a red light when Coco saw someone walking, his arms filled with shopping bags.

"Ain't no store open where that nigga going with all those bags, yo?"

"Coco you think everyone out late at night is a crack-head who's ripping someone else off?" Deedee chuckled.

Her eyes were still on traffic while Coco kept staring at the figure coming out of the shadows. Glare from the street lights hit his face, and she immediately recognized the man.

"Back up, Dee," Coco shouted excitedly.

"What now you're gonna stop and frisk him?" Deedee asked sarcastically.

"No, don't be a silly chick. He's that crack-head Madukes was with. Remember that time when your uncle first was arrested and we wanted to find Rightchus?"

"Yes, but what does that—oh, that's right. He's the guy who was at your mother's apartment when we ah—" Deedee exclaimed.

"Yes, exactly."

Deedee threw the car in reverse and Coco was about to get out. She saw the man looking at her, and hurrying to get in a taxi.

"Dontay... Hey yo," Coco shouted.

The man glanced around and looked nervously at Coco. Then he raced for the next gypsy cab and took off. Coco stood with a confused expression and got back inside the car with Deedee.

"That nigga just jumped in a cab acting like I was trying to rob him, yo."

"You want to talk to him right?"

"I wanna give him that message Nurse Roberts told me to tell all my mother former... You know...?"

"Sex partners...?" Deedee asked.

"Yuck! Pew... I can't even say it, yo."

"Is your message urgent?"

"It's urgent. The nurse is always asking me about it, yo."

"Okay, let's go give that bastard his urgent message then," Deedee said.

"How we gonna do that? He's out, yo."

"Coco, this is a BMW 525i, capable of going from zero to sixty in less time than you can say—"

Deedee suddenly gunned the engine, and the car accelerated with such force, Coco's Afro had blown back. She held onto the dash for dear life while staring at Deedee with great concern as the BMW burning rubbers left tire tracks in the street.

"I'll—oh shit!"

Before Coco's scream was completed, the five-speed automatic transmission hit its peak, and they were behind the cab with Dontay inside.

Deedee glanced at Coco, smiled, and said, "There's no cab in the city that can outrun us.

"I hear that, yo," Coco said, visibly impressed.

"Now let's give him this urgent message," Deedee said, honking at the cab.

"Dee, I swear you're crazy, yo."

"Somehow I have to make this cabbie stop," Deedee said.

Halogen headlights flashed wildly, and honking horn, Deedee tailgated the cab. Minutes later, the cabbie pulled over, and Deedee drove up alongside the cab. The girls sat and waited for a couple beats while an argument between passenger and the cab driver ensued. Finally Dontay rolled his window down.

"Dontay, you scared or sump'n? You've gotta go to Harlem hospital and get tested. Ask for Nurse Roberts, she's on the eighth floor," Coco said, coldly staring him down.

"And where did you get all those bags? I didn't know designer stores opened this late?" Deedee chuckled.

"Yeah, whose house you done broke into now, you bum-ass nigga?" Coco laughed.

"Are you gonna sell those for a couple of jumbo?" Deedee laughed.

"Ain't none of either y'all's damn biz," Dontay said, looking at the girls. "That's it, Coco?" He asked. Then he turned back to the driver and said, "A'ight driver, I think we done here. Break out," he continued.

"Now I can visit madukes without the nurse harassing me, yo. Let's go speed racer," Coco said.

Both girls laughed and tires screeching loudly, the BMW shot off around the cab. Music pumping loudly, the fast-moving European sports auto disappeared into the morning traffic. The cabbie and his passenger were both left staring in awe.

Kim and Tina were still partying in a Hell's Kitchen nightclub. Sitting down to have a drink, they chatted and caught their collective breath.

"Shyt! It's jam packed up in this piece," Kim said. "Some cute guys up in here too and shyt," she laughed.

"Uh-huh, I seen the one you were dancing with, ho. That's Flack from uptown. He cute but he ain't nobody," Tina said, grabbing her cell phone. "I don't want him. I can do way better than him," Tina laughed and started to walk away.

"Where you going, bitch?" Kim asked.

"None of your beeswax, ho. But since you must know, I'm going to make a call to check on my son. Do you mind?"

"Go on, bitch. I'm a get my groove back with Flack," Kim said, shaking her ass, and heading to the dance floor.

"Shut your face, bitch. Do you. Just don't be giving up that big ass on the dance floor," Tina said.

By the time Tina returned three guys were all over Kim's wiggling ass, moving round on the dance floor. Tina was stopped in her tracks by the sight of the guys drooling over themselves for Kim. Teasingly, Tina joined the revelry, dropping it like it was on fire.

It was beginning of the weekend. Kim and Tina were having so much fun partying they paid no attention to the time. Kim was slow dancing with one guy while Tina danced and flirted her way into the forefront. She was now the center of attention. She smiled as four guys circled her like hunter to prey. They were completely unaware they were playing her game.

Kim kept an eye on Tina, and saw the way she took over the floor. A flash of mound here and there. It didn't take a long time for all the unattached men to be in Tina's zone. She was queen and everyone yearned to yield to her bidding. Feeling a hint of jealousy coupled with inadequacy, Kim held onto the guy she was dancing with. Grinding her hips against his crotch, she opened her legs, and made him feel her ass. He looked longingly at Tina, but stayed with Kim.

"You wanna join her, Flack?" Kim asked.

"I ain't going nowhere, Kim," he said, his hands caressing her. "I wanna boom-boom in your poom-poom, baby."

"Shyt, I like that, babe," Kim said, smiling seductively.

Later on they left the club and made out while waiting outside in his car. Kim was biting his lips while his tongue roamed inside her mouth when she spotted Tina.

"Shyt! There goes my girl," Kim said, breaking their lip-lock position.

"Hmm okay..." Flack smiled. "Damn baby, you gotta leave?"

"Yeah, I came here with my girl. I gotta leave with her. You know how that is. Call me, you got my digits," Kim said, jumping out the car.

She met with Tina, who had her eyes on Flack sitting in the car. He winked at Tina before driving away.

"How you gon' be sitting in a hooptee, making out with this nigga, and have me looking for your ho' ass up in da club?"

"Bitch, I waved at you when me and Flack was walking out da club—"

"Shut your face! You messin' 'round with that bird-ass nigga Flack from uptown...?"

"Shyt bitch. He cute and dress nice all the time. And he smells good too," Kim said.

"Shut your damn face! That nigga drives a Hyundai. Bitch, get it together. Who you know got money and be driving sump'n like that?"

"Bitch stop playin'. It takes him from A to B," Kim said, laughing.

"And that's all it's gon' do, ho," Tina said, joining the hilarity. "He was gon' give you a ride home in the hooptee?"

"My life is too precious. I wouldn't think of goin' anywhere with his drunk ass. I was just lettin' him smell me."

"Shut your dirty mouth, ho! Let's catch a cab before the sun starts shining," Tina said.

"Let's do it, bitch," Kim said.

Kim and Tina hung out until the early Saturday morning. In the city that never sleeps, two pretty girls, in the shortest of dresses, waving for a cab presented a golden opportunity. Three cabs raced over to where they stood on the corner.

"Shyt! They trying to run us over," Kim shouted.

"Damn near killed us," Tina said, getting inside the first cab.

"Y'all cab drivers are the worst. Please!"

"Where to ladies...?"

"Don't try to be nice after you just tried to kill us," Kim said.

"We're going uptown East A Hundred and Six Street," Tina laughed.

"But on da real, drive safely. Shyt! I wanna get home alive. I have a beautiful son to live for," Kim said. "So be easy, my man. I'm expensive luggage."

"Shut your expensive ass and let him concentrate on taking us uptown, ho."

"I'm very sorry, Miss," the cab driver said. "I'm a careful driver."

He glanced at the girls in the back seat through his rearview and couldn't remove his eyes from what he saw. Tina had opened her legs, and she was wearing no panties.

"Bitch, you're really OD'ing on that shyt, right now," Kim said, shaking her head.

Tina giggled provocatively at the cabbie's reaction. He smiled, staring at the center of her opened legs. The driver's vision returned to the road. It was too late. His reaction time was shortened by Tina's shaven mound. Suddenly the cab hurtled forward, slamming into the back of another car.

"Oh shyt! See, this da fuck I'm talking about!" Kim shrieked.

"Shut da front door! This muthafucka done got us into an accident!" Tina shouted, making the sign of the cross.

"I-I-I sorry—he stopped short and—"

"Shyt! This exactly what I was talkin' 'bout!" Kim said, trying to get out of the car. "Shyt! The door is fuckin' stuck! Get us outta this bitch!"

"Shut your face, and calm down, ho!" Tina said, checking her door then making the sign of the cross. "Both doors are stuck. Driver please let us out, now!" Tina shouted,

Jumping out, the driver assisted Kim and Tina out of the back of the taxi. They were physically uninjured, but mentally bruised. The driver of the other car was none other than Flack.

"What da hell were you doing? Couldn't you see that I had to stop short? There's a traffic jam up ahead, man. Where da fuck are you racing to go...?"

Flack's six-foot, athletic frame was hopping mad. He was enraged until he saw Kim and Tina. Then his mannerism softened. He was glancing at his rear bumper, but Flack seemed more concerned about the welfare of Kim and Tina. The girls were appreciative.

"Shyt look its Flack," Kim said, pointing.

"Shut your face, ho! Stop acting like he somebody. How we gon' get uptown?"

"Kim, Tina," Flack exclaimed, walking to where the girls stood.

"I-I-I—" the cabbie was still baffled.

Ignoring the cabbie's excuses, Flack was standing with Kim and Tina. He hugged them both then he turned to cab driver. Flack was the perfect gentleman, checking to make sure both girls were not hurt.

"Hey man, you could've killed these beautiful women," Flack shouted, admiring both Kim's and Tina's derrieres.

"Yeah, he damage your bumper driving reckless—"

"He should just pay us so we can be on our way. I got places to go," Tina said.

"Shyt, that's true rap," Kim joined in, her neck was moving and her arms were in motion.

Kim and Tina watched carefully as the cab driver looked at his bumper. It wasn't badly damaged. Then he examined Flack's car and saw there was some damage. He turned to Flack.

"How much...?"

"Give me seven hundred and we keep it moving," Flack said.

"It's minor damage, my friend. I give you six hundred," the cabbie said.

Flack got on his knees and closely inspected the damage to his bumper. It was being held up by a screw. Flack undid the screw and bumper fell to the asphalt. He stood and looked at the cabbie who was pulling out a wad of cash.

"Okay, give me six-fifty. The fifty's for the girls," Flack said.

"Okay," the cabbie nodded, counting the money and handed it to Flack.

"Shut da front door! That's all we get... Fifty...?" Tina asked.

"Shyt, that's all?" Kim echoed. "We suffered bodily damages too."

"I feel all kinds a pain in my back," Tina said.

The cabbie glanced at them and placed the money in Flack's hand. He quickly turned and ran back to his cab.

"Hell, he must be an illegal alien or sump'n," Tina said, laughing.

"Is that enough money to fix your bumper?" Kim asked Flack.

"More than enough," he smiled.

Flack counted the cash and waved at the nervous cabbie, in the midst of driving away. Then Flack picked up his damaged bumper and stuck the state tags inside the rear window. He was able to fit the bumper inside the back of the car. With the bumper occupying the backseat area, both Kim and Tina squeezed into the front with Flack.

"Everyone in?" he asked, laughing and driving off.

"Shyt nigga, why you lookin' soo damn happy?" Kim asked.

"He must be feeling your big ass rubbing up on him," Tina said.

"That feels good," Flack smiled. "But I'm glad it's y'all."

"Really," Tina grunted sarcastically.

"Why's that?" Kim asked.

"I just made me six hundred and fifty dollars with y'all. It must be good luck," Flack said.

"Okay, because we up in the front of your Hyundai and Kim rubbing her ass all over you—you call that good luck?"

"Yes, that and the fact that I'm a mechanic and fixing this car won't cost me nada."

"Shut da front door! I love this guy."

Tina reached over and gave Flack a high-five. Kim wiggled her body and made sure her thigh was touching the side of Flack's leg. Tina saw Kim being protective and smiled, relishing the competition.

"So Flack how much we getting'?" Tina asked.

"Yes, Flack you best break us off good. Shyt..." Kim smiled, accidently touching his crotch.

"We'll split it three ways," he said.

"Shut da front door! You mean we each get two hundred and sixteen dollars apiece?" Tina excitedly asked.

"Y'all two get a hundred and sixteen apiece and I get the rest," Flack said.

"Oh," Tina said, sounding disappointed.

"Shyt, give me my cut. It may not sound like a lot, but it is good since it didn't cost us anything," Kim said. "We got our own, right bitch?"

"Shut da front door ho! There you go just thinking the way poor people do."

"Shyt, please, bitch! Does that radio work, Flack? Kim asked.

"Why...?" Flack asked.

"I just need to drown out the sound of a bitch in my neck," Kim said, brushing off her shoulder.

"Shut your face ho! No you didn't!" Tina said.

"I don't think so," Flack said, trying the knobs.

They drove in silence. Kim avoided looking over at Tina. She kept her thigh rubbing against his, enjoying the feeling of his strong thigh. Then there were his accidental touches on her exposed legs.

"Right here, Flack," Tina said.

She got out of the car and started walking to the door. Kim kissed Flack, and was about to get out of the car.

"Here, give Tina her share," he said, shoving money in Kim's hand.

Kim smiled at him, and closed the door. Flack waited until they were both inside the building then he stepped on the gas, and drove away. Kim and Tina took the elevator to the sixth floor.

"Bitch, just cuz you got that cash stashed, don't mean you can't take a hundred here or there," Kim said.

"Shut your face! That nigga could've given us two hundred a piece. He was being selfish, keeping all that dough. He can keep his scraps. Greedy-butt nigga," Tina said, opening the door.

What they saw shocked both Kim and Tina equally. Kim ran to where she left the bags and they were all gone with the money. She threw herself on the sofa and screamed loudly.

"Kim, Kim shut da fuck up!" Tina shouted. "You're gonna wake up the whole neighborhood, bitch!"

"I don't care. Fucking thieves broke in and stole everything including the ten thousand dollars you gave me and shyt."

"Shut da front door, ho! Why da fuck would you leave all that money in the bag?"

"Shyt I thought it was okay, bitch. How was I gonna know that these grimy neighbors that you have were gonna break into the damn apartment. They took all the clothes, and I had just stashed the money in one of the bags," Kim cried.

"A'ight bitch! Shut da fuck up and stop sniffling like a bitch ass. You da one who left the dough carelessly," Tina said.

"How was I gon' know, huh bitch? Tell me how?"

"These muthafuckas don't care, Tina said, walking to the window before continuing to speak. "They probably saw us with all 'em bags and came here to steal."

"I didn't know—"

"Bitch you were raised in this city. Thieves find a way to steal your shit. They must've come through the kitchen window. It has the fire escape. And you left all that money here. That's what poor people do. They leave money carelessly laying all over damn the place."

"Shyt! I'm a call the police," Kim said.

"Nah, I don't want nobody to shoot me for snitching. Fuck being a rata. I can get you some more money, but you gonna have to put a lil' work in," Tina said.

"What kind a work you talkin' 'bout...?"

"Just a lil' sump'n, sump'n," Tina said.

"As long as it ain't no illegal shit, bitch. I'm through doing that type o' shit with you," Kim said.

"Shut da front door, ho! It ain't nothing illegal."

"When you want me to do this work?"

"I'll let you know soon. In the meantime, I'm a give you two G's out of my fifteen thousand—"

"I thought you said it was twenty thousand and you gave me half which is ten? Remember your story bitch, cuz now you got me thinking."

"Shut your mouth, ho! You acting like you ain't the one who lost your dough!"

"Yes, but I left it in your apartment, bitch. Your fucking neighbors are a bunch of thieves!"

"Ain't nobody's fault, but your own ho! You can't blame anyone else—"

"So you're sayin I should've took all that dough to the club, bitch?"

"I'm sayin' you should've hid it. Put it somewhere safe like under the bathroom sink like I did."

"Shyt bitch! I wasn't expecting a robbery!"

"I gave that ten thousand to you out of the goodness of my heart. So, it don't even matter if it's ten or fifteen thousand. That was from my heart, ho."

"You right, bitch. You're right. Thanks again. When you want me to do this for you?"

"I'll let you know, ho. And just shut your face—didn't I say that already. Didn't I?"

"Just checking, bitch," Kim said.

Tina went to the kitchen and closed the window. Then she poured two drinks and offered one to Kim.

"Here drink this ho," Tina said. "By the way, you sleeping over tonight?"

"I might as well, bitch. Cuz I'm go home and all I'm gonna be thinking about is losing that money. And I ain't gonna be able to sleep either," Kim said, gulping the drink down.

"A'ight, you know the lay of the land. I'll take the sofa. When you're ready, you can have my bed, ho," Tina said.

"Why are you being soo nice, bitch?"

"Shut your face! Who said I was being nice?

"Then what is it then, bitch...?"

"I just don't want your fat ass to break down my sofa," Tina said.

"Good night, bitch," Kim wryly said, swallowing her drink and walking away.

"Good night, ho," Tina said, raising her glass with a cunning smile on her face.

While Deedee leafed through an edition of *Uptown* magazine, she munched on fruits from a variety neatly set out on a tray. She glanced up now and again to hear her uncle who kept correcting Coco. Eric Ascot, music producer extraordinaire, was helping Coco revise her lyrics. He worked with a strained patience, stopping often to give Coco pointers. The teen seemed to labor in vain at her craft.

"Play it back for me again," Coco requested.

Listening to the recording, Coco changed her pronunciation and rhymes based on Eric's recommendations. They were in the recording studio of Eric's apartment. "Home-base studio" was what he had dubbed the place he now worked one-on-one with his new artist Coco.

Mumbling softly, the talented teen bopped to the beat, trying to get the verses right in her head. Eric watched her for a few moments, glanced at the diamond-crusted Cartier on his wrist, and turned the volume down.

"Are you ready to go in yet?" he asked Coco. "Don't be scared," Eric added with a hint of sarcasm.

Coco's head was nodding like it was on a spring. She twisted her body and neck in rhythm to the beat, but her body language expressed doubt. Coco didn't have the hook to the song completely set in her mind. Eric could hear the doubt in her tone when she made the request.

"Could I hear the first verse again?" Coco asked.

"C'mon already—if you don't have it down by now, Coco, you just ain't got it. I can't be fuckin' around with a three-line hook all day!" Eric shouted.

He should have had the music on full blast, but the volume was down, and the ensuing silence was made tense by Coco and Deedee's shock. Fingering the controls, Eric glanced at the expressions on each of the teens' faces.

Biting his lips, he shook his head at the realization of how offensive he sounded. He shouldn't have let his emotions run uncontrolled. Coco was a new artist going through tough times and he should be more nurturing. Silently he wished no one had heard him. Coco and Deedee continued to shoot him stares of disbelief. They heard him loud and clear.

"I'm sorry. That wasn't supposed to come out like that, Coco," Eric said in an apologetic tone.

The six-bedroom apartment was huge, but at the moment it felt smaller than a tiny closet. "Maybe we should just break here and continue tomorrow," Eric said, walking out.

Coco and Deedee glanced quizzically at each other. Saying nothing, Deedee could read the smirk on Coco's face.

"My uncle's intense, but I don't think he meant it to come out quite like that," Deedee said.

Walking to where Coco stood in the small recording booth, Deedee pushed the microphone from her face, hugging the talented teen. Coco's mind was still wrapping around what had just gone down. Her body stood frozen stiff in Deedee's arms.

Deedee planted a deep kiss on Coco's sensitive lips and breathed life into her. Tears came easily. Her lithe body jerked in convulsions, and Coco sobbed quietly with her head resting on Deedee's shoulders.

"I gotta go see my mother, yo," she said.

"I'll go with you—"

"You don't have to, yo," Coco shrugged, walking away.

"Coco, I want to go with you," Deedee shouted, running after a seemingly seething Coco.

They both ran by Eric who was pouring a drink. He saw Coco storming out of the apartment door with Deedee quickly behind her. Eric drank his drink then pulled out his cell phone and called his security.

"My niece and Coco are on their way out. Detain them until I get there," he said, and finished his drink.

Coco walked out of the building and Deedee was still behind her. The teens exited the elevator at the same time, but Coco's pace increased.

"Wait up!"

They both turned around when they heard the voice. Two beefy guys came huffing toward the girls, and Deedee recognized the security.

"Do you have somewhere to go in a hurry?" he asked.

"Well, I—"

"I gotta go see Madukes. My mom's in the hospital, so I'm out, yo."

Coco attempted to walk away but the second burly security guy moved closer to her. He blocked her path.

"You ain't going nowhere until Mr. Ascot gets here," he said.

"A'ight chill, yo," Coco said, sizing up the security. "Don't look so insecure. When Ascot comes I'll make sure to tell him what a great job you did," she continued, her tone dripping with sarcasm.

Coco took one too many steps and the security was in her face. Deedee pulled Coco back from the staring contest with the determined-looking security guy. Coco reluctantly back down. A few minutes later Eric Ascot walked out and the guards turned over the enraged teen girls.

"Where are you running off to Coco?" Eric asked.

The sigh of exasperation escaping Coco's lips was the only the response. Eric let the question hung in the air for a couple of beats while looking at Coco's face. Then he turned to Deedee.

"Where is Coco—" he was about to ask Deedee, but Coco interrupted.

"I can speak for myself," Coco said, raising her voice. "I'm going to see my mother in the hospital."

"Okay, that's not a problem. I think we'll all go and visit your mother in the hospital," Eric said, nodding to the security.

In no time they were all loading in the back of the black limousine. Eric and the girls were heading to the hospital. Coco felt mixed emotions. She spent the time staring out the window, trying to figure out if there was any truth to what Mrs. Jones told her. Coco couldn't wait to talk with her mother.

They entered the hospital and Eric stopped in at the gift shop again.

"I'll call you back—the famous Eric Ascot just walked into the store!" a store clerk said. This time he even posed for a picture with the gift-shop employee.

Eric chose a huge bouquet. He walked to the cashier, who was staring at him and seemed eager to wait on him.

"Anything else, Mr. Ascot...?"

"Flowers that's it," Eric said.

"I know that trial's coming soon, but I know you're gonna beat all that. They ain't got nothing against you but made-up trash," one of the employees said.

"Government always trying to jam up the Black man," a customer shouted.

Eric looked around and saw that other customers were becoming involved in the discussion. Preferring not to be the focus of the commotion, he quickly paid and rushed to join the girls waiting by the elevator. Hospital security waved the group on and they entered the elevator.

Coco led the way to the hospital room with her mother. The frail woman was sitting up in bed with Nurse Roberts at her side when they walked in. Nurse Roberts was busy checking Ms. Harvey and turned to see the group. She directed her stare at Coco.

"I've got a few words to say to you Coco," Nurse Roberts said, and continued to check Ms. Harvey.

"My boyfriend! Oh you always bring me flowers," Ms. Harvey gushed. "He's nice right, Nurse?"

"Yes, he's a good man," Nurse Roberts smiled.

"Okay, take your googly eyes off him. I know you wish you had a one like him and you trying to steal him," Ms. Harvey said. "Take it easy, my dear. If I wasn't married, you would definitely have some competition. Hi, Mr. Ascot. Coco, I need to speak with you." Coco looked at her. "Now, Miss."

Unwillingly, Coco walked out with the nurse, leaving Eric and Deedee with Ms. Harvey. The feeble woman was back to lying in the bed, and peering from her moist swollen eyes. Life sustaining machines were hooked into her main arteries and veins. Straining to look directly at Deedee, Ms. Harvey said, "I just meed a few minutes to talk adult talk with your uncle."

Surprised by the request, Deedee stood and looked at the

ailing woman then at her uncle. Wishing she could stay, she walked out of the room into the hallway and spotted Coco talking to the nurse.

"And you did what...?" the nurse asked.

By the uneasy look registering on the nurse's face, Deedee could tell that the discussion was about something very serious. She tried to move closer, but Coco and the nurse walked further down the hall. Determined to find out what was being discussed between Coco and the nurse, Deedee followed until she was within earshot.

"I'm telling you that it wasn't real liquor. It was only fruit juice in a liquor bottle," Coco said.

Nurse Roberts saw penitence on the teen's face and the nurse's disdain faded. She was now concerned about Coco's actions.

"But why...?" she asked.

"Madukes... My mother's always stressin' about me bring her lil' sump'n," Coco said. "She was killin' me with all her feignin'."

"So you decided to give her—"

"Fruit juice—cranberry and grape," Deedee said, butting into the conversation.

"Dee was there. She knew," Coco said.

"Okay, but Dee is your best friend. Were there any adults around?" Nurse Roberts asked inquisitively.

"Yes, my uncle was there. He bought the bottle and Coco poured out the liquor then replaced it with the juices," Deedee said.

"Then let's go find out from your uncle," Nurse Roberts said.

They walked back down to the room. Coco was thinking about the trouble her little trick had caused. They arrived in the room and overheard Eric talking with Ms. Harvey. They were holding hands as if sealing an agreement.

"Everything will be alright. Don't you worry, Ms. Harvey, I'll take care of her make sure everything goes right. You just get your rest and recover from this, alright?"

"Thanks, Eric. You understand me. And I can see you're an

honest man," Ms. Harvey said.

"Speaking of honesty, may I speak to you for a brief moment, Mr. Ascot?"

"Sure," Eric said to the nurse. Standing, he continued. "I'll talk to you again, Rachel baby. You take care of yourself, girl."

"Yes, boo. And you don't worry about them judges, and the prosecutors. They're all legal thieves just trying a rob you blind," Ms. Harvey said. "They won't win."

A smiling Eric walked outside the room with the nurse. Ms. Harvey was lying on the bed with her eyes closed while Coco and Deedee watched silently over her. Several questions hovered in Coco's mind. She tried not to sound angry when she began talking to her mother.

"Mom, I have to talk—we have to talk," Coco said, patting her chest, and pointing at her mother.

"What's up with all that bass in your voice? You better check that at the door," Ms. Harvey said, wheezing loudly.

"You know Mrs. Jones?"

"Yes? From the east side...?"

"Yes," Coco answered.

"What about her?"

"She told me that ah... Rightchus is my father and she wanted me to know for my own good—"

"That woman don't mean nobody no good. She just be letting her mouth flap off da hinges," Ms. Harvey said.

"She said she used to babysit me, and that Rightchus and you—" Coco began, but her mother interrupted.

"That nosey woman chat too damn much! Always mindin' other people's biz," Ms. Harvey said. "Never minding her damn own! Just look at her. She has six children and you see how they turned out. Two dead and two in lockup, and the other two are damn sluts!"

"Yeah, but Mom, he was coming around and you and him were

cool," Coco said.

"If you must know why, it's because I asked Rightchus to keep an eye on you. He was always in da streets and—"

"Ma," Coco shouted. "So you asked this crack-head to check up on me? Yuck!" Coco said in disbelief.

"I been known Rightchus for a long time. He wasn't always a crack-head. Back in the days, none of us were, Coco," Ms. Harvey said, and started coughing.

"That may be true, but this ain't back in the days, yo."

"You best mind your lingo, girl," Ms. Harvey said.

Her coughing continued even when Eric and the nurse returned to the room. Nurse Roberts walked to where Coco stood. The teen turned to face the nurse.

"Well Coco, I checked out things with Mr. Ascot and I'm happy to say it makes me feel better. We were all wondering where the bottle came from," the nurse said, smiling and shaking her index finger at Coco.

"I told you so," Coco said excitedly.

"What's going on? Everyone's just jumping around. Tell me why. Did someone win the lotto or what?" snapped Ms. Harvey.

"No Rachel, the nurse just had to straighten some things out with me," Eric said.

"Thank you, Eric," Ms. Harvey said, and started to cough again.

"But next time please consult with me," Nurse Roberts said, hurrying past Coco and going straight to Ms. Harvey's bedside. "You've gotta take it easy, Rachel."

She examined the ailing woman. After poking here and there on Ms. Harvey's bony structure, Nurse Roberts addressed the pensively waiting group.

"I'm gonna have to curtail this visit; I'll have to administer sedatives and she'll be asleep soon. So you can always come back tomorrow. Maybe she'll be feeling better. Even though she's over the worst hill, her condition still is critical," Nurse Roberts said with a disappointing tone.

"Okay we'll be back," Eric said.

He put his hand on Deedee's shoulder then walked away. Deedee glanced at Coco, who was still staring at her mother. There was pain in her eyes. Deedee knew Coco wasn't satisfied with the conversation she had with her mother. Coco wanted to keep asking questions, but she would have to wait for another time.

Deedee reached out and embraced Coco. With her arm around the distraught teen, she guided her out of the hospital room. Eric was waiting and hugged both girls. As they walked toward the elevator, Coco seemed deeply saddened. She wished the truth about Rightchus being her dad would have been learned today. The talk with her mother only seemed to cause further confusion.

Her mind was spinning when she walked in the elevator. Coco kept thinking maybe this part of her life was a bad dream. She wanted it to be over badly and quietly she cried. Deedee saw her tears and gave her a hug.

They stayed that way until the elevator reached the lobby. Eric walked out and made a call.

"We're at the front of the hospital," he said on the cell phone. Before hanging up, he turned to a grieving Coco, and saw Deedee still embracing her. "You girls feel like eating?" Eric asked. They both nodded. Eric returned to his cell phone and said, "Take us to dinner."

Eric waited until after dinner. Then he notified both girls that he had made an agreement with Coco's mother to care for Coco, just in case, he had told them. Coco looked at him and knew what a generous offer that was—but she wanted her mother to survive.

"That's really nice, Uncle E," Deedee said.

"Yes, good looking out," Coco said quietly, holding her head up.

"You'll be alright, Coco," Eric said

It was a squally day. The rain seemed like it was about to fall, but the sun kept peeking from behind darkened skies, and rays shed light. It was in this uncertain weather that Coco and Deedee drove to the doctor's office.

"No matter how it turns out, you gonna be a'ight, yo."

Reassured by Coco's support, Deedee walked into the waiting room of the doctor's office and was seen immediately. The nurse smiled and ushered Deedee inside an examination office and proceeded to complete a battery of tests. Later the doctor sat with Deedee, and an assisting nurse.

"I have the results of your pregnancy test," he said.

Deedee glanced cautiously at the gray-haired man and felt the knots tightened in her stomach. She wanted badly to get out of the chair and run out of the office. Sweat poured her face while the doctor spoke. She shook her head unable to hear him clearly.

"Would like your friend to sit in on this?" the doctor asked.

Biting her lips, Deedee nodded her head and the nurse walked out to get Coco. She walked in seemingly confident. There were a lot of problems on her friend's shoulders, but Deedee was sure Coco's presence would be helpful. It was.

Her self-confidence returned and buoyed the troubled teen's mind. She leaned her head against Coco and they walked silently to the car. There was nothing else to be said. It was a done deal, Deedee's mind was made up even though she had not told her uncle. She was planning on breaking the news to him. There was now a certain urgency attached to the news.

"I'm glad you decide on what you wanna do, yo."

"I guess you wanna go visit your mother now?" Deedee asked and Coco nodded.

It had been their ritual. Accompanied by Deedee, Coco made daily visits to the hospital. Hope stayed lodged firmly in her heart every time she saw her mother, even though the news never improved. Rachel Harvey's health was in fast decline, the nurses and doctors treating her mother at the hospital tried to prepare Coco for the worse.

Over the past few days, Rachel Harvey's condition took a turn for the worse. Doctors and nurses worked around the clock in an attempt to keep her alive. Eric Ascot had opened his checkbook, offering to foot the hospital bill. Even with his enormous generosity, Ms. Harvey failed to react to treatment and she continued deteriorating.

The teen, convinced that her mother would recover, kept constant vigil at her mother's bedside. Shoulders hunched, heart drawn, smile gone, Coco held unto her mother's bony hand. Ravished by the medical treatment, needles constant poking, Rachel Harvey's flesh seemed wounded. Her body was swollen and Coco massaged the wounds with her hands, wishing her mother would open her eyes just one more time.

At the end of the visit, she would ride back from the hospital feeling cheated. Nothing had changed. She was able to deflect some of the energy she felt and put it into her music. She was working intensely with Eric on finishing her first album.

It was late evening and Coco was riding from visiting her mother in the hospital. She turned up the volume on the music coming from the car stereo. From the driver's seat, Deedee immediately nodded her head to the beat.

...I feel so alone cornered by the four walls of my room
staring at the ceiling hearing voices I'm ready to go nuts
but I see All eyes on me, I got the media, po-po watching me
My mind playin tricks on me getting skitz homey
Somebody trying to murder me like they trying to plot on me
I gotta tighten up my circle before they put all this hurt on me
Riddle my flesh with bullets before they hand me 99 problems
I'll check their body language and see what strings they pull
rush that puppet master spray 'em fuck 'em bastards
I gotta play my cards and continue against all odds
Keep on shooting for the moon if I miss I'll be floating with stars...

"I'm so feeling this one, Coco," Deedee said. "I think that Biggie hook goes well with it too," Deedee continued.

"Yeah, I hear that, yo."

Steering the car through traffic, Deedee sang along with the hook from Coco's new single. "Back in the days, our parents used to take care of us. Look at 'em now, they even fuckin' scared of us... Things done changed cuz this ain't back in the days... Muthafucka this ain't back in the days, but you don't hear me though..."

Coco nodded her head to beat. Her lack of enthusiasm wasn't lost on Deedee, who had spent enough time with her best friend to know she was really feeling in the dumps.

"Wanna smoke sump'n?" Deedee asked, trying to cheer up Coco.

Coco glanced at Deedee and the realization hit her. Deedee was trying to cheer her up and Coco appreciated the effort. She went along with the suggestion.

"That sounds cool. Let's do it, yo."

"We gotta go cop the weed," Deedee said.

"Okay, let's," Coco said.

"Is that all you're gonna say? I mean you could sound a little bit more cheerful, Coco."

"I am cheerful. You know where you gonna cop?"

"No idea. I was kinda waiting on you to let me know. You know all the spots, Coco."

"I don't know all the spots. But you know what?"

"What...?"

"I've got some, yo."

"Pull it out then," Deedee said excitedly.

"It's at Madukes apartment, yo."

"Okay, let's get it," Deedee said, steering the car in the direction of uptown.

A few minutes later they pulled up and found parking near the apartment building. Coco and Deedee were walking to the entrance when they spot Kim with her son. Smiling, she waved at them.

"Hey y'all," Kim greeted.

"Hey Kim," Deedee answered.

"Whassup, yo?" Coco deadpanned.

"Is this your son?" Deedee asked.

"Yes, this is my Roshawn. Say hi to the rich and famous, Roshawn," Kim said.

"Hi Rich and Famous," Roshawn mumbled.

His reply was close to being inaudible, but the smile that he wore sent laughter through the air.

"He's a cutie," Deedee gushed.

"Yes, he got all that from his mother," Kim laughed. "How's it going, Coco?" she asked the silent Coco. "How's your mom?"

"She ain't too good, yo."

"Oh, I'm sorry to hear that shyt..." Kim said and immediately put her index finger to her lips. "Uh I mean.... Say hi to her fo' me the next time you see her."

"Sure, we ah, I'll..." Coco started and Kim cut her off.

"Shyt... I mean shoot. Things ain't too good all the way 'round," Kim said. "Where y'all going...?"

"Roshawn really got bigger since I seen him last, yo."

"Yes, it's been a minute. Right, Coco... What since his father got shot...?"

"Yeah, it's been a minute—"

"So what y'all getting ready to get into...?"

"Just chillin'—" Coco started out coyly, but was interrupted by her best friend.

"We were gonna smoke and chill for a minute," Deedee said.

"Y'all gonna be at Coco's place? I'll come by after I take Roshawn to the sitter."

"We don't know how long—"

"Okay," Deedee said, interrupting Coco.

She waited until they were out of earshot before she spoke again, but even then they weren't alone. Coco saw the regular crowd in front of the building. They rushed to greet her in their usual manner.

"Whassup, superstar...?"

"Coco, you're all that and your girl, damn! She could get it too."

"Y'all both fine."

Coco held up her two fingers in a V-formation. The peace sign stayed in her face while she went by the crowd. Deedee smiled at the compliments, but Coco had other things on her mind.

"Why did you invite Kim to chill with us, yo?"

"I really didn't. She sort of invited herself," Deedee countered.

"I thought you and I were chillin'. Not with her, yo," Coco said with disdain.

Coco and Deedee were in the stairwell, walking up to third floor. Before they could get to the landing, Kim was already knocking on her mother's apartment door.

"Damn! That was quick," Deedee said walking to where Kim stood waiting.

Coco opened the door and they all went inside the apartment. Kim pulled out a large plastic bag of weed. She took some of it out and placed it on the center table.

"Wow!" Deedee exclaimed, looking at the bag. "I've never seen soo much weed in my life."

"Shyt this for me and Tina, we spilt it with her brother," Kim said.

"That's a lot of weed," Deedee said.

Coco twisted the blunt and soon they were all smoking while the TV played videos in the background.

"So you still working with Eric, Coco?" Kim asked, pulling out a bottle of champagne. "I copped this for Tina, but I can buy her another," Kim continued and popped the cork.

"Yes we're—" Coco started but Kim interrupted.

"Just remember me when you making the video. I wanna shake my ass in your video," Kim laughed. "Shyt, I gots lots of ass to shake."

"Lemme get some glasses," Coco said, walking away to the kitchen.

"I love Coco's new song. It's really good," Deedee said.

"Aw shyt! Well lemme hear it, girl," Kim said.

"I don't have a copy with me," Coco said, handing a glass to both Deedee and Kim.

"I do, I do," Deedee said. "I took it out of the car and carried it just in case we needed background music," she continued.

Kim poured the drinks and they toasted. Smirking, Coco shot Deedee a look without saying anything. Deedee put the CD into the player, and they all listened as the song played.

I'm alone cornered in a room
It ain't paranoia just thoughts
Start poppin' off like hammers
I'm ready to go bananas beatin' on my chest
Feelin' I'm ready to go off like 2 techs verbal hammer
Problems hangin' from my neck like extra clips
My mind ain't playin tricks I ain't goin' skitzo
Nobody slip me a mick oh just voices from the past in my head
Coco go loc they said hurt 'em 'fore they do you
Even the ones who swear they know you
Others comin' at you just to know you
Whatever you do know who you're puffin' after
Just play your cards right against all odds
You'll succeed superseding all expectations
Shoot for the moon missing will only make you a star

Deedee sang along with the hook from Coco's new single. "Back in the days, our parents used to take care of us. Look at em now, they even fuckin' scared of us... Things done changed cuz this ain't back in the days... Muthafucka this ain't back in the days, but you don't hear me though..."

Alcohol and weed had Kim listening with fervor to the music. Nodding her head to the beat, she ad-libbed the lines she caught. Puffing the weed, they laughed, enjoying the song.

"That's some hot shit right there!" Kim shouted. "Coco, you on fire girl! You killing 'em!"

"Good looking, yo."

"And she's so fuckin' modest. I wish I could rip the track like that. The beat is grrr-eat and that's the perfect song for all the shit that you're going through right now," Kim said. "I love it. Like I said, just remember you-know-who when you ready to shoot that video," she said.

"Sure yo," Coco said with wry smile.

"I see you wearing those jeans. They fit you well," Deedee said.

"Shyt! I would be wearing my new designer shyt but these muthafuckin' thieving-ass bitches robbed Tina's place a couple weeks ago!"

"That's fucked up, yo."

"Yeah some crack-head stole all my new gear. Gucci, Versace, Vuitton and Valentino all gone. Like they got up, and walked away and shyt," Kim said, throwing up her hands. "You just gotta make sure your shyt is locked down or else!"

"That's true, yo."

"And you know some muthafuckin' crack-head walking 'round in my shyt."

"That's like the other night, Coco and I were traveling uptown and we saw that guy... What's his name Coco?"

"Who...?" Coco asked, noting nervously that Deedee had become vociferous.

"Home boy that you trying to give the message to... Ah?"

"What message, yo?"

"The message from the hospital, Coco," Deedee said, jump-starting Coco's memory. "And we saw him carrying all those packages. Then he jumped into a cab and tried to run away and we had to chase him..."

"Oh you mean, Dontay, yo."

"Yes him," Deedee said.

"He was carrying packages?"

"Yes," Deedee laughed. "Coco was even saying it was too early in the morning and that the stores weren't even open and it—"

"Shyt, Dontay...? Y'all remember exactly when that was? That nigga's a crack-head, and that muthafucka cannot be trusted," Kim said. Looking directly at Coco, she continued. "No disrespect meant, but you can't trust no crack-head! They'll fuckin' steal all your shyt!"

"It was that same Friday night when I saw you and Coco... Actually early the following Saturday morning..."

"Lemme find out that nigga broke into Tina's apartment! Oh my God! I will put my hands on him and break him and shyt!" Kim shouted. "Tell me, where you saw him at?"

Deedee glanced at Coco. She was wondering if Dontay had stolen the merchandise when they had seen him. Coco didn't care, but Deedee's mouth had drawn her into the fire.

"He was coming from the park side on the east side—"

"Shyt! When...? Oh my gosh! That's the same day Tina took me shopping downtown!"

There was long pause as Kim tried to recount the exact moment they left Tina's apartment, and what time Coco and Deedee had seen Dontay. Kim quickly summed it up in her brain and shrieked.

"Oh shyt, that nigga had all that time! I'm going to find him, and put a whopping on his ugly ass," Kim said.

"If it's actually him," Deedee cautioned.

"It had to be him. Shyt, y'all saw him with the packages like bags from a store. They were new, and that's why you could tell sump'n was up. Who else but a damn crack-head thief gon' be walking 'round at that time of the morning with all 'em packages," Kim said.

"You might be right, yo."

"I'm out," Kim said, getting her bag together. "Shyt, y'all can finish the rest of the champagne. I'll buy Tina another one."

"Here's some money to buy another," Deedee offered. I'm sure Tina's gonna want to drink some when she gets back."

"It's all good. You slow—you blow," Kim said.

"You sure...?" Deedee asked.

"Shyt, it's all good. It was for her new car, but she ain't back yet. She told me she was going with her father to buy it and that was since about lunch time," Kim said. "I'm gonna look for Dontay. He better not be the one. I swear that the monster will not be his only issue."

"Hold up. He's got AIDS, yo?" Coco asked.

Kim stared at her for a beat too long. Coco remembered that both Kim and her mother were connected to the rumor mill. She stared at Kim.

"It's only gossip, but Tina knows him better. I really don't know him too well like that and shyt," Kim said, backtracking.

She quickly gathered herself and hurried out of the apartment. Her jeans were so tight her ass cheeks were exposed. That was all they saw. Coco and Deedee both had the same look of surprise all over their faces. Kim's revelation about Dontay meant more since he was a former lover of her mother.

"That was kind of weird," Deedee said. "Maybe he did break into Tina's apartment. He was probably lying, watching them bring all those bags into her place. Then when he saw Kim and Tina leave, he chilled, and waited to make sure they didn't come back right away," Deedee said.

Expressionless, Coco listened intently to Deedee theorizing. Coco remained silent, but when Deedee started revving her for an answer Coco became agitated.

"Look, don't get me involved in their he-say-she-say BS. I just wanted to know if that nigga knew he had the monster before he got with madukes, yo."

"Yuck, bite your tongue, Coco. You're messing with my high," Deedee smirked.

"I'm telling you, Dee. Kim already blew my high, letting that piece of info slip. I'm a get at the nigga and find out, yo."

"Find out what, Coco?"

"If he had AIDS before he got with madukes. If so, then he murdered Madukes. It's as simple as that, yo."

"What you're saying, Coco...?"

"I'm sayin that nigga doesn't deserve to live any longer than madukes, yo. Madukes goes—Dontay goes."

"You're definitely right. He must be stopped or he could infect the whole neighborhood."

"You feeling me, yo?"

"Yes, but we must make sure, Coco," Deedee said. "You already know it's no good killing the wrong man. We need to make sure. But how do we do that?"

"That's real simple, Dee. In the hood, all you have to do is hang out in front of the building and you can find out everything about everyone coming and going in the building."

"So we're gonna be hanging out in the front of your building, Coco?"

"Not we... I am gonna hangout in front of my building, yo."

"But Coco, what if someone—"

"Dee, chill yo. Those people out front of the building are bitches, ho's, and niggas and they ain't gonna say nada to you 'bout nothing. They gotta know you and or respect you, yo."

"And you're saying they wouldn't talk to me. They all try to kick it to me, Coco."

"True, but you gotta understand. Niggas just trying to get up in your dress... Ho's they just like how fly you dress. And bitches hate but deal with you cuz they know you got status, yo."

"Status? What's that and how they know that?"

"By the way you dress, yo," Coco deadpanned.

"Uh-huh, Coco—are you saying I'm dressing whorish?"

"No Dee, don't be silly. I'm saying that the people in front of the building judge me and you on different standards. I'm Coco from the hood. You're Deedee, niece of Eric Ascot... Long money," Coco said, extending both her arms.

"All that money you're talking about I don't see. I have to start taking care of lil' Dee from the hood," Deedee laughed, patting her stomach. "All that money might not be there for Lil' Dee from da hood, she may have to go rap and dance or sing with Aunt Coco," Deedee laughed.

"I swear you're the illest, yo," Coco said, joining the laughter.

"Dontay, open up its Kim, I wanna talk to you," Kim repeated. "Open the door. Someone told me you're home. She just spoke to you a second ago. I asked her to call you. So don't front, my nigga. Open up the door now!" Kim shouted.

She banged couple more times and rang the doorbell. There was no response. Kim moved closer, putting her ear to the door. She could hear the rustling from behind the door.

"Shyt, if you don't open the door right now I'm gonna blow your spot up and you..." Kim lowered her voice when she heard the door being opened.

"Kim, I wasn't expecting you. I thought Tina was with you?"

"No, she ain't. I asked her to call you and tell you that we were together, my nigga," Kim said.

Dontay swallowed hard when he was greeted by Kim's cold,

scrutinizing stare. He was trying to crawl away with a bag of excuses. Kim sensed his weakness and slammed the door after him.

"Let me get straight to the point, Dontay," Kim said, sniffing around the apartment.

She walked around looking here and there. Searching, she opened a closet door, and peeked in the bedroom while Dontay stood in fear watching her. He stood in the middle of the tiny living room, and trembled while Kim circled him. She glanced around the apartment before swooping down on him. The salvo was something awful.

"What da fuck you did with all the shyt you took outta Tina's place?"

"I don't know what you talkin' 'bout!"

"Listen, you piece-a-shit-sick-ass-disease-carrying crack-head, I don't have time to waste!"

"I swear, I don't know what you talkin' 'bout!"

"Do not fuck around with me bitch-ass nigga. You know how I can spread a rumor—all I gotta do is tell the right people and everyone in the city will know you have the monster. Don't tempt me, Dontay!"

Eagle to a prey she ripped into his chest and dug out his heart. Her sharp talons pulled out her cell phone, a symbol of communication to the world and started dialing.

"Shyt, I got some news for you, girl. Know that nigga that be walkin' round the hood, calling himself 'pimpin''? Hmm-hmm... Yeah him he got the—"

"It was Tina's idea," Dontay said.

Kim's conversation came to an abrupt pause. She slowly looked Dontay up and down from his fake alligator shoes to his hairdo. She noticed for the first time that his curls never quite curled. Dontay was rocking a badly done perm and Kim let him know.

"You fuckin' bad-hair-having nigga naps-for-curls! How da fuck you gonna bring my girl in this convo like that...? Shyt, this between me and you my nigga, don't even try to bring Tina's name up.

Shyt, me and her went out that night, my nigga!"

"Put the cell phone down, please. I'll tell you," Dontay pleaded.

"I'm a call you back, Mommy. This gon' take a minute," Kim said, ending the call.

She eyed Dontay with fury. With shaky hands, he was reaching to get a cigarette. He groped to retrieve the pack and a book of matches at the same time. Kim shook her head as he put the cigarette to his mouth and lit it.

"Fucking loser, you best be tellin' da truth..." she said and her voice trailed when she heard him speaking.

"I know that. I know y'all went out together. She called me and told me to go check if her was window open. And then told me to take all the bags, she was gonna return them to the store or sump'n. She ain't told me that your bags were there, too."

"Really nigga, and what about my money that was in one of the bags and shyt?"

"What money? I ain't touch no money. I gave her back the bags the next evening!"

This revelation left Kim speechless. She blinked rapidly several times, trying to digest the information. She processed the facts slowly while Dontay smoked.

"You sayin' Tina came and took all the bags and that was it?"

"Yes, that was it. She hit me with a lil' dough and I swear that was it, Kim."

She stared at Dontay with a menacing look. There was evil in her eyes and he shuddered in fear, but Kim was deep in thoughts. She glanced at him, looking him up and down. Then Kim turned to walk away. She looked back with a smirk when she heard Dontay.

"Kim, please. I'm a pimp under pressure, there's a monster on my back. I don't wanna take my life, but if you get on your horn, and start talkin' then that shit be all over the place. I don't want that stinkness following me around," Dontay pleaded.

"I could care less, my nigga. Ain't karma a bitch...? A pimp with AIDS... Life's a bitch and then you die."

"I'm still tryin' to live like Magic, and die respectable is what I'm sayin', Kim. Please don't blow up my spot," Dontay said, sucking nervously on the cigarette.

"You know, Dontay, when I was a teenager, I really thought I loved you. Remember those times, back in the days when you used to roll up in your big phat whips? Oh man, you used to make me wet. I ain't mad atcha, my nigga. If what you're sayin' is true then you ain't got shyt to worry 'bout."

"Kim, Kim I remember, back in the days I was big time. Now I'm trying to repeat it. I'm a be on top again, Kim. It's my body that's got the monster in it, not my mind," Dontay said, pointing to his dome.

Kim took a couple steps back, and quizzically stared at Dontay. She was summing him up. He appeared physically alright. A lot of women may find him handsome, she thought. But she knew he carried a deadly virus. Kim continued to listen to the excitement building in Dontay.

"They got drugs for all that. Look at Magic Johnson, Number thirty-two—that's me. I'm starting with this... My modeling biz about to jump off, Kim, I'm also doing camera work, videos and so on," he said, winking lecherously at her. "Kim, you got all the right assets to be my bottom... I mean my top model, and you'll get prime spots in videos and—"

"Nigga, I'm good. I just came here to find out that shyt with Tina's. So I just want you to know that you can drop me from your list of candidates, my nigga."

"A'ight then, Kim. I respect that."

"Do your shyt just don't include me in it."

"But you should check your girlfriend real good. She might be trying to do you wrong. Check the facts and you'll see," Dontay said, exhaling smoke with a sigh of relief.

"Yes, I'll do that. Like I said, if you're tellin' da truth then pimp on, my nigga. But I find out your ass up to no good, then its gon be ho's up, and pimp's down, my nigga. Believe that!"

With a swish of her ass, Kim walked past a stunned Dontay. Pulling out her cell phone, she was out the door, and down the hallway. She got on the elevator, thinking about what Dontay had told her. She dialed on her cell phone, no service. Kim's hectic mind couldn't rest until she called Tina. She had her on speed dial and hit the button as soon as she got off the elevator. Kim listened intently as her call went straight to voicemail.

She walked out to the corner and waved her arm to hail a cab. Three gypsy cabbies immediately responded. Kim jumped into the first one. A couple of minutes later, the taxi rolled to a stop outside Tina's building. After paying the driver, Kim jumped out and ran inside the building. Kim pulled out her keys, and fidgeted with them to find the spare keys to Tina's apartment. Kim walked quickly to the lobby, and got in the elevator.

Soon after, Kim was standing outside Tina's apartment door. She tinkered with the keys, trying to figure the right one. Kim tried to open the door, but couldn't figure out the right combination of keys.

"I'm gonna wait right here or wake this bitch outta bed," she sighed ringing the doorbell in frustration.

There was rustling behind the door and she heard Tina's voice. Kim impatiently waited with hands on her hips, while tapping her heels.

"Who...?"

"It's Kim, bitch!"

The door opened and Kim barged in past a surprised Tina. She walked down a short hallway to the living room and saw Flack pulling on his clothes. Tina, clad in a housecoat, was walking behind her.

"We gotta talk, bitch!" Kim said.

"It wasn't what I planned, but—" Flack started chatting

nervously, but Kim waved her arm, cutting him off.

"Shyt, I don't give a fuck about your bitch ass!"

"I ain't seen no tags on him, ho," Tina said.

"I never meant to hurt—" Flack started again, but was rudely by Kim.

"Shyt nigga, please!"

"As you can see he just had to skin my kitty cat alive," Tina said, letting her housecoat slip just enough for Kim to see her nudity beneath. "He ate the shit outta my pussy," she laughed, looking at Flack.

He slipped into his pants, and seemed to relax when he saw that Kim was not yelling at him. Maybe she wasn't mad at him. Maybe he could have them both. Tina was standing practically naked, and Kim sat down on the sofa. She was looking around at the empty liquor bottles, and clipped blunt in the ashtray when she felt Flack sitting next to her. He reached over, trying to hug her.

"Shyt, if you ever touch me—they be calling you numb nubs, okay?" Kim said in her nastiest tone.

"You better leave her alone, Flack. That ho' mad as hell. And ain't no calming down a mad ho'," Tina laughed, lighting a cigarette. "Why you so mad, ho'? Duh, he wanted this pussy more than yours. You know that's how niggas are. They always want to have the best pussy, ho."

"Look, I don't give a shyt about this fucking bitch-ass nigga! I just wanna know why you fuckin' tried to play me, bitch?"

"You mean Flack? You said you fuckin' with Eric Ascot. How many fuckin' men you want for yourself, ho?"

"I'm really not talking 'bout this piece a shit of a nigga!" Kim said, her tone getting harsher. "Who gives a fuck about what he do... This' between me, you, and Dontay, bitch!"

"Y'all ain't gotta notice that I'm here while y'all busy arguing about some other nigga and all," Flack said.

Kim and Tina both stared at the shirtless man with contempt. Then they looked at each other, and shook their heads simultaneously.

"Shyt, get da fuck outta here. Bird-ass nigga!"

"Who you think you talkin' to like that, bitch? This ain't your crib!" Flack said to Kim.

"It's mine. And nigga, you ain't gon' be up here callin' my girl a bitch. So muthafucka you gotta get da fuck up outta here right now!" Tina said, signaling with her thumb conspicuously in the air like an irate baseball umpire throwing out an anguished batter. "Fuck that, nigga!"

Flack jumped up, and put on his shirt. He quickly fixed his clothes. Then without saying anything, he angrily stomped out the door. Kim and Tina kept their eyes on him, waiting for him to leave. Flack stared at them for a beat then he left, slamming the door. Kim and Tina both shook their heads. Then they resumed their conversation.

"So bitch, word has it that you sent Dontay to rob the place, and take all the shyt," Kim said. "Is that true?"

"Shut da front door, ho! Whose words? Dontay...? He ain't nothing but a wanna be fake-ass pimp-dying of AIDS."

"And he also knew that we went to the club and your ass called him and told him to go take the bags outta your place, like you been robbed. Shyt, I can't believe you tried to play me by going through all that trouble, bitch. If you didn't want me to have the money—all you had to do was not give me it to me, bitch!"

"All that screaming must make you thirsty. You want a drink, ho?"

"Don't try to appease me with no drink, bitch. You actually tried to play me. I still can't get over that, bitch. Of all the dirty schemes you played on other people, I mean you tried to do your girl Kim dirty?"

"Shut your face, bitch! It ain't even like that," Tina said.

"Okay, I guess I better roll up a blunt and get comfy for this one. Here comes bull-shyt," Kim said, undoing the straps on her espadrilles and unbuckling her name belt.

Then Kim stood and shimmied out of her tight jeans. Folding it and laying on a cluttered side table, she poured a drink and sipped. Then she pulled out a bag of weed.

"Shyt! That tasted like piss. Yee-uck! What's that?" Kim said, making a gas-face.

"It's Brugal, some type of cheap-ass Dominican rum," Tina said. "That nigga bought it. I told you 'is ass was cheap."

"Fuck all that other shyt. He already showed his true colors."

"I'm just sayin' that nigga is not the one. He—"

"I'm already onto the next nigga," Kim said with a smirk.

"You don't have to get defensive, ho!"

"Trust me, I'm not defensive, bitch. I just wanna hear your explanation of this whole shyt. What you thought you'd accomplish with all this scheming, bitch?" Kim said, pouring a drink from another bottle.

Nodding in delight, she said, "This da shyt." She continued rolling the blunt while listening to Tina.

"I really wasn't trying to do anything. I just had to ah... You know? Justify the numbers. Money was going out and nothing coming in, and I, ah figure if I can make some on the money we already spent then you know?"

"But you forgot one thing, rich bitch. Kim is smart. Okay, you remember that," Kim said, and lit the blunt.

"Shut da front door! It's how rich people think, ho. I don't want to ever go back to being a broke-ass bitch from the projects."

"So you were thinking like a rich bitch, huh?" Kim asked, taking a sip and puffing.

"I gotta make that dough work for us, ho. And I have to make moves."

"Let me get this shyt straight. You was gonna use poor ol' stupid nigga-ass Kim. She ain't gonna know the difference 'bout shyt.

Kim so damn dumb she'll eat her own name written on a piece of paper, huh? Tell me that was the plan?" Kim said.

"Shut your face! That was not no plan, ho!"

"Damn right it wasn't cuz that shyt is not gonna work. My mommy didn't raise no dumb-ass-kids. Maybe my middle brother that's locked up. But I can read between the lines, bitch," Kim said, puffing on the blunt.

"And I got us more money, ho," Tina said.

"Oh really...? You did, huh?"

Tina disregarded Kim's sarcasm. Under her veneer, Tina's wily mind was busy at work. She was already thinking of a way to repay Dontay. Kim was her best friend. Neither of them graduated but they went to high school together. From murder to stripping, Tina had done everything illegal and legal to make money. She did all she wanted to do and always felt like the leader. Kim adored her free spirit, but was more conservative. She wanted the money and rewards, without doing the dirty work.

"Only thing is we have to do this one thing," Tina said, watching Kim licking her dried lips, preparing for another blunt. "You not gonna share?" she asked.

"You already got my nigga what else you want? My blunt...? Nah bitch go roll your own shyt."

"Shut you face, ho'! My money in that ounce too," Tina said.

"I ain't sayin no to that, bitch. I'm saying you gonna have to roll your own shyt!"

"Okay, I remember when... Hold up, hold up," Tina said, walking away.

Returning in a hot minute later, she carried two bags. She handed Kim the bag filled with money. Kim skeptically gazed at the shopping bag then at Tina.

"Whatcha got in the other bag?" Kim asked and passed Tina the blunt.

"I'll tell you later, ho'."

Kim opened it and a wide smile lit up her face. She stuck her hands in the shopping bag and fingered the money stacked in it.

"Hmm, my money," she hummed.

"I done told you, ho'. We gotta do sump'n for that dough," Tina said, puffing the blunt and watching Kim.

"Okay, bitch, break that shyt down while I count how much is in this bag," Kim said, emptying the shopping bag of money.

"It's all there, ten thousand dollars, ho'."

"I'm still counting this shyt."

"I should've taken some of that money for paying all your tabs, ho'."

"Bitch, lemme hear what we have to do for this?"

"First of all it ain't we—it's you, ho'. You have to put this listening device in his apartment," Tina said, reaching into the second bag.

"Huh-uh, who the hell wants to spy on this man, now...?"

"Max said he's been trying to get Eric to call his ex-fiancée, and Eric been refusing to do it. So he just wanna keep an eye on Eric because he's been actin' kinda tough, and now he doesn't even wanna return Max's calls, and they have to work on this for the court case."

"There has to be a reason for Eric not calling him back. And as for his ex, shyt I read the newspaper. That bitch just turned on him."

"How you know, ho'?"

"It's all over the news, bitch!"

"Shut your face, ho. A lot of that shit is pure gossip. I just wanna hear about stocks and bonds," Tina said, grabbing Kim's ass."

"Shyt bitch! Stop pinching my assets," Kim said.

"Exactly, use all that assets to complete the mission. Get this device planted in Eric's place."

"How bitch...?" Kim asked.

"Well, ho', you're friends with his niece and artist. How 'bout you think like you're a good singer, lie and tell her you wanna be on her track?"

"That's not a lie. I'd love to be on a track with Coco, produced by Eric Ascot. Shyt that would be a dream come true," Kim said.

"Don't wet your panties, ho'," Tina laughed, passing Kim the blunt.

Eric sat quietly in the studio replaying the song over and over. He drank black coffee like he had been up all night. His frustration wedged deep into the lines above his brows. Eric turned to something stronger than caffeine to ease the thoughts. He poured from the bottle, then raising the glass to his mouth, he flung the heavy liquid to the back of his throat. He repeated the action over and over.

He left the bottle of Louis XIII Le Jeroboam and staggered away with his cell phone held tightly in his hand. The rich taste of cognac did nothing to erase his thought of calling her. It remained like a stain on his mind, still there after wetting his whistle. Eric wanted to skip this episode, but it seemed like the more he tried, the more he felt trapped in a web. Sophia had betrayed him and that was it. Ignoring the wish of his attorney and his better sense, Eric steadfastly refused to call Sophia.

The attorney warned him that her testimony could be damaging and jeopardize his defense. Eric winced at the thought of his freedom being taken away based on statements by someone he helped through law school. He shrugged to the irony and flipped a switch. A heavy bass guitar solo banged loudly. Eric let the rhythm fill the air before adding kettledrum and handclaps.

"Oh yeah, Houston I think we have a liftoff that makes me feel real charged... Wanna rip this to shreds, and bring it to y'all..." Coco sang, walking into the studio.

"I think we're ready for it. Not a lot of people can do something with this beat right here. Maybe you can. Are you ready, Coco?"

"Yeah, let's get it, yo. I'm amped."

Deedee smiled at the pair. Watching them working closely together, she realized that her uncle had found a real protégé. Coco went with all his beats—good and bad, his hiccups—she was now learning from his unique experience. An excellent student, Coco sang, rapped and started feeling full confidence in her ability.

"Lift off taking my coat off gotta go off into my zone
lifting off my coat I gotta get up into my zone...
this Harlem swagga is rolling back,
gotta let you think renaissance swing made it back again live
I live it daily writing like Langston Hughes in my verses,
Zora eyes watching 'em not ba,d huh?
I'm gonna make it live Apollo in my blood
running down 1-2-5 black on blacks back door at Club Savoy
struttin' when me and Mr. Ascot connect...
what can I say are you feeling these changes
or are you just stuck on this champagne
flow like delivering what you need to your home town...
Gotta go off into my zone, lifting off my coat clearing my throat...
I gotta get, get up in my zone...
Over-stand Bobbie Seale inside George Jackson action

I'll shed blood but why die when I'd murder you several times
my third rail flow on this track,
activist Angela Davis wanna end lives in a revolution
but then get a prayer fell on my lips
I cannot go that route now spreadin' rhymes like
    Lovin' all my peoples living and dealing survivors of life's
struggles...
cocaine swagger let these niggas know they outta
 they minds tryin to sway my rhymes every time I pause...
I change time drugs coming from Madukes' loin..."

Coco went silent and biting her lips, she nodded her head to the rhythm of the beat. Eric watched her closely and waited for a few minutes before he turned down the volume.

"You good...?" Eric asked.

"Yeah, I was just thinking about what I was saying and—"

The phone next to Deedee buzzed silently and Deedee picked it up. She walked out and closed the door of the studio then she answered.

"Hello...?"

"Hey Dee," Kim said.

"Hi Kim," Deedee said. "What's up?"

"Yeah, I was wondering if I could stop by and you know chill...?"

"I'm afraid my uncle and Coco—"

"Coco and Eric are working together? I could stop by and watch and shyt. You know say hello to Mr. Ascot and..."

"Okay, okay Kim come on by. You've got the address, right?"

"Yeah, I can't wait and shyt. I'll be there soon, Dee," Kim said.

Tina thoughtfully stared at Kim when she hung up the phone. Kim checked her makeup and got out of the cab. Tina waved at her entering Ascot's building. Making sure that her plan was in effect, she went off in the cab across town.

Kim continued upstairs and was met by security's inquisitive eyes. They nodded as she sashayed by them and went inside the apartment. Coco and Eric was busy getting the lyrics right, the collaboration was filled with creative energy.

"Take it from the second segment. You started at 'Gotta go off into my zone, lifting off my coat clearing my throat... I gotta get, get up in my zone...'" Eric said, humming the lyrics.

"Okay, gotcha... Hit it..."

Uh ha... Gotta go off into my zone,
lifting off my coat clearing my throat...
I gotta get, get up in my zone...
Over-standin Bobbie Seale inside George Jackson action
I'll shed blood but why die when I'd murder
you several times third rail flow on this track,
activist like Angela Davis wanna end lives
revolution but then get a prayer fell on my lips
I cannot go that route now spreadin' rhymes
like love to all my peoples living and dealing
survivors of life's struggles... cocaine swagger
let these niggas know before they utta
minds tryin to sway my rhymes every time I pause...
I change time drugs coming from madukes' loin...

Again, Coco paused. She was not being able to complete the line. She nodded for a couple of beats then she looked up, surprised by the voice. The beat was still rocking and Kim shouted above it.

"That was sounding really good and shyt, Coco!" Kim loudly exclaimed.

Both Coco and Eric turned their attention to the newcomer. Deedee stood next to her and smiled, shaking her head.

"Is it alright, Kim was, ah, in the neighborhood," Deedee said. "She wanted to say hi to your uncle."

"Hi Kim," Eric smiled.

"Kim was singing something she said could be used as a hook to the song," Deedee announced.

"I didn't know you could sing, Kim?" Eric smiled, getting closer.

"There are a lot of things you don't know," Kim said, returning Eric's smile.

"I heard her do her thing before," Coco said.

"You want the beat or—"

"Nah, I'm good. I was singing as soon as I heard Coco rhyming and shyt."

"Go ahead, Kim. Sing the hook," Deedee said.

"Huh... This is for my bitches and ho's who been waiting for a long, long time just to get into their zone all this time been waiting for a long, long time just to get into this for long, long time..." Kim sang, snapping her fingers in rhythm. "Something like that, you know...? It's just a lil' sump'n and shyt," she said.

"It could work," Eric said with no hesitation. "Your voice sounds just right and everything. Coco, what you think?"

"Yeah, I mean, I've heard Kim's voice before. She can blow it down. So we can do it. I'm totally with it," Coco said.

"Yes, I agree with both your opinions," Deedee smiled.

"Oh my and that's a just a little taste—"

"Alright it's minimum talking, Kim. I already know you so I'm a need you to sing that hook again," Eric said.

Coco and Deedee walked outside of the studio. Deedee closed the door and handed Coco her cell phone.

"Damn she come up here and jumped on the track, yo. I mean why didn't you warn me at least?"

"She just called then she was here. I'm sorry I had no time to warn you. You were in the midst of doing the song," Deedee said, handing Coco a cell phone. "Coco, later for that—you've gotta call the hospital," Deedee said with urgency.

Coco could hear Kim's voice still coming through the insulated studio. She looked at Kim then at Deedee holding the cell phone.

"Huh... This is for my bitches and ho's
been waiting for a long, long time
to get into their zone all this time been waiting
for a long, long time
just to get into this for long, long time..."

Kim was singing the hook when Coco barged into the studio. Eric glanced up at her and saw the pain all over her face. There were no tears, but Coco's breathing was coming hard like she was running a race.

"Deedee, get her some water," Eric shouted, rushing to the teen.

Coco collapsed in his arms. Eric held her and Kim held the door as he carried Coco to the sofa. Deedee arrived with the water and looked down at Coco's frame.

"She passed out?" Deedee asked.

"Yeah, she did the same damn shyt ... Ah... thing at mommy's place when I gave her the news about Rightchus. But we were puffin' weed and shyt..." Kim said and let her voice trailed. "Were y'all puffin'?" she asked, looking at Deedee.

"No we weren't," Deedee said, walking away.

"Mommy used Robitussin. That's ghetto. I don't know if y'all got any of that."

Deedee returned and saw Eric checking Coco's vital functions at her wrist. She found some smelling salts for them. She ushered her uncle out of the way and waved the capsule below Coco's nostrils.

The teen stirred then tried to push Deedee's hand away. Coco shook her head as if she had just been punched out. She tried to get up.

"I gotta get to the hospital, yo. It's Madukes, yo. She—"

"Oh my God...!" Kim screamed, running to her bag.

Eric was on his cell phone dialing then calling. Deedee was comforting the weeping Coco and Kim took the opportunity to plant the electronic device the way Tina had instructed.

"Let's go," Eric said.

Eric and Deedee helped the devastated Coco as they walked out. Coco's head was spinning so much that she thought she would pass out on the elevator. Eric held the door as Deedee, Coco, and Kim filed in. There were hushed tones filtering between Deedee and Kim, but Coco made no sound during the ride to the hospital. Jumping out of the limousine when it came to a stop, Coco raced to the entrance, Deedee, Kim and Eric were following closely behind her.

Hospital security seemed nicer, even letting the group upstairs immediately. Coco's expression appeared to be calm, but everyone could tell she was trapped in a current of emotion.

The elevator seemed to move slower than usual, but eventually they reached the seventh floor. Coco watched the door slide open. She seemed confused for a second.

"It's the next floor, yo."

It took only a few minutes to reach the next floor, but for Coco and the group with her, it could have been a lifetime. They arrived and the elevator doors slid away. This time Coco jumped off and immediately saw Nurse Roberts.

There were tears in her eyes when she embraced Coco. The teen flopped lifeless against the white uniform of the dedicated nurse.

"It's no use, Coco. The doctors did all they could—her system just rejected all the medications. She left us about fifteen minutes ago," Nurse Roberts said, still holding to Coco's seemingly lifeless frame.

Deedee was weeping. Kim hugged her and started crying. Eric sighed and tried to help Deedee. Coco stood sobbing.

"She passed away peacefully. There was no pain," the

compassionate nurse said.

"Can I see her?" Coco asked, tears slowly falling from her eyes.

"Sure, I'll arrange it for a few minutes," the nurse said.

There were no dry eyes as the nurse, and Deedee supporting Coco's wobbly bop, walked to the deceased woman's room. Eric hugged Kim against his body and she stuck with him like glue as they followed behind. They waited quietly outside the room while Coco disappeared inside.

Nurse Roberts turned to Deedee and asked, "Do you know if she gave that man, ah—"

"Dontay...?" Deedee asked.

"Yes, I think that's his name. It's imperative that he come in and get himself checked. He's a potential carrier of the virus. It's our responsibility to—"

"You talkin' Dontay, Dontay? That fake pimp?" Kim asked Deedee. "Shyt if you talkin' 'bout that Dontay then he already got the monster."

"What...?" Nurse Roberts asked.

"He's positive. He got AIDS," Kim said.

"You mean he's already tested and knows for sure?" The surprised nurse asked.

"Yes, he used to do this big-time pimpin' and got caught up in the system and went down for about five or six years for forgery and embezzlement of a lot of money. I don't know for sure what he did when he was there. Cuz them men be tossin' each other on the reg when they in lockup. He came outta the feds with the A-I-D-S monster and shyt."

They were all stunned, Coco walked out with tears in her eyes and Deedee hugged the distraught teen.

"I'm sorry, Coco," the nurse said. "Please get her home safely. I was told you'd be responsible, right Mr. Ascot?"

"Yes," Eric said.

"There are a few papers to be signed for the death certificate," Nurse Roberts said. "If you would like to do that now then—"

"Sure, okay," Eric said and left the girls.

Coco leaned against the hospital wall, banging her head. It wasn't hard enough to knock her out, but Deedee moved to pull her form the wall.

"Coco, don't take out your frustration like that. Guess who was already positive while messin' with your mother?" Deedee asked.

Coco stared at her with a perplexed expression. She said nothing to Deedee and heard Kim joining into the conversation.

"Dontay—"

"He had A-I-D-S this whole time," Deedee eagerly said. "He's the one who passed the virus to your mother, Coco," she continued. "I think Tina had it all setup to happen."Coco stood for a beat looking in the direction of her mother's room. She saw the gurney with her mother's body being rolled out by hospital's orderlies.

"What da fuck? Are you serious, yo?" Coco asked and the anguish in her tone echoed through the hospital's corridors.

The cab stopped and the driver was still busy petting Tina's exposed pussy. He had one hand on the steering wheel. The other was fingering Tina's exposed clit. She leaned back smiling as he tried to keep one eye on the road, and the other on her panty-less crotch. They had almost side-swiped another driver, came close to running over a pedestrian in the crosswalk, and twice nearly rear-ended another driver.

"Ah hmm, yes-s-s, right here is fine," Tina said. "No not your fingers. This is my destination," she laughed.

The cabbie stopped the car, and drooled while licking his fingers. Tina laughed watching him succumb to her feminine powers. It was all a game to her, and she gave him one last look. Then Tina seductively wiggled her backside on the way out the cab.

It was a humid day and her extra-short tight-fitting clothes made her desirable to any man. She could hear the trail of whistles following her. Tina flaunted her resources while walking to Dontay's apartment. She rang the bell. After a stall, he opened the door.

"My queen," he smiled, swinging the door to greet her.

She sashayed inside without saying anything. Dontay dutifully followed behind her. Tina glanced around the place and looked at Dontay.

"Dontay, Dontay, Dontay, you're gonna have to learn to do what I ask, and not as you like," Tina said.

He immediately knew what Tina was talking about. She walked close and patted Dontay's sweating cheek.

"She was gonna expose me. You know what kinda mouth that bitch, ah your friend has. I mean one word outta her and everything I'm building goes out the window," he said.

"Shut your face! You've already said too much. It ain't about Dontay. This is way bigger than you and me. I keep tellin' you that," Tina said. "Now your bitch-ass-ness got you in trouble.

"What you mean, Tina?"

"You fucking up," she deadpanned.

"But she was gonna expose me. It would've been all over anyway."

"Stick to the script, Dontay. You ain't that important!"

"What was I supposed to do? You said you'd handle Kim. That was your words to me, Tina."

"These people I'm working with—they serious, Dontay. They are not playin'."

"So what's gonna happen now?"

"You're out, Dontay. You've gotta get up out of the city by the end of the day," Tina said. "That's what I was told to tell you."

"Damn, Tina!" Dontay exclaimed jumping up. "We had sump'n. You used to be my bottom ho'. My girl..." Dontay's voice trailed.

He saw her poker face, and knew she wasn't phased by his

pleas. Dontay slowly realized his begging was falling on deaf ears. Tina reached inside the Birkin bag on her shoulder and pulled out a wad of money. She offered the wad to Dontay while she spoke.

"You're right, Dontay," Tina said with a chuckle. "Back in the days, I used to be all that for you. But you fucked all that shit up. You created me, Dontay. You taught me how to look out for myself. You should feel good. Cuz now you're sick and I feel sorry for you," she said. "But things ain't always what it seems," she continued, attempting to hand him the money.

Dontay was about to take the money then suddenly changed his mind and slapped the wad from Tina's hand. He stepped back, holding his head. Dontay closed his eyes when Tina tossed the rest of the money at him and started to walk out.

"I don't want your pity," he shouted, looking at the money scattered on the floor. "I ain't running out like Rightchus did!"

"Dontay, you taught me a few tricks in this game of life, and I'll never forget them. But you see what those peoples did to Rightchus. They'll be coming for you," Tina warned.

"Whatever, let them come. I ain't scared," Dontay calmly said. "I'm dying of AIDS. What do I have to live for, huh? So let 'em come. I'm already dead. "

"These people 'bout their biz, so just pick up the money and get out of town," Tina said, and strutted out the door.

When Tina reached outside, she dialed on her cell phone, the phone rang a couple times before her party answered.

"Hello...?"

"Max... I delivered the message... Yes and the dough," she said. "He didn't take it too well."

"Good, it will be handled from here."

Tina hung up the call and dialed another number. She waited for a few moments before she asked, "How's it goin, ho'...? Meet me uptown later. Let's get a mani and pedi..."

Later that day Kim and Tina met at the hair-and-nail salon. They were both sashaying in the tightest of dresses, walking like they didn't see the other women staring evilly at them. Needless to say all the men in the vicinity had their eyes riveted on the pair of derrieres going by. They stood outside, and finished smoking their cigarettes while chatting.

"Shut da front door, ho! You singing on Coco's song for real. Then what happened? I know you tried to fuck that nigga," Tina said.

"I didn't get a chance. I was only up in there for a few then we had to go to the hospital and shyt."

"Shut your face, ho! Why you had to go to the hospital?"

"Coco's mom, bitch."

"She's still in the hospital?"

"I'm telling you it was sad and shyt. Everybody bawling for Coco and her mother," Kim said, shaking her head.

"Shut your mouth! She dead?

"Dead, dead, dead, and shyt, bitch."

"So did you at least do what I ask, ho?"

"Yes bitch. I left the device in Eric's apartment and shyt. I forgot how huge that damn place was. He needs me up in there helping him decorate and shyt," Kim said.

"Shut your face! What you gon' do ho', be the housekeeper?"

"Nah bitch, we'd hire your mira-mira ass for that shyt. I'm talkin' bout being Mrs. Ascot and shyt."

"Shut your face, ho'! Eric Ascot marrying your poor ass, not happening—definitely not," Tina said, shaking her head.

"Leave me alone. A ho' can dream can't she?"

"Shut da front door, ho!"

"Lemme go get my mani and pedi done and shyt."

"Pay for mine, I'll give you the money back, ho'," Tina said.

"Nah, nah, not the rich bitch asking poor ol' Kim for a loan...?"

"Shut your face! I got money, ho. I had to give Dontay money earlier and I ain't got no more cash on me."

"I thought you stopped doing that shyt for him. I didn't know you still his ho'."

"Shut your face! He had to leave town in a hurry."

"He told me he was starting all this model and video biz. Where he had to leave for in such hurry and shyt—Cali?"

"That nigga was too busy leaving. He ain't had time to say where he going."

"Shyt, that's hurrying. What he smell your stank ass and shyt?

"Shut your face, ho'! You gon' give me the money or what?"

"Okay bitch, come on let's get our nails did. I gotcha on da dough and shyt..." Kim said and they both strutted into the nail salon.

It was later that evening and Dontay still had not picked up the money scattered on the floor. He sat drinking whiskey from the bottle and fiddling with the thoughts in his mind. He heard the knock on his door. Dontay paid no heed to the knocking, but the banging grew louder, and he could no longer ignore it.

"Who da fuck is it?" he slurred.

"It's the police. Open up in there!"

His brain jumped into panic mode and Dontay grabbed his shirt. He picked up the bottle and took a last swig. Then he ran to bathroom and popped the window opened. Dontay jumped out the window and swung his body across to an adjoining building. He lost his footing and attempted to brace himself on an air conditioner.

Night had darkened the evening sky and the whiskey saturated his system. Dontay miscalculated his leap. The air conditioner was not secured to the window and easily gave way under his weight. Dontay found himself falling from the eighth floor.

"Oh shi-i-i-i-t!" he shrieked.

His body landed in a heap with the trash behind the building. Dontay realized that the stacked garbage bags had cushioned his fall. Out of the blue, Dontay smiled, happy he was still alive. Then all of a sudden, the weight of the air conditioner crashed into him. With blood leaking from the wound on his head, Dontay's twisted, lifeless form mixed with the garbage in a strange, macabre collage.

The next day, news of Dontay's fall was all over the building. People were gathered in front of the building talking. Dontay's name was warming their lips. In a hot minute, the debacle of Dontay was in the rumor mill and traveling around the neighborhood. Kim immediately called Tina after receiving the news.

"Bitch, you heard that Dontay threw himself off the building and shyt last night...?"

"Shut da front door, ho'! He did what?"

"Come over here—mad drama on this side, bitch. I gotta call Mommy and let her know Coco's mother died and shyt."

"A'ight, ho. I'll be there later," Tina said.

Coco woke up with her head swimming in a deep sea of emotions. There were so many thoughts swirling, her mind was confused. She stared at the room and for a minute she forgot where she was. Startled by her surroundings, Coco rapidly blinked her eyes trying to clear her head. Then she rubbed her eyes and felt the tear stains. Slowly she remembered that she was at Eric's apartment. She heard Deedee's voice.

"Coco...? Are you okay?"

"I feel like I was in this horrible nightmare... And madukes..." Coco's voice trailed as her feelings consumed her. Coco's body shuddered when she continued. "Madukes was dead, yo."

Deedee heard Coco's tone of despair. She stared at her best friend's puffy, red eyes. Coco had cried herself to sleep. A look of confusion clouded her face. Coco was shaking her head.

"It's true, huh? Madukes is dead, right Dee?"

Deedee ran over to Coco and threw her arms around her. They both stood crying in each other's embrace for a couple of beats.

"Tell me..."

"Yes," Deedee whispered. "She passed away yesterday at the hospital."

"So it really happened, yo?"

"Yes, we went to the hospital and—"

"I remember going to the hospital and then I was talking to the nurse..."

"You fainted, but don't worry. Uncle E has everything covered. He's making all the arrangements for the funeral. And you're staying here. So you better get used to staying here," Deedee said.

"I gotta go to Madukes' apartment... I mean. Well, you know what I mean, right, yo?"

"Let's freshen up and get brunch then we'll go over to your former apartment," Deedee said trying to keep Coco's mind on track.

"Cool, let me take a shower, yo."

Coco stepped inside the shower and selected "Massage." The warm water soothed her body, but the pain was growing deep down inside her. She felt the sting of the water hitting her skin as her lithe body heaved with sorrow. Coco sobbed.

Later, she slipped her dark shades on. Coco stepped out dressed in all black from head to toe. Deedee was waiting for her and she too was wearing an all-black outfit. Together they walked to a small café on the corner. There was a midday rush, but the girls were seated immediately. Coco ordered hot chocolate and perused the menu. After a few minutes, Coco put the menu down and went blank.

"You should try to eat something," she heard Deedee said, but Coco's mind was caught in her sorrow. "Try the fruit salad. It's always good."

"Okay, yo."

The waiter came by, took their orders and walked away.

Coco sat with the weight of her mother's death like a boulder on her shoulder. She was tired from not sleeping and yawned several times. Coco fiddled with her hand, wanting badly to make this a dream, but it was her reality. Thinking about her mother's passing, Coco bit her fist and let the sadness drive her to tears. Coco quietly removed the shades and wiped her eyes.

Deedee saw her pain and reached out. She held Coco's hand and tried to provide some measure of support. Sometimes being best friends was just not enough. Deedee quickly paid the tab when she realized that Coco really needed this moment to cry. She guided her out of the café as onlookers stared. Coco's body shuddered while they walked out. She felt Deedee's hug, and the distraught teen laid her head on the shoulders of her best friend.

They sat in Deedee's car and smoked cigarettes. Coco was massaging her temple with her fingertips.

"What's bothering you soo much that you can't talk, Coco?" Deedee asked.

"What's bothering me?" Coco repeated. Inhaling, she waited a beat before saying, "I feel angry. I feel so fucking angry when I think of the way my mother died," she said, exhaling with a loud sigh. "Let's go uptown, yo, I wanna go see that nigga, Dontay," she said, composing herself. "I wanna smash that nigga's face so bad... Hmm!" Coco hissed.

They arrived there in a flash and the people were out in full force, milling in front of the building. News of Dontay's death was making the rounds. Coco and Deedee walked smack into the hubbub of hearsay.

"What up, Coco?" the usual greeting came, and Coco held up two fingers. Deuces! Then she heard a question she never expected.

"You heard wha' happened to Dontay?"

Coco wore a zombie-like stare and the person asking the question was unsure whether to continue. Then after a beat, Coco said, "No, what happened, yo?"

"He dead, fell off the roof, running from the police."

"You can bet that them cops threw him off the roof," another person said.

Deedee saw the look of surprise on Coco's face. She knew Coco had wanted to talk to Dontay, but now that was impossible. Maybe it was better, because Coco was angry, and Deedee didn't know if she had the courage to stop her from killing Dontay. In a strange twist of fate, he had already died.

"That's fucked up, yo."

Coco and Deedee continued inside the building. They walked in silence up the stairs. Coco opened the door and they entered the apartment. The place seemed smaller and Coco stood in the middle of the place looking around.

Drab furniture placed around the new sofa, the draperies didn't match, but the place appeared tidy. The two-bedroom apartment contained many bittersweet memories for Coco. She had lived here with her mother for most of her life. Her memories of being raised by her mother in the apartment started a waterfall of feelings, flooding her confused mind.

"I remember some crazy things about this place," Coco said.

Coco shook her head and wore an expression that was puzzling to Deedee. She felt the urge to find out what was behind the sarcastic smile.

"What're you thinking, Coco," Deedee asked.

"Just thinking about back in the days how I used to come in with my attitude, yo," Coco smiled. "Miss Katie used to keep an eye on madukes," she continued soberly.

Damn! She almost said it out loud. The bus lurched forward, and Coco fell back into the seat. Her thoughts switched to home. *What kind of mood is Madukes' gonna be in?* She wondered, getting off the bus and moved toward the broken glass doors of the dirty brick building. There were always people outside while crack-heads lurched in and out. *Home, sweet home,* she thought as she pushed by them and into the building.

"Hi Coco," they greeted.

"Peace," Coco said.

She continued inside the building without looking back. Coco headed for the elevator, but the sign on the door read "Out of Service."

"The usual bullshit," Coco said, trudging to the stairwell.

At the third floor she walked down the hallway, and reached the apartment door where—she thought—a sign should be posted: 'You're now entering hell.' By the way it looked, a stray shotgun shell must have made the peephole.

Let's see what the devil's gonna cook up this evening. Maybe she'll be too drunk to deal with life. Coco's mind tried to enter before her body. This type of mind-game prepared her for whatever came next. *Think it's worse maybe it'll be better.* She was preparing herself when another door squeaked open.

It was Miss Katie, the widow from 3D. Her apartment was toward the entrance of the building and from her window she could see both corners of the streets below.

"Hi Coco, how are you doing?" Ms. Katie asked. "It's been about a month that she's been home, right Coco?"

"Yes, Miss Katie," Coco answered politely.

It was not her usual style to talk to the neighbors. Coco hated gossip, but Katie Patterson was different from the other neighbors. She was in her fifties and still looked young and bright. "My husband was killed in Vietnam," she would say during times she allowed herself to talk about him. Coco knew him only as Sergeant Patterson. But Miss Katie didn't sit around moping; she went back to college and earned her bachelor's degree.

Coco admired her greatly for accomplishing that. Miss Katie did this while raising and sending her children, Roxy and Robert, to none other than Princeton University. Coco smiled at Miss Katie, who deserved a lot of respect and love. "Well, I'm pleased to report that she didn't go down to the dens today," Miss Katie reported.

"That's good news, Miss Katie," Coco beamed.

Ever since her mother came out of drug rehab, Miss Katie provided a daily account of her mother's activity. Her mother was continuing counseling on an outpatient basis and Coco wanted to know if her mother was out drugging with friends.

"How's she on the inside?" Miss Katie asked.

Coco flipped her right hand up and down, wrist loose. "She's a little crazy but I guess it takes time, huh?"

"Yes, it does, Coco. How's school, and your tests coming along?"

"Really fair to fine, Miss Katie," Coco replied, enthusiasm in her voice.

"Good, good. Keep it up, Coco." Miss Katie called after the girl as she walked away.

"Coco, is that you?"

She heard her mother's voice and saw her standing in the doorway. Coco turned and waved at Miss Katie.

"Yes, I will, Miss Katie. I'll see you later."

"Bye, Coco. Take care."

Coco entered an apartment that was well worn. It appeared every stitch of the family's clothing was laid out in the tiny hallway.

"I was gonna do laundry," her mother said, lighting a cigarette. "But I just couldn't make it down them goddamn steps. Elevator's still out?"

"Yeah, Ma," Coco said, shaking her head. "I'll get them in a few. Just sort 'em out..."

The teen knew that it would be an opportunity to go downstairs and sit with the pay phone. It would also prevent her mother from going outside.

"Any mail...?" Coco asked.

"Girl, you constantly asking the same question... What you hoping for? Publisher's Clearinghouse told you that you gonna be their next first-prize winner, huh?"

"No, Mom. Just checking, just checking," Coco said, grabbing a bag of chips.

Under her mother's watchful eyes, Coco slipped a couple into her mouth and crunched. The woman took a couple of drags from the cigarette. Then she exhaled and spoke.

"The mail's over by the kitchen window."

Coco sauntered to the window, bopping with excitement and even her mother's rebuke didn't curb her enthusiasm as she sorted through the mail.

"Why can't you walk ladylike? You're getting older, and you've got to learn to conduct yourself proper, like a lady."

"Mom, please save the sermon," Coco sighed.

She continued checking each letter. There were only bills and junk mail. No college acceptances, no record contracts. She looked down through the window. People were milling around. From above, they looked like robots, moving a few steps at a time, pausing as if trying to reach something, but never succeeding. Coco saw beggars with turned up palms stained with dirt. The working people moved faster, walking quickly with noses turned up in disgust. Just across the side of the building, a torch was sparked—a fiend scored.

Coco turned her back to the window. Her mother plopped herself down on the soiled sofa. Everything was worn out just like the sofa. A mouse scuttled from underneath somewhere and disappeared through a hole in the wall. Well, maybe not everything.

"I guess I better start the laundry."

Coco grabbed the keys along with the cart. Just as Coco started out the door, her mother approached and Coco saw her expression. The woman was itching for a fix.

"Get me a pint of Hen," she said and handed Coco a ten-dollar bill.

The whole time she was looking the other way. Coco knew there would be no eye-to eye contact.

"You can bring it after you put the clothes in the washer, okay?" Mrs. Harvey said, using her sincerest tone.

Coco noted that her mother's demeanor was like that of a little girl asking for candy.

"Okay?"

Coco wished her mother was more like Miss Katie. No, she wanted to answer. No more candies for you. Instead she smiled, shaking her head, and said, "Yeah, yeah. A'ight."

"Don't be giving me that 'yeah, a'ight' street lingo. Just be careful with your mouth," Ms. Harvey said.

"To the dungeon," Coco said.

The door slammed shut and Coco stopped in the hallway outside the door. She quickly checked her pockets and realized there was something that she had forgotten.

"Nah, nah. Not yet. I need my smokes."

Coco started banging on the door. Mrs. Harvey came to the door. From the outside, Coco could see her clearly through the damaged peephole. She opened the door and threw the pack of cigarettes. Coco caught them in her left hand easily.

"We've got to get 'em to fix this hole, yo," Coco said.

"Yeah, when you get back, hurry. And I'm not gonna tell you again to stop da street slang. I'm not your 'yo-yo'. I'm your mother, alright? I don't know how many more times I've gotta remind you of that fact."

Calm down, mother. Cuz right now you just whinin' like a little girl. You'll have your candy soon, Coco thought.

"Okay," she blurted out instead as she started for the stairwell, dragging the cart of dirty laundry.

+

She had always wanted to move her mother out of this apartment and into better digs. Coco felt incomplete; she didn't finish the job.

"I never got her out, yo..."

"Coco you did a lot of great things. And even though you've been through hell, you're still here."

"I feel like the drugs won, yo."

"No, drugs only win if you let them. It's up to you to not let her life be in vain, Coco."

"I failed her, cuz I couldn't save her life, yo."

"She was unable to save her own life. You can't beat up yourself over that one," Deedee said.

Coco glanced around the apartment, and said, "I still feel like I let her down, yo."

Her dreams were big, but reality slowly set in. She wanted her mother to be a part of her success. Now what did it all matter? Coco felt stuck in depression. She wanted to strike out, but with Dontay dead, she had to defuse the thought of talking to him. Deedee watched her walk to her mother's room and started searching the drawers. She was unsure what exactly Coco was seeking to find, but Deedee joined her.

"I want to help you, Coco," Deedee said. "What're you looking for?"

"I saw some photos here before. I just wanna see them now, yo."

She pulled out the drawer and came across some photos hidden in a corner. Coco took out the collection of snapshots and glanced at them. Deedee joined her and together they scanned Rachel

Harvey's collection of photos. Most of them were from when Rachel Harvey was younger. Then she saw one of her mother and someone else, but the person's face was ripped out of the photo. Coco examined the photo closely and her musings took over. It could've been Rightchus, she thought, but couldn't know for sure.

"Who do you think was in this shot, yo?"

Deedee took the photo and examined it. She twisted it and looked at the photo from different angles, trying to identify the person, but still couldn't.

"This photo is old and it's torn badly. So I don't think anyone could tell," Deedee said.

"Yeah, maybe just the person who took the picture, yo," Coco said, sighing in frustration.

"Try to let it go, Coco."

"Dee, do me a favor and call Rightchus, yo."

"Are you sure you want to do that?" Deedee asked, removing her cell phone from her handbag.

"Yes, I'm sure, yo."

Deedee searched the directory of the cell phone, found the number, and dialed. The phone on the other end rang once then went to voicemail.

"Rightchus, this is Deedee. Please answer this message and call me back. It's very important," Deedee said and ended the call.

"It ain't that important, yo."

Coco continued searching the apartment and finally walked out. She still had the collection of photos.

"What're we gonna do with all this, yo," Coco said, looking around the apartment.

"Uncle E is busy making all the arrangements. I'll remind him about getting rid of all the furniture."

"Damn, yo! I feel like they part of me, you know?"

"I understand, Coco. I mean you can donate them to Salvation

Army or have a sale," Deedee said with an inquisitive look.

Coco walked around, touching the television, glancing at the new sofa. Then she went into her room and returned carrying only a small duffel bag and the photo. Then she walked out of the apartment and stopped in the hallway, looking at the door.

"I think I'll give it all to the Salvation Army, yo."

They walked downstairs and saw the people milling in front of the apartment building. Slowly the crowd started drifting toward the surprised girls. Coco was eyeing the crowd suspiciously then someone spoke.

"Sorry to hear about your loss, Coco."

What was said triggered her uncontrollable emotions to rush to the surface. Coco felt her heartbeat quicken and her body heave with sadness. Deedee saw Coco's reaction and knew the teen didn't want to start crying. She held her shaking arm and led her away.

"Let us know about the funeral," another person said.

"Okay will do," Deedee said, hugging Coco.

"Keep your head up, Coco," someone shouted.

"She'll stay alive through you, Coco," another person shouted.

Coco flashed the peace sign at the waving crowd and Deedee sped off. Then her tears flowed. Coco sobbed heavily while Deedee slipped Coco's new song into the CD changer and pumped up the volume. She started singing along with the song.

"*Uh ha.. Gotta go off into my zone, lifting off my coat clearing my throat... I gotta get, get up in my zone...Over-stand Bobbie Seale inside George Jackson action I'll shed blood but why die when I'd murder you several times my third rail flow on this track...*

Listening to her new song eventually lifted Coco's spirit and she joined Deedee. They both sang, and laughed. Deedee steered the car through the city's evening traffic.

"*Activist like Angela Davis wanna end lives in a revolution
then a prayer fell on my lips I cannot go that route now spreadin'*

rhymes like love to all my peoples living and dealing
survivors of life's struggles... cocaine swagger
let these niggas know they outta they minds
tryin' to sway my rhymes every time I pause...
I change time drugs coming from Madukes' loins...
supercharged shit I spit with put you in orbit
got 'em spacemen ducking... liftoff..."

"Eric, Eric, you're not listening to me," Max Roose said to Eric Ascot.

Both men sat in the very comfortable midtown office of the attorney, discussing the case against Eric. He had reluctantly agreed to meet with the attorney, but Roose was even more adamant about Eric's complete participation. With the trial date set, Max Roose was trying to convince him to cooperate with the preparation of his legal defense.

"You must call your ex-fiancée. It's vital to your defense, Eric. And if we're not prepared for what she aims to reveal—we might as well give up now."

"What about Rightchus? I thought you said—"

"Rightchus is gone. We tried but can't reach him. He cannot

be found, so he's out, Eric."

"Did you use the number I gave you?"

"Yes, we tried. We traced it to an address in South Carolina. It was a Baptist church and they told my people that he left, but not on good terms. He apparently ripped off the church funds."

"Are you serious? How can Rightchus rip off funds from a church?"

"It really doesn't matter," Max Roose said. "We must get to Sophia so she can shed some light on this Busta thing or it's going to ruin our chances."

"Cornered...?"

"Yes Eric. Cornered. The police had undercover agents around you and they're gonna testify that you talked about Busta and you killing the wrong man," Max Roose said, clapping his hands and jumping up. "That's why this call to Sophia is imperative, Eric."

"What's so fucking important about that?"

"For one thing, how long have you known her?"

"Ah since she was twenty-two or twenty-three or so," Eric said, scratching his head. "Why?"

"She has been around and probably knows everything about your affairs, right?" Max Roose said, pointing at Eric.

"And so...?"

"And so I want to know what she's willing to testify to. If she corroborates the other side's idea regarding your alliance with Busta then they could charge you with at least one count of murder in the first degree. And I don't want that mess," Max Roose said. "I want to know how much she knows," he continued and shuffled papers on his desk.

"She was there from the beginning. She knows everything," Eric said, seemingly lost in his thoughts.

He was thinking about the first time Sophia broke off their engagement. They were at the Long Island mansion in the Hamptons and he had gone outside to pick up the newspaper. It was still fresh in Eric's mind.

Clothed in a white terry-cloth robe and Sean Jean blue boxers, Eric Ascot dragged his Hermes sandals to the front lawn. Pulling out a mini recording device, Eric mumbled into it. Then he turned it off and returned it to his pocket. He was always ready for a new din.

He glanced at the newspaper in his hand. He saw in the headlines an investigation concerning dirty cops. The next page contained a picture of himself, Sophia, and Mariuchi taken last night at the restaurant. The caption read, "Cozying up to mob boss." It mentioned Eric and Mariuchi by name.Sophia joined Eric on the lawn. He quickly folded the newspaper and tucked it under his arm.

"How'd you like this to go on for about a week or so?" he asked leading her back to the house.

"A week or so? Don't tempt me Eric—you know I could use a vacation, baby," Sophia said, placing wet kisses on his neck.

"Let's take one," Eric said.

"Eric, I haven't had a real one in a long time."

"So, let's start planning something, somewhere, maybe San Tropez..."

Sophia's eyes sparkled when she looked at him. She kissed him and walked away. The legal eagle went straight to her laptop and logged on to the Web. Before long she was sighing at the tourist attractions.

"I need a few winks," Eric said as she walked into the house heading toward his bedroom.

"All right, big man, but you can't sleep all day. We've got book our flight to San Tropez," Sophia sang while grabbing the newspaper.

Hours later, when he finally awoke Eric was greeted by an evil glare from Sophia. Despite her obvious anger, Sophia looked resplendent in her Channel skirt suit.

"What's the matter, hon?"

"You didn't want me to read about you being a damn mafia earner and all the other names they were calling you. You have some nerve, Eric, sweet-talking me to go on a vacation with you," Sophia said accusingly. "What were you going to do? Have me with you on the lam, running from the law? Cause that's who will be coming after you, Eric. Why can't you be honest with me?"

"There's nothing honest about that. The article dealt with two bad cops who got killed. In fact it referred to them as rogue cops. Whoever took the picture was only trying to link me with Mariuchi by saying what? I'm part of their organization. I'm not a member of the mob. You know you can't believe anything in the news. You know those people only write partial truths." Eric looked serious and concerned.

"Eric, this is serious. They have you under investigation. Can you please tell me why?"

"I make good music and they have to know where all the deadly sound coming from." His response was lighthearted, but his fear and need showed plainly through his awful joke. He watched Sophia sadly shaking her head. By now she had almost convinced herself that what wasn't working in the relationship was Eric's fault.

"I don't understand—if you love me, why can't you just trust me and tell me what's really going on, Eric?" she asked sobbing.

"This shit all started when I, ah...well you know how close me and Busta was? Before he got killed we had ah...taken out this contract for the ones who raped Deedee. I told him about the rape and he was mad. He's Deedee's godfather. Then bullets started flying. Before you know it, he's dead and the cops..."

"Eric, wouldn't it have been better to go to the police in the first place?"

"Yeah, maybe—I mean in retrospect I should've, but what's done is done," Eric said in a flat, bored voice.

"Why didn't it stop there? Why was there bloodshed? There are men chasing you..."

"Maybe it's connected, maybe it's not. Like I said, I really don't know the details of what Busta did. I know the first one turned out to be the wrong guy and eventually we got the right guy."

"I don't want to hear anymore. Eric. You could go to jail for life. Conspiracy to commit murder, solicitation to commit murder, and at least about two counts of murder, oh my God! How could you Eric? Now you've aligned yourself to... ah, these people with mobster connections and you actually think things are going to be easier? I'm an attorney. How do you think this makes me look? I could get disbarred," Sophia angrily said.

"That's it," Eric said in the flat voice of defeat.

"I don't want to hear from you until you resolve this Eric. You cannot be serious about getting married under these conditions. Call the car, Eric, I've had enough."

Sophia had made a veiled threat, but then she went and actually did it. Eric was not only put off by what he considered a betrayal by Sophia, but he was also deeply hurt. Sitting in his attorney's office, Eric Ascot pondered the possibility of following his former fiancée's advice. He was still thinking about Sophia when Max Roose's voice jarred him into the present.

"Then we've got to be prepared for her as a hostile," Max Roose said. "This would all be easier if you sink your manly pride a bit and speak to her. Get close to her, you know...?"

"I don't think she wants me to do that, and you're asking me to beg her? I won't, Max. We just gonna have to go another route that's all there is to it."

"Eric, I'm trying to spare us going that route. It could be handled, but would be a costly trip."

"Freedom ain't a cheap thing, Max," Eric said with a wry smile. "I got a funeral that I have to attend," Eric said, glancing at a clock and looking at the Rolex on his wrist.

"Whose, your own?" Max Roose joked.

"Very funny, Max," Eric said, standing and walking to the door. He waved at his attorney. "We're in trouble, huh, Max?"

"No. *You* are going to be buried alive in that courtroom if you don't call Sophia so we can find out everything she's going to talk about," Max Roose said, getting up from his chair.

His mind was still thinking about Sophia when Eric walked out the office. He met his chauffeur downstairs and they drove away. Eric Ascot's mind returned to the scene with Sophia. It had been such a pleasant relationship until he hired the shooter. Then it all crumbled. Accompanied by his bodyguards, Eric Ascot walked inside his apartment and started to get dressed.

He was nattily attired in a black suit, having a drink in his living room when he saw Coco and Deedee.

"Are you guys ready?" he asked.

Two pairs of red eyes silently stared back him. Then both girls nodded and they walked out. All three got inside the back of the limousine and it drove off. Even though Eric Ascot had the weight of his legal problems on his shoulder, he was still able to make all the final arrangements for Rachel Harvey's burial.

They arrived at Ortiz Funeral Home and saw the place was packed. Residents from the apartment building, some known others unknown, were there inside and outside. Most were dressed in black, but there was a group of individuals wearing T-shirt with a picture of Rachel Harvey emblazoned on the front. It was the same photo Coco had kept of her mother. "RIP Rachel" was inscribed on the back.

Inside, the place was buzzing with talk of how Rachel Harvey died. Some were angry and others saddened, and by the time Coco walked in, there was solemn silence. She walked down to where her mother lay in a white coffin awaiting interment.

Rows of onlookers and mourners walked by and Coco sat quietly in front with Deedee and Eric Ascot. They watched Kim and Tina, along with Mrs. Jones stopping for an observance. Other residents from the neighborhood stopped and stared at the deceased woman. They were all quietly surprised when Sophia made her way down the aisle and stopped to pay her condolences.

Eric Ascot harrumphed and got out of his seat when Sophia walked over. He hurried away without making eye contact as Sophia hugged both Coco and Deedee. Eric returned to find that she was sitting in a seat between Deedee and Coco. Then there was a slight commotion and heightened buzz as Silky Black, The Chop Shop Crew, Lord Finesse, Show Biz and AG, Jigga Man, Fat Joe and other music royalty drifted into the hall. They sat in the front along with Coco and listened intently.

"She was a beautiful and kind woman..." the preacher started saying and the place was dead silent. The service got going with the preacher's oration, and the introduction of Coco drew a loud, long applause. Dressed in black, she walked somberly to the platform.

"I'd like to thank everyone of you for coming out," she said. "And I know you didn't have to because y'all are busy, but thank you," she continued speaking and her statement drew applause. "My mother would appreciate this very much. Some of you knew her very well and others knew her better," Coco said. Then Coco invited Kim up to the platform with her. "I'd like to sing a song and I want you to sing along with me and Kim, " Coco said.

"That's my mother You got in Your arms oh Lord
so please make me understand why you had to take her
back so early, yeah she wasn't always good but she was always
there

and I remain bias cuz her love was all I had
sometimes late at night watching her hold on to her addiction.
Pain feel when she was high but
escape from a world you create she felt was unfair,
she said back in the days they didn't have AIDs
nowadays they got diseases for all the seasons
Are you to blame or are we doomed from the beginning
this time another child born another life on the line
That's my mother you got in your arms oh Lord
please make me understand why you had to take her
back so early help me to speak clearly,
hold her thoughts with me on earth so dearly
That's my mother you got in your arms oh Lord
please help me understand clearly,
speak my heart fairly keep love on my mind
please remind me why I'm still here what am I doing here
That's my mother you in your arms oh Lord,
please make me over-stand I wanna find answers to questions
oh Lord why Lord tell me why I'm here floating with the stars."

There wasn't a single dry eye in the funeral home by the time Coco was finished singing. The captive audience sang along with Coco and Kim. Long after the duo had stopped, the audience kept humming the song. After the service, most of the attendees were transported in limousine vans to the gravesite in Yonkers. It was Rachel Harvey's final resting place.

Darkness had set in when they arrived at the burial ground. Each person was given a rose and a lit candle in a holder carved with the same old photo of Rachel Harvey. This was Deedee's idea and she made sure the picture was given back to Coco. Mourning with a black veil on her face, the teen walked to her mother's grave and placed the photo inside. Coco sobbed loudly. Deedee hugged Coco as the teen shuddered in sadness and her tears flowed.

In the chorus of *Amazing Grace*, Rachel Harvey's coffin was closed. The candles lit the dark sky while the pastor prayed. Through the flickering lights held high, Rachel Harvey's body was finally lowered into the darkness of the earth.

"Ashes to ashes and dust to dust..." the preacher man ended his eulogy.

In honor of Rachel Harvey, a huge feast was held at Sardi's restaurant. All in attendance were provided transportation to the eatery. They all hugged Coco before getting back in the limousine vans and were transported. Sophia waited with Coco and Deedee. They were huddled together when Eric Ascot saw her. He finished shaking hands with some of his friends from the music world, walked over and nodded politely.

"Are we ready to go, Deedee... Coco?"

"There's another person also present, Uncle E," Deedee said, looking at Sophia.

"Ah yes, Sophia are you coming along?" Eric casually asked.

"I ah—"

"Oh, I think you should come with us," Deedee said, sounding excited and hopeful that there would be a renewal.

Sophia was watching Eric's reaction and seemed to have developed second thoughts as they walked to the limousine.

"I've got a long day ahead of me," she suddenly said. "You guys go along without me," Sophia said.

She wore a compassionate smile despite her choice. Eric wore a smirk of uneasiness during the limousine ride. The unhappy trip ended abruptly outside her apartment. Sophia gave Coco and Deedee a hug before staring pensively at a sour-faced Eric.

"We'll talk some more Dee," she said, getting out. "Coco take care, honey," Sophia continued and got out.

Eric Ascot wore a sneer on his face all the way to the restaurant.

They rode in ominous silence to the popular eatery, and arrived to see that most of the people were still there. The attendees, made up of mostly people who stood outside the building, were seated.

"We have thirty-three guests here, reporting for your feast," the maître d' said.

"Make sure they're all fed well," Eric smiled.

"Whatever you say, Mr. Ascot."

Waiters carrying trays of fried chicken, fish, and steak, were busy serving the many guests. Drinks were served and all ate and drank heartily in celebration of Rachel Harvey's life.

"Life's tough, but you gotta keep on living," Mrs. Jones said, looking at both Coco and Deedee. "I don't think we've met. I'm Kim's mother, Mrs. Jones," she said, reaching a hand out.

"I'm Coco's friend, Deedee," Deedee said, shaking the woman's hand. "Nice to meet you."

"You're Eric Ascot's niece. Nice to meet you too. I heard so much about you and your uncle that I feel like I know you. How's—"

"Mom, let's go, the limo is waiting," Kim said.

"Well, good night Deedee. Coco, you take care baby-girl. Stop by when you can," Mrs. Jones said.

Coco nodded politely then the elderly woman left with Kim and Tina. Later all the attendees filed out and were transported to their various destinations. Many of them had never left the four squares of the projects, but in one evening had traveled all the way to Westchester County and downtown, all because of her mother's death. Their bellies were full so they left and went back to the front of the building to talk about the event for the rest of the evening.

Coco hugged Eric who was smoking a cigar with the owner. Then Coco and Deedee sat quietly on a balcony overlooking the city's busy streets. Lights lit up the night sky and the girls both smoked cigarettes. Deedee fiddled with her cell phone while Coco stared straight ahead.

"Coco you just have to eat something, dear," Deedee said. "Are you coming to Uncle E's trial? It starts today."

Coco awoke and glanced around the place. She realized she had been dreaming and had overslept. It was a day that Coco wished would come. It was here, and she wasn't sure if she was ready for it. She sheepishly watched Deedee's naked ass running around trying to get dressed.

It had been a tumultuous week for Coco, who had seen her mother buried, and was still reeling from the epic emotional saga. She had not been eating, and her best friend, Deedee, was constantly getting on her case about this. The grieving teen was down since her mother's funeral, and wasn't doing too much to get out of the sadness. She had spent the past couple of days sitting around reading magazines and watching *Sanford and Son*. Coco kept her headphones on and hardly spoke.

Deedee tried to help her regain her zest for living, but to no avail. Coco remained sad and her melancholic outlook weighed on Deedee. She often tried to get Coco going by playing her songs or singing, and in general attempting to entertain the distraught teen. Nothing seemed to work. Coco remained despondent and moped around the apartment.

Deedee wandered into the room, dressed and ready to go to Eric Ascot's first day of trial. She glanced at Coco who was still lying in the bed.

"So, are you gonna move today? If you are, we've got to get breakfast and then go to the courthouse," Deedee said.

"Damn, you're in a rush, yo."

"Of course. I have to go and see what's gonna happen to Uncle E," Deedee said.

"I mean ain't nothing good going down, yo."

"Yeah, but I have to support my uncle."

"A'ight, already. Give a few minutes let me go and get dressed," Coco said.

"Okay, you got it Coco. Let's go," Deedee said.

She sat on the bed, and lit a cigarette while Coco prepared to get dressed. Deedee picked up the same tattered photo of Rachel Harvey and stared at it for a beat. There was a great resemblance between Coco and her mother. Staring at the photo made Deedee sad and she put it away.

A couple of minutes later, Coco was dressed and ready to go. They walked out of the apartment and out to the café on the corner. Both girls drank hot chocolates and later left for the courthouse. Sharing a cigarette, they walked to the car and Deedee drove downtown. After leaving the car in a parking lot, the girls walked toward the crowded courthouse.

There was a media frenzy. It seemed like all the news outlets and curious bystanders came out to see the trial. Cameras went off and photo bugs ran to different points of entrance trying to catch any sightings of celebrities going into the courthouse. Coco and Deedee walked inside the heavily secured place.

They were thoroughly searched and allowed to enter. Coco and Deedee walked inside the courtroom and immediately spotted Sophia. She was sitting with the prosecutors. Coco and Deedee sat behind Eric Ascot and his attorney Max Roose. There were several assistants at the table talking with Max Roose. Eric turned and acknowledged his niece and Coco.

The trial was just getting on the way, and the prosecutor addressed the judge. She was good-looking, organized, and appeared meticulous. The prosecutor presented the opening arguments in the case against Eric Ascot.

"At the end of this trial, you will see that this man, Eric Ascot, is responsible for taking the lives of three people including an officer of the city police force. He has, through a ring of organized terror, brought mayhem into the lives of many people, and deprived justice from being served by attempting to cover up his illegal and ruthless acts," she said.

"Wow, she's really making Uncle Eric out to be an evil villain," Deedee said.

All eyes were on Eric Ascot, who sat nattily dressed in a dark suit and blue shirt. He seemed out of place amongst the legal minds. When the prosecutor was finished, his attorney, Max Roose, wearing his usual pinstripe suit, got up and spoke to the court.

"This is another conspiracy chump-up by the prosecutor to hook us into believing that a musician—and a very successful one at that—has gone out of his way to rain terror on the city and to commit murder. And I will prove beyond the shadow of any reasonable doubt that he is innocent of all charges, and should be allowed to go back to doing what he does best—making music, and providing entertainment for us to enjoy..."

Eric stared straight ahead and seemed to be unfazed by the direct line the prosecutor had taken. Referring to him as a murderer several times in her opening statement, she was trying to annoy him from the beginning. Eric sighed and quietly shook his head. His mind went back to the time when he first became involved with the crime he was being accused of.

He had been out of town and received a call from the police about his niece being raped. Eric remembered rushing back to the city and immediately going to the hospital where he saw his niece being questioned by investigators. Lying in the hospital bed, her lips were badly bruised, and she had cuts and scrapes on her face. He was angered and wanted revenge on the person who had done this horrible crime, immediately. Eric wasn't about to wait for the police, who had let him down after his brother was murdered. He had walked into that hospital with revenge on his mind.

"It will get better. It's going to take some time. You'll have to come back for a follow-up, or you may see your family doctor. Call this phone number for the results of your HIV tests. Your uncle is here." The last words sent a chill through Deedee.

"My uncle is here?" Deedee echoed and took the card with the phone number.

Her mind lingered. How was she gonna face him, she wondered. He was gonna be so mad at her. Deedee felt ashamed and instinctively covered her body with the hospital robe. This was not enough. She glanced around the room. It seemed everyone was staring at her, or talking about her. They all knew. She could see it in their eyes, even though they were all in the hallway, and she had a screen around the stretcher.

"Nurse, where are my clothes?"

"Oh, I'm sorry. Here you are. Your uncle brought these," the nurse said, handing Deedee fresh clothing. They were her gears, but somehow it didn't feel right putting them on.

"Thanks," Deedee said. She sat on the stretcher, and a younger woman in a dark suit approached. Here we go again, thought Deedee.

"Hi, I'm Maxine Singleton and I am a rape survivor counselor," the woman said. Her stare made Deedee uneasy. "Here's my card," the woman continued. "Feel free to call me. I know you've had an awful and scary experience. I can provide the help that you need. All you need to do is call the number on the card and I will call to check on you periodically. But you should call me whenever you need someone to talk to, and I'll try to help," the counselor concluded.

Deedee took the card and stared past the fast-talking counselor.

"May I leave now?" she asked.

"I think the police have some more questions. I'll stay with you if you don't mind."

As if on cue, a policeman and a woman came around the screen. Deedee's uneasiness returned. She lay back on the stretcher and crossed her legs.

"My name is Officer Brown. I'm from the District Attorney's office," the woman said.

She was dressed in a blue suit with black shoes. She looked more like a lawyer than a cop. She even smelled like one. Her perfumed hand was highlighting every word.

"How're you feeling Deedee?" The male officer asked.

Deedee mumbled something inaudibly. Everyone peered at her when she cleared her throat. "Can you tell me what happened?"

"We know it's a very difficult thing for you to do, but please, you have to try and help us catch the men who did this to you."

Deedee was close to tears. The query made her go back to the ordeal, which she sought to escape. It assaulted her mind, and started an ache in her stomach that rose to her throat. She cried uncontrollably.

Her uncle, standing just outside the screen, dashed in and grabbed Deedee. She sobbed into his chest. He held her close, reluctant to let go. But Officer Brown interrupted.

"We need to find out what happened, sir. Who are you?"

Eric kept hugging his niece. He ignored the officer's presence and focused all his attention on his niece.

"Uncle, uncle, I'm sorry," Deedee cried. "I'm so sorry," she said, and the tears continued to flow.

"It'll be alright," Eric said.

He held Deedee, hoping she believed him. He wasn't sure, but the phrase seemed to fit. He loved his niece. Eric had raised her since she was six years old, when her father, his brother and partner, was killed.

"Are you the uncle?" Officer Brown asked. "I have a question about—"

"What's your question?" Eric asked, interrupting her.

"Did you loan your niece the car tonight?"

There was a long pause. Eric smelled the stench of the hospital and it brought back a rush of memories about his brother's death. The police had rejected Eric's argument that the killing took place during a robbery. His brother's death had been labeled a drug-related incident. There was no trial. The police didn't care enough to pursue it.

Eric had done some research on his own, paying an informer to do the research he needed done, then took the information to the police. He was certain they would find and prosecute his brother's killers. But the authorities saw no reason to reopen the case, and Eric couldn't produce the informant. As far as the record went, Dennis was just another dead drug dealer. Eric knew this was wrong. This was a dishonor to his brother's memory, and Eric felt cheated. Fuck these cops, he thought.

"I am not answering any questions until I speak to my lawyer," *he said.*

"Listen," the officer said. "We're asking real simple questions here. Your niece was raped and beaten up, according to this report. I know you're very angry, but we'd like to catch the bastards who did this sick thing. So it would be very nice if you would just cooperate."

"We don't have to do shit! Matter of fact, we're not gonna do shit, because you guys have never done anything to help me," Eric said.

He turned to his niece who was staring at him, bewildered by what she had just witnessed. My uncle never gets angry, she thought.

"Let's go, baby," Eric said, grabbing Deedee by her arm and stomping past the surprised counselor.

"We're trying to conduct an investigation. A carjacking and rape. You can't let the scum who did this get away," the officer pleaded.

Eric wasn't listening. He rushed out the doorway, into the hallway and out of the hospital, dragging Deedee along. They hurried to the parking lot. He quickly found the green Range Rover and helped Deedee into the passenger seat.

Eric Ascot drove, paying close attention to the morning traffic. He tapped his thumbs frantically on the steering column. Deedee heard him breathe loudly through his nostrils, but neither said anything to the other. Her usually talkative uncle had secluded himself in the quiet of his thoughts. He didn't even look at her. Maybe he was ashamed of her. She shuddered and looked away.

Sitting in the courtroom Eric Ascot remained poker-faced throughout the prosecutor's arguments, depicting him as a murderous imbecile. All he wanted to do was to get even with the culprits involved in the abduction and rape of his niece. Eric glanced back at Deedee and Coco, and he was satisfied that she had recovered. Nothing but the best for her was what he sought, and sometimes obstacles got in the way. Eric realized that the court scene was just another obstruction. He could hear the prosecutor tearing into his name, disavowing his fame as a musician, and didn't even flinch.

"You may present your witnesses," the stone-faced judge said.

Then the prosecution paraded a litany of police officers, all attesting to reports that Eric was involved in a murder-for-hire scheme that backfired. The idea was preposterous, and Eric at different points in time, stared directly at Sophia. He could see her shapely legs wrapped neatly in a tight-fitting blue pant-suit. Sighting her cleavage rising and falling when she leaned, he saw flashes of her flesh. Eric wondered when she would be called.

Sophia was easily the most beautiful person in the courtroom, but she had betrayed his trust. Eric was surprised that he still harbored feelings of adoration for his ex. He tried to dismiss the thoughts, but they devoured his mind. Eric found himself reminiscing about when Sophia stood by him right after the rape. He had overheard Deedee crying. She was really upset over the whole situation, but especially hard on herself. He didn't know what to do.

Deedee stood in front of the oval mirror on the back of the door. She stared at her reflection. This is what happens when you take something without permission. You have to pay. But why is there such a heavy price? Tears welled in her eyes. Deedee's chest heaved uncontrollably; then she cried hard and loud. Her uncle heard, and froze to the spot where he stood in the kitchen.

"Where is Sophia? I need her now!" Eric said, talking to the ceiling. "And Deedee's damn drugged-out mother. I don't even know where she is. Dammit! I swear on my brother's grave, whoever did this fucking shit, I'll

personally take care of them. I want no help from those fucking police."

Eric was almost on the verge of tears as he collapsed in an easy chair. When he couldn't stand hearing his niece cry for help going unheeded, Eric drank couple glasses of Louis. He settled, but it wasn't so with Deedee's sobbing.

Later, as he sipped another brew, Eric heard the keys turning in the door and the sound of Sophia's footsteps rapidly approaching. They embraced briefly.

"I could hear her from outside. What's wrong? Why's she crying so loud?" Sophia asked.

"Listen, I really don't know. She came in and went straight upstairs and locked her door. I didn't get a chance to talk to her."

"What? You haven't even spoken to her? Well..."

"I didn't know what to say."

"She may have wanted to say something to you."

"She had a chance when we were driving from the hospital and—"

"Eric, get me two glasses of cold water, please."

"For what? I don't need to cool down."

"Who said anything about you? They're for me and Deedee."

Sophia took the first glass and drank a mouthful. She set the glasses on a tray and took her black pumps off, then made her way up the short stairway to Deedee's room.

"Dee? May I come in?" she asked knocking gently.

"Hold on. Just a second, Sophia," Deedee said then opened the door and headed toward the bed.

"Hey, girlfriend," Sophia said, trying to sound upbeat. Deedee mumbled, but Sophia ignored the inaudible response.

"I brought some water... Cold water, with a few ice cubes, I thought you could use a little. I know I could."

"Mr. Ascot's culpability is made even clearer and shows that his hands were dirty and involved in the deaths..."

The prosecution was still rattling off evidence that Eric was involved in a murder for hire conspiracy that resulted in the killing of several people. Her name came up again as a key person with close knowledge of an alliance between him and Busta. Eric glanced at Sophia when she was introduced.

After an emotionally shaky start, Sophia eloquently articulated her story. Her soft lips were assisting the prosecution, and Eric stared at her sexy features. He couldn't resist reflecting on their sexually charged encounters, even when he was late for an important event and tried to make it up to her. Everything seemed to turn out just right.

"Good. Just the way we planned this, Mr. Lateness," Sophia said.

"I won't be late..." Eric said.

Eric massaged Sophia's thigh. The fabric felt supple in his hand, her flesh warmed to his touch. She put the car in gear and zoomed out of the parking lot. Eric and Sophia, a little drunk from the evening's activity, crept up the stairs like kids who had broken curfew. They dashed into the bedroom, where Eric's hands quickly encountered the silk panties covering Sophia's ass.

"Take it easy," Sophia whispered.

"I'm just trying to be on time."

"You don't have to try. The loving ain't going nowhere. It's right here, waiting for you," Sophia said in a throaty whisper.

She turned to face Eric, and he watched with fascination. Sophia reached up and made the black dress clinging to her toned, five-foot-eight-curves-in-the-right-places, svelte body, disappear with her arm movements. Eric kissed her gently, biting Sophia's earlobes while his hands moved smoothly all over her ass.

"Ooh. Oh my, are we the impatient one..." Sophia sighed as her body clung to Eric's.

"Ah," she moaned as her heartbeat galloped, making her breath come in gasps.

Their bodies fell entangled on the huge waterbed. The bed swayed slightly. Sophia rolled on top. She peeled off the rest of her clothing. Eric kissed and sucked at her nipples. Sophia's naked body came in contact with the wool covering his erection.

"You're not out of your clothes yet, good looking? Late again, huh?" whispered Sophia.

She straddled Eric. He could feel her soft skin. His hands roamed, kneading her taut hot brown body. His touch made her skin burn. Her tension uncoiled into mush. The heat ignited Sophia, raising her temperature to dizzying heights.

"Ah, uh, I can't wait on you, honey. I want you inside of me now," she whispered, pulling Eric's zipper down.

His erection was unleashed and Sophia easily mounted his hardness and began rocking back and forth.

"Oh, oh, ugh yeah, baby," Eric grunted.

"Oh baby," Sophia whispered as she kissed Eric's face.

She wrapped her arms around his neck. The cheeks of her buttocks were cupped in his large strong hands. Her gentle rocking brought him to the gates of ecstasy. She felt his body in a spastic dance ritual signifying Eric reaching his orgasm.

"That's it? That's all?" Sophia grunted with Eric on top of her.

She flipped Eric over on to his back. Then sucked until his dick head pointed proudly to the ceiling. Sophia straddled him. All the time Eric grunted while he enjoyed the view of Sophia her breasts bouncing up and down. He saw the way she bit her lips to prevent from screaming. She sweated as she continued to ride.

He was like a kid in classroom with a crush on the sexy teacher. Eric was afraid of being found out. Lips that once kissed him softly, were now testifying in a court of law against him. Eric realized he had attained a full-size erection while sitting in the courtroom listening to Sophia's deposition. He was still enamored by Sophia. His incandescent sexual excitement with her continued blissfully, until he heard his attorney shouting.

"I object. That's hearsay, your honor," Max Roose said, interrupting Sophia's answer and Eric's sexual musing. "This witness has no actual knowledge of any conversation between this man known as Busta and my client regarding shooting anyone."

His lawyer's verbal tirade brought Eric back to the reality of his situation. The attorney was arguing the validity of the evidence. Busta had his apartment wired with three cameras from different angles and the police were able to get a copy of the recordings.

"Apparently this man had a recording device installed, and we have a copy. Your honor what you're about to see is real," the prosecutor said and signaled to an assistant.

Eric Ascot watched the screen lowering, and the video started to roll. It was lights, camera, and a lot of trumped up drama.

Vulcha rang the doorbell. Lil' Long stood guard next to the stairs. He swayed as if drunk. Vulcha rang a second time. He heard sounds within the apartment, but the door did not open.

"Busta, whassup? Got some biz to see you on, big man," he called

through the door.

He rang the bell for the third time, nodding to Lil' Long. The rattling of the door caught his attention. Vulcha stood and waited. He was uneasy now. Just as nervous as on that cold morning when he was released on parole after serving nine months of a one-year bid. Back then, it seemed like every day was cold. He was trying to survive on the streets. Snatching chains was all he knew. It was a street specialty that yielded long ropes of gold, but he was still short on cash.

Busta had owned and operated many weed spots back then. He hired Vulcha immediately when he saw the young Vulcha stalking his victims.

"You gonna have to keep getting up after getting your swerve, kid. Doeth unto others, know-wha' I'm saying? Why take his shit in violence? Take it in peace, see? You don't have to hurt the brother. Come, I'll show you," Busta had told him.

Vulcha had listened. His eyes grew wider as Busta peeled a crisp hundred-dollar bill from a thick wad of bills.

Busta smiled and said, "Niggas will pay for all types of entertainment, cuz we love that type o' shit. Nobody else love that shit like we do. We wait on long lines on the coldest of nights, searching through our pockets trying to get into a nightclub."

The he placed the clean bill on top of a public phone, damaged by an angry user. Vulcha took the bill, and several more from Busta. Vulcha eventually ran one of Busta's weed spots. It kept him indoors, out of the cold, but it also landed him another stretch in jail for parole violation. He had never repaid Busta for his kindness. Vulcha remembered as he waited.

"Who dat? Who is it? Ooh, uh, ugh. Shit."

Vulcha heard the hiss of passing bullets. He turned in time to see smoke departing the silenced, shiny muzzle of the Desert Eagle held in Lil' Long's left hand. He turned and stared at the space carved by the bullets. They had ripped the upper half of the door nearly to shreds and mutilated Busta's heavy body with holes the size of baseballs.

"These rhino shits are really bad, dogs. I'm telling you, da rhino rounds will penetrate anything. Don't sleep, nigga. Damn!" Lil' Long excitedly shouted.

Vulcha realized what had transpired. He pushed, and the door swung open. He stood back as if to admire the handiwork, awed by the damage done by the bullets. Vulcha walked slowly into the apartment without speaking. He glanced around, guns clenched tightly in each hand as if he expected Busta to rise.

Busta's bleeding body moved in slow convulsions. Thick red blood flowed, staining the soft, plush, earth-hued rug. Vulcha ambled over to Busta's jerking body. He dropped a one hundred dollar bill in the spreading blood-stain. He fired twice and Busta's body jerked for the final time. Vulcha slowly shook his head as Lil' Long spewed his venom.

"All weak muthafuckas must die in order for me to achieve immortality. Niggas must perish. That's why we still here, kid. I don't joke when I go to smoke a mo'fucka!"

Lil' Long held his Desert Eagle high. Vulcha gaped, grasping for words. They came in an uncontrollable outburst.

"I--I thought...I thought I was da one to take care of this fucking problem. It was my problem. He was my man...remember? We go way back. What—What, you don't trust me, or sump'n?" he asked.

"You're heated, nigga. I saved your fucking life and you don't even..." Lil' Long began his search, lifting long gold chains with heavy medallions, rummaging through drawers. "Let's go, Vulcha. This fat muthafucka kept everything in da fucking bank. All I see is bank receipts. Let's get his producer friend. You can shoot his ass. But are you getting soft, nigga?"

Vulcha looked at his old friend's apartment. He fired one of his nine-millimeters twice into Busta's head. Then he leaned down and removed a diamond-encrusted ring from Busta's twitching left pinky.

"I knew your ass would want that shit, yo. Let's go before po-po start hitting the doors."

"Yeah," Vulcha said. "Let's use da fucking stairs."

"Let's find us a music producer, and you can shoot him, dogs," Lil'

Long said. He pounded his fist against Vulcha's.

The video clip brought a chilling effect. Several lives were affected and Eric knew he had directly involved Busta. Busta's death had been clearly motivated by Eric's need for revenge. Busta was just trying to help out a friend and he was killed. He had not been charged with that particular crime, but Eric Ascot sat wondering if he wasn't already guilty by association.

"Well, I think we've seen enough for the day. Let's adjourn this proceeding until tomorrow at 9 a.m.," the judge said, looking bored.

It was an exhausting hump-day for Eric. He wanted badly to lounge at his apartment with a drink. He was about to do just that when his phone rang. "Max Roose," the caller I.D. read.

"What's going on?"

"Eric, sorry to be calling you at this time. Is it a good time—uh—can you talk?"

"Yes, sure Max go ahead," Eric said looking at the bottle of Louis.

"I wanted to talk earlier but you left quickly to avoid all that press and stuff, huh?"

"Yeah, but you handled it."

"That's what I do Eric. That's exactly what you pay me to do. But Eric, we can't get clobbered tomorrow. I don't think Sophia's testimony was very damaging. The prosecution will be bringing out the detectives who overheard your conversation with yourself while you were locked up—"

"That's bullshit, Max!" Eric shouted so loud, the cell phone almost fell out his grasp. He recovered it just in time to hear Max Roose.

"Not to worry. We can counter with Tina Torres. She'll be a very reliable witness. Stick with me Eric and you'll be fine."

"Okay, Max. See you tomorrow at nine."

"Good night Eric."

Eric poured the drink, but couldn't help but think of Busta and how he drew his friend into the fire. If only he hadn't made that call, things would be all different. He flung the shot of Louis XIV to the back of his throat. Eric sucked his teeth while going through the possibilities. Eric was in the midst of second-guessing how he handled the rape situation, and Deedee walked into the living room carrying a bowl of ice cream and almonds. He could see her from the corner of his eye. She had really grown up and as Deedee leaned against the marbled wall, Eric saw something else.

"All this legal stuff getting you down, huh Uncle E?" she asked, shoving a spoonful of ice cream in her mouth and chewing some nuts.

"I don't really know if it's boring me to death or agitating more. I don't know."

"Yes, I could imagine. And it's only the first day," Deedee chuckled. "Wow, uncle, I know she wasn't on our side, but Sophia really looked fly in that courtroom. Her outfit, anyway..." Deedee's voice trailed.

"I mean...she did. Anyway Dee, do you think I'm doing the right thing with Sophia? I mean I don't hate her or anything like that but," Eric said, and there was a loaded pause. "Forget about it. You know what, it's really adult business and—"

"But uncle, that's not fair. You started to ask me a question and then you just tell me not to bother answering. Why did you ask in the first place? Well since you already asked, I think you should talk to her. But let it happen casually. Don't be too intense, because you can be intense,

Uncle. And if you guys really love each other then I think it can happen. You know a rekindling of some sorts..."

Deedee kept shoving ice cream in her mouth and eating almond nuts. Eric watched her for a beat while she enjoyed her snack.

"Take it easy with that ice cream. You don't wanna eat too much of that..."

"Uncle E!" Deedee screeched and quickly walked out.

Eric Ascot scratched his bearded chin, smiled and said, "Dee must be growing up. She's so sensitive."

He continued drinking and thinking about his trial. Then he hummed a tune and walked over to the piano, banged out a few chords and just like that, Eric was caught up in the creation of a new song.

Deedee hurried down to hallway to Coco's room. She knocked then walked inside the room. She was aware that Coco was still in grief. She found Coco at a desk writing with headphones on.

"Coco, Coco, do I look I'm gaining weight?" Deedee asked.

"Huh, yo?" Coco asked, removing the headphones. "What you said, yo? I couldn't hear you."

"Coco, I'm sorry to be bothering you, but do I look like I'm gaining weight?"

"I mean I guess... Somewhat, yo. It's hard to tell. But if you're pregnant then more than likely you'll gain weight, yo."

"Anyway, Uncle E was like, 'You're getting fat, Dee,'" Deedee said with disdain.

"That was a good time to mention to him that you're carrying a baby inside your stomach."

"Coco, you're right. But I'm—I don't know where to begin."

"That was your opportunity right there, yo. And opportunity only knocks once."

"Well, there's always a second chance. I'm wishing that Uncle E gets back with Sophia and then she can sort of break the news to him and you know—"

"Butter him up...?"

"Yeah, get him lathered up... Hmm, how do I go about arranging that?"

"You're still a beautiful person, Dee. But you're crazy, yo."

"So what are you getting into? Uncle E is drinking, and that made me want one of those drinks, too. Anyway, what're you up to?"

"Just messing with these beats Uncle E gave me, yo," Coco said, smiling.

Deedee glanced at her smile and realized that it was the first one in a long while. Coco had been brokenhearted and barely spoke, so her smile was a welcome relief for Deedee. She embraced Coco and kissed her.

"What you wanna do, Coco?"

"Let's take a ride uptown. I wanna go see Mrs. Jones."

"Why?"

"I just wanna talk to her, that's all."

"You sure?"

"That's it, yo."

"Okay, let's go uptown, and see Mrs. Jones then."

They girls left the apartment and were uptown in minutes. Deedee found parking, and now the people in front of the building volunteered to look out for her car.

"Hey Dee, don't worry 'bout it. We got you," someone said.

Deedee flashed the peace sign while the people in front of the building ran over and gave Coco hugs. It was a good feeling. She had not returned since her mother's funeral and they were happy to see her.

"We got mad love for you Coco," someone said.

They walked to Kim's mother's building which was not far away. Coco and Deedee waited on the elevator.

"That's mad love they show you Coco. I mean they always show you love but that was like wow. Over the top," Deedee smiled.

"Yeah, but they gave you props. You ain't gotta worry 'bout your car getting touched out here. That's real right there, yo."

The elevator came, and they got inside. Before long they were standing in front Mrs. Jones' apartment door. Coco rang the doorbell several times, and Deedee gave her a strange look.

"She's got a hearing problem, yo."

"Okay..."

The door opened after a few more rings. Mrs. Jones stood at the door for a couple of beats before recognizing Coco and Deedee.

"Coco, it's you. For a minute there, I thought you were your mother. My, my, my, you're as beautiful as she was when you're all dressed up. Girl, come in, come in," Mrs. Jones greeted.

"You remember my friend Deedee, right?"

"Oh yes, how's your uncle, Deedee?" Mrs. Jones asked.

"Thank you, my uncle is fine," Deedee smiled.

"Y'all come and sit down with me. Coco, you know Kim just left not too long ago," Mrs. Jones said, closing the door. "Yes, she was here all dressed up saying she's going to hang out with Tina."

"I came to talk to you about my mother," Coco said.

Kim was on her way to Tina's apartment after dropping her son off to the babysitter. They were going out clubbing after an evening of shopping. Kim saw Flack on his way out of the apartment building. He was moving too fast to see her slip inside, heading to the elevator.

Tina was inside her apartment getting ready for another night on the town. She heard the doorbell, and went to open the door.

"Use your key, ho'," Tina greeted.

"I wasn't trying to be all up in your biz like that. What if you had a man up in here or sump'n, bitch...?" Kim said.

"It wouldn't be the first time your nosey ass catch me giving some ass to a nigga. You ho," Tina said.

"Uh-hmm... Guess who I saw running out your building just a while ago?"

"I don't fucking know ho'," Tina said.

"Flack, bitch. You still fucking that nigga?"

"Shut your face! You saw him. That nigga was up here and his cell phone was ringing off the hook."

"He still gave you some ass. And then he ran home to his wife. I heard she jealous as fuck. She some fat Dominican chica from da Heights."

"She ain't gotta worry 'bout me. I only need her nigga every now and then to bang me out," Tina laughed.

"You love fuckin' other bitches' man and shyt, huh? Make you feel like you got better pussy than the other bitch?"

"Shut your face, bitch! Why don't you make yourself useful? Stop analyzing me and roll up a blunt."

They continued sipping a champagne-and-Hennessy mix while Tina put on her jewelry and Kim adjusted her makeup. Finally they completed the process by smoking weed, grabbing their handbags, and heading out the door.

Strutting their stuff outside, Kim and Tina couldn't take a step without a man greeting their presence.

"Damn, you looking good, mamis. Twin delight, let me be your papi tonight..." a passerby said.

Kim and Tina laughed and waved for a cab. Before the taxi could arrive a short Latina woman walked hurriedly to them.

"Hey are you Tina?" she asked.

"Shyt, what is that to you, bitch?" Kim asked.

"I just want to know that's all," the woman answered.

"I'm Tina. What about it?" Tina asked, walking a few paces toward the woman.

"I just wanna make sure you're the right bitch, that's all," the woman said. "The man you been fucking. I'm his wife and I don't like it."

It happened in a flash. By the time they saw the glint from the knife's blade, it was already too late. In one swift motion, the woman lurched forward, shoving the knife deep into Tina's chest. Then she took off running. Kim was behind Tina and was unaware of what had taken place until the woman was already way down the street. Tina turned facing Kim. The handle was the only part of the knife visible. A trickling of blood showed where the blade entered and disappeared into Tina's flesh. For one horrific beat Kim stared at her friend in disbelief. Then she let out a blood curdling scream.

"Shyt! Bitch she stab you!" Kim shouted.

"Help me," Tina said, clutching at the knife's handle with both hands.

Stainless steel was lodged inside her and Tina didn't have the strength to pull it out. She collapsed in Kim's arms and they both sat on the asphalt as Tina faded. Kim pulled out her cell phone and dialed.

"Help! I need help. Some bitch just stabbed my friend and she's dying," Kim screamed into the cell phone.

"What's the victim name?" the 9-1-1 operator asked.

"Tina Torres," Kim said.

A small crowd had formed by the time the ambulance showed up. They scooped her and started to immediately working on Tina. She was carted off to the emergency room with her life dangling on a string.

The following morning Eric Ascot sat with his attorney and listened to the grim news. Their defense had been dealt a crushing blow. Tina Torres was in critical condition in the hospital, and they didn't know when she would be available. Max Roose was incessant in trying to convince Eric to pay the judge.

Eric listened attentively and realized that his defense was crumbling. Witnesses were disappearing left and right. First Rightchus then Tina. He stared at the facts thinking about Coco and Deedee. Besides Sophia, they were the only ones there inside the apartment. Eric never wanted to get his niece or Coco involved in this caper.

Sure life wasn't always a bed of roses, but he did not want to jeopardize his niece or Coco's lives. Eric had made a promise to care for each of them like a father, and wanted to stick to that. Yet protecting his freedom was dependent on putting them in harm's way. Sitting in the interview room at the courthouse with his attorney, his coffee had gone cold. Eric's mind revisited the fateful incident that could cost him. He thought those events were dead, but they seemed to be resurfacing right at his doorstep.

"Everyone listen, this is the story. We were having guests over and this thug broke in trying to rob us. I shot him to protect mine. These are my guns and I have the right to use them. I was defending my guests, my property, and myself. All everyone has to do is please just stick to the story, all right?"

"Honey, honey, please! I mean, are you in your right mind? How're you gonna explain the guns, huh? This is not a project building. There are no armed looters randomly visiting you. There is absolutely no reason for you to be sitting in your living room with guns," Sophia said worriedly.

"I was in the bathroom when he broke in. That's all. He didn't know that I was home so I surprised him. That's it, sweetheart. It's that simple."

"I don't like it, Eric," Sophia said regaining her senses. The blow to her head had initially rattled her. "Why don't we just tell the truth, Eric?"

she asked. "The more you lie, the more you're gonna have to keep lying in order to cover up the other lies." Sophia appealed to Eric. "I'm just afraid somewhere along the line someone might..." There was a long silence as Sophia paused. It was as if she was the voice of their deepest fears. "What if one of us breaks down? Or some key thing is overlooked? Then what?" Everyone heard the question but no one dared answer. Sophia continued, "I just think we should tell the truth and take our chances." She pleaded with Eric but he shied away from looking directly at her face. He looked to the floor instead.

Eric already had his mind made up. He had defended himself against a violent and illegal intruder, someone who not only wanted to rob his guests but who had also shot and killed Kamilla. Eric knew it was the best story and he defended it.

"The truth, honey, is that the police ain't gonna hear anything I've got to say. They're gonna hear what they wanna hear, then they're gonna start questioning and dragging this case out trying to bring me down. The cops, they're all about bringing the next Black man down. It's not happening here," Eric said, hoping for sympathetic ear. "Everyone just has to stick to the story. It's easy. I mean, is everyone on the same page or what?" Eric asked looking at everyone's face but paying close attention to Sophia's body language.

"I'm with it. If we decide that's it then that's all that po-po is getting outta me, yo," Coco said.

"Deedee, are you okay? Do you understand what is going on, sweetheart?" Eric asked. Immediately, she knew the reason for his inquiry. He wanted to make sure he understood the worried look that had spread across her face. He moved to comfort her. Wide-eyed with alarm, she recoiled when Eric tried to touch her. He eventually was able hold her and felt her heartbeat slow down from triple time.

"But Uncle E..."

"It'll be all right, sweetheart. Everything will work out," Eric said patting his niece's shoulder and nodding as he looked at Sophia. He knew *she didn't want it like this but this was the only way no one would go to jail. If it didn't go the way he planned then the question would be, was he prepared to go? The thought fast-forwarded through his overactive mind. He would be ready.*

"We have to make this deal with the judge while the chance is still available, Eric. Our indecision could cost us," Max Roose said, as if he was counting his words.

Eric considered all aspects of his circumstances and figured whatever was done in the dark was slowly coming to light. Eric hoped to remove the boulder that was now weighing heavier than ever on his mind. He smirked when he spoke.

"Okay, make a deal," Eric said.

The case was temporarily adjourned for the day. This gave Max Roose a chance to meet with the judge. Eric Ascot escaped the paparazzi by leaving quickly in his limousine. This allowed Max Roose to do his other job, communicating with the media.

"We're going to settle this very soon and hopefully make a deal..."

Eric Ascot was busy finishing Coco's album and together they had already done twelve songs. Eric's focus kept Coco's artistry stimulated and she delivered a combination of songs that offered a great sampling of not only her singing voice but also her command of rapping.

The collaboration was dynamic, and the pair often spent heavy hours laboring on the collection of songs. Eric gave Coco his full and far-reaching musical experience, sampling not just beats and R&B vocals, but also rock guitars and other sounds. He wanted the album to be different—not just an average, run-of-the-mill rap album. Hence, he experimented with Jimi Hendrix–styled guitar riffs and Talking Heads organ samples. Coco was eager to learn the nuances of recording and became the consummate professional. With deep and thoughtful lyrics, Coco poured her soul into the recording sessions and gave her all to the performances. She was slowly blossoming into a superstar.

No one was prouder than Deedee. They became tighter, and often slept in the same bed. Awaking in each other's arms they would kiss and hug. Sometimes they just chilled, staring into each other's eyes. Deedee enjoyed having Coco living under the same roof with her. They were in the room when Eric received the call from Max Roose. Twenty million was a very steep price to pay, but it would guarantee no jail time and Eric would have made friends in high places.

Eric made his way to the café to think. He quickly did the math and realized that he would have only a million left. That wouldn't be enough to do a movie and the album. He gazed at the waitress and thought of the figure. Twenty million dollars was a very high cost for freedom. He was contemplating the prospects when his cell phone rang.

"What's your answer, Eric? It's now or never."

Eric felt hounded by Max Roose, but knew he had to pull the trigger, and authorized the requested money to be wired to his attorney's account. Then he walked back to his apartment in a zombie-like state, thinking about all that he was giving up. The pain didn't come cheap, and neither did the relief of his sorrows. Eric headed straight to bottle of Louis XIII and poured himself a couple of shots.

Coco was in the studio listening to her recordings. She saw Eric walk in and smiled at him.

"Uncle E," she greeted. "How're you?"

"I'm fine, Coco," Eric smiled.

"I just wanna say thank you from the bottom of my heart for all you've done," Coco said.

"You're welcome from the bottom of my heart," Eric smiled and hugged the beaming teen. "Are you ready to work?" he asked.

"Oh, no doubt," she said, checking her lyrics written on the notepad. "I'm fired up, yo."

Eric Ascot got busy making songs. The process of creativity altered his mind state and before long he was thinking of how big Coco could become. She was a hard worker and a fast learner. Coco became the prodigy he always knew she would develop into. Eric sat at the controls listening to her do her thing. Singing, rapping, she owned the songs and made it easier for him to see the finish line.

His cell phone rang and Eric glanced at it. The number was one he didn't know and Eric hit the reject button on his phone. He went back to listening as Coco rap. Then he came up with an idea to do a video. It was a long shot. With all his industry connections, Eric felt he could not only pull it off in a couple days, but also have the video aired nationally. Eric hurried out of the studio and dialed on his cell.

"Nick," he said.

"What up, E?"

"I need a favor," Eric continued.

"Go ahead..."

"You know how you used to use the artist's hood as a background when you used to direct rap videos?"

"Yes, I showed the QB in Nas' videos," Nick said.

"Yes, I need you to recreate one of those like back in the days for my new artist."

"Who's that?"

"Coco," Eric said with a smile.

"I heard about her. You got it. Tell me when and I'll make it happen."

Eric was smiling when he ended the call and returned to the small studio. Deedee was listening to Coco go through her lyrics in acapella style. The renowned music producer signaled for a timeout.

"We're gonna make a video," Eric shouted.

"When...?" both Coco and Deedee chorused.

"Tomorrow afternoon," Eric said.

Both girls jumped with joy. Coco and Deedee ran over to where he stood. They both hugged Eric and he smiled at their unwavering affection.

"I'm gonna have to get your outfits ready," Deedee said.

"Yes and we'll set up at Coco's old building and use the people who were at the funeral for extras," Eric announced. "We'll use the song you dedicated to your mother," he smiled at Coco.

She hugged him tighter and there were tears in her eyes. Deedee smiled and they were caught in the moment.

"Alright, okay, Deedee. You got wardrobe, and Nick will bring all the necessary equipment. Coco, you chill out, and just be you. Your real work will start tomorrow. I have to make a couple calls. So let's get the show on the road," Eric said and both girls cheered.

Coco and Deedee could hardly wait for the day to arrive. They spent most of the evening preparing for the video shoot. Deedee collected all the items of clothing that were necessary. She went into her closet and brought out Gucci, Prada, and Dolce & Gabbana outfits with the tags still hanging,

The next day involved, "Lights, camera, action!" In the making of Coco's first music video-shoot. It took place center-stage in front of Coco's old building. Eric, Coco, and Deedee were transported in the limousine site and cameras were already rolling when they arrived.

"Hey Nick, what's good?"

"Cool man. Eric how're you?"

"I'm good. Nick, this is Coco. Coco this is director extraordinaire, Nick Quest," Eric said.

Kim was there, dressed and ready to go. Just like Eric planned, the shooting of the video brought out the entire neighborhood, and he gladly welcomed the participation of the people. He took time out to address them. Then he walked over to the director's chair, and spoke with Nick.

"You're really taking this shoot like what we used to do back in the days, E," the director said to Eric. "It's a great day to use the raw natural light, and the landscape looks good for the backdrop."

"Yes you got it, Nick. I want you to use all that footage. From the moment we arrive and all..."

"I got you, E," Nick said. "I already shot some footage of the area."

"Great," Eric said, nodding in agreement. "So let's do it."

"Are you ready Coco?" Nick asked.

Deedee had been working on her makeup and fixing Coco's wardrobe. She looked up and answered.

"The star will be ready in a couple seconds," Deedee said.

Nick took over the video shoot and Coco performed her song. She did it several times on several takes, but eventually she got the knack. She held the audience in her hand, Coco performed brilliantly.

"Dedicated to all the people out there who lost a loved one—uh, uh," Coco started rapping. Kim sang the hook and Coco flowed. It was a perfect duet.

That's my mother you got in your arms, oh Lord

Please make me understand why you had to take her back so early

Help me to speak clearly,

Hold her thoughts with me on earth so dearly

That's my mother you got in your arms, oh Lord

Please help me understand clearly,

Speak my heart fairly, keep love on my mind

Please remind me why I'm still here what am I doing here

That's my mother you in your arms, oh Lord,

please make over-stand I wanna find answers to these questions oh Lord

why Lord tell me why I'm here floating with the stars."

It took an anxious couple of days for the video to be completely ready to go. There was enough footage for two videos, but Nick and his staff expertly trimmed hours of footage to five strong minutes of Coco.

The gifted teen was adding the finishing touches to her debut album. As soon as the video premiered, it went viral. Her message was simple, her rhymes easy, and Coco became a big hit. She was poised to take over the music world. 'Sins of My Mother," the video, was released with a major splash.

Coco was interviewed on a popular local morning show to coincide with the release of her video. With Deedee along, Coco arrived promptly and Deedee made sure she was photo-shoot fresh for her interview. She was courteous and smiled easily throughout the process.

"So Coco, you have a hot video and album coming soon. We want you to come back and talk soon," the host said.

"No doubt. And I just wanna thank Eric Ascot and Nick Quest for making a hot video," Coco said.

"And we have that video coming up right now. The new video from Coco," the host announced.

"I absolutely love this video," Deedee said when Coco joined her in the listening room.

It was a huge launch. That same day, Coco and Deedee were chauffeured in a limousine to different television stations, and Coco gave multiple interviews. The buzz had been created and Coco was performing and going live on all the popular video channels.

"Are you ready to eat? I am," Deedee smiled, rubbing her stomach.

"I hear you, yo."

"Please find us some place to eat quickly," Deedee said to the driver.

"No problem," he said.

Eric had spent the seed money, and knew he was making the right decision. Now all he needed was the returns so he could fuel the machinery. The video was the bait to attract the right suitors.

He was watching Coco's interview and Eric received the call he had hoped to get. Because of the stir the video had caused, a mysterious person had contacted Max Roose.

"They wanna do business with you, Eric," Roose said. "You're going have to make the call."

Eric made the call, and agreed to meet with the potential investors. Checking the big face Rolex on his wrist, Eric walked inside the restaurant. He was immediately seated in a quiet corner away from the lunch-time crowd enjoying their meals. After waiting for half hour, Eric was nursing his second martini then signaled for the maitre d'.

"I was supposed to meet someone here," Ascot said.

"Oh, so sorry, Mr. Ascot. Mr. Mariuchi will be here shortly," the man said in a deep Italian accent. "Can we get you anything else?" he asked, signaling the waiter. "Bring Mr. Ascot another Martini," he said, bowed and walked away.

They walked in like a team of basketball players, and it was clear they were familiar with everyone in the restaurant. There were five of them, and one approached the table Eric Ascot was sitting at. He saw the youthful face and thought he was a fan.

"Mr. Eric Ascot, I'm Joseph Mariuchi. Friends call me Joey. May I sit down?"

Eric silently waved his arm and the kid sat down in front of him. Meanwhile his friends took up a table not too far away.

"I was expecting your brother or father," Eric said.

"Maybe you were expecting my granddad and dad. Neither of

them could make it. So I'm here. Do you mind?"

"No, go right ahead," Eric said cautious of the teen's swagger.

Joey waved his hand and the waiter rushed over with drinks for the tables. Then he waited until all the glasses were filled and the waiter walked away before he started speaking.

"I represent the Mariuchi family Mr. Ascot. Can I call you Eric? I know I may seem real young to you, but that's beside the point. We want to become the sole investors in your company. Fifty-fifty, everything even and legal," Joey said and sipped.

Eric remained tightlipped, analyzing the young man sitting in front of him. He had known the Mariuchi and done business with them but never the grandson. He was completely new to the ways of the chain-wearing, fast-talking man sitting in front of him. Eric understood exactly what was being said, but wondered about Joey's authority.

"How much are you prepared to offer?" Eric asked, testing the water.

"Eric, just in case you haven't heard. My father was setup by a certain man, whether you know him or not is not important. His name is Rightchus. Correction, was," Joey said, watching Eric's reaction. "We already took care of him. But because of that fucking rat, my grandfather can't come back to this country that he loves and my uncle is a paraplegic."

"I'm sorry to hear that, but—"

"That doesn't answer your question," Joey finished the sentence and Eric sat back and sipped his martini. "If you agree and we think you will, we will start with a one hundred and twenty million split."

Eric almost choked on his martini and reached out to grab the young man. He quickly let go and smiled.

"You're bullshitting me, right?"

"You're very a smart and talented man. Why would that figure seem such a big deal to you? It's not just money it's a partnership. We want to operate through you and attract others like yourself. Eventually...

you can see where this going, right Eric?" Joey said with a knowing smile.

"So what do I have to do?" Eric flippantly asked.

"That's simple. Meet with our check writer, our representative, at her office tomorrow and we can begin business."

"That's it?"

"She'll have the particulars such as the project names, movies, music, and whatever else you're working on. She'll have the paperwork and you just sign on the dotted line and we're in business, Eric."

Eric looked up at the young kid possessing all the acumen of a wise guy. Joey wore athletic gear and appeared to have just crawled out of a pickup game of basketball. Maybe he had been sniffing coke, Eric mused, staring at his face and seeing the redness of his flared nostrils.

"Alright, let me have the address," Eric said.

"Here you are, sir," Joey said, handing a business card to Eric.

Eric took the card and quickly glanced at it. Suddenly he started laughing, and pointing at Joey. "No way! Where are the cameras? Is this some type of reality show you're involved in?"

"No, Eric, what you see on the card is very real. That card is worth one hundred and twenty million dollars guaranteed," Joey smiled and stood.

He held out his hand and Eric accepted the handshake. Eric was still nervously glancing around looking for a camera. He looked at Joey expecting a punch line.

"This is real, Eric," Joey said, walking away with his friends.

Eric slammed the martini to the back of his throat, and raced after the young man and his friends. Outside, he saw them loading up in a Benz truck.

"Hey Joey, is this some kinda joke, man?" Eric shouted.

Music blasting, tires screeching, the Benz was gone. Eric was left in their wake, closely examining the card in his itchy palm.

"Oh no, not her," Eric said, scratching his head.

Standing outside the restaurant, Eric could hear the heavy bass of the music thundering loudly from the car's speakers. The chorus rang from Coco's song.

That's my mother you got in your arms oh Lord

please make me understand why you had to take her back so early

help me to speak clearly,

hold her thoughts with me on earth soo dearly

That's my mother you got in your arms oh Lord

please help me understand clearly,

speak my heart fairly keep love on my mind

please remind me why I'm still here what am I doing here

That's my mother you in your arms oh Lord,

please make over-stand I wanna find answers to these questions oh Lord

why Lord tell me why I'm here floating with the stars.

EPILOGUE

Six months later...

"Hey Dee, what's good?" Coco said walking out the door of the huge library.

"Coco whassup, girl...?"

"Just chillin', trying to study and doing this college girl thing, yo," Coco answered, walking across the Quad heading to the Yard where the freshmen lived and congregated.

She was in the process of completing her first semester at Harvard. Coco stood outside her dorm room, looking at the manicured lawn. The phone call swung her into an upbeat mood, and put a smile on her face as she chatted on the phone.

"Guess what?"

"What, you're about to have the baby, yo?"

"Yes, but it's time for you to play superstar again..."

"The movie is gonna finally be released?"

"Bingo, and there's an airline ticket waiting for you at Logan

Airport..."

"That's great, Dee," Coco said jumping up with excitement. "I'll be home soon."

It was close to Christmas break and she was set to travel back to New York city. Coco was so excited, she spent the entire night listening to all twelve songs on her album. Morning couldn't come soon enough.

Deedee and Sophia were awaiting her arrival at La Guardia Airport. There were a few paparazzi flashbulbs going off as Coco walked through the airport. They screamed and ran when they spotted one another. Then they laughed during the ensuing hugfest which occurred between Coco, Deedee and Sophia.

"Hey you look very pregnant, yo," Coco laughed.

"Isn't she?" Sophia said, joining in.

"Coco, you look fabulous. I must say college is becoming you," Deedee laughed. "No more ghetto girl," Deedee continued and they all laughed.

"When are you—?"

"In a couple of months," Deedee said. "You'll have to come back for his birth," she laughed. "But seriously Coco, you're gonna be too busy right now. I have your itinerary. We got a wedding on our hands."

"A wedding?"

"Yes, a wedding," Sophia laughed and raised her hand.

"Oh my! What a huge rock," Coco said, admiring the engagement ring on Sophia's finger.

"It's a 3-carat and don't ask how much it cost," Deedee said.

"Well, it's is a marquise hand-crafted to the highest level of excellence," Sophia bragged. "It was worth every bit of time," she continued.

"Nice..." Coco said, she examined the ring, visibly impressed. "So when is the wedding, yo?"

"A week after the movie premieres," Deedee happily said.

"Congrats," Coco said, hugging Sophia.

"And congrats to you, Coco," Sophia said.

"Yes, tomorrow after the movie opens, you're gonna be a real superstar," Deedee said.

"You're gonna be star too, Dee," Coco smiled.

The chauffeur gathered Coco's luggage. Then hugging, they all walked to the limousine. The chauffeur packed the bags away then quickly whisked Coco, Deedee, and Sophia away to the Manhattan apartment.

"Welcome home, Coco," Deedee said with a smile.

She handed Coco a set of keys. Sophia walked in front leaving Coco and Deedee behind. Coco glanced at the building then she hurried to catch up with Deedee. They embraced and Deedee kissed her passionately.

"You're soo sweet. Thanks for everything," Coco said.

"You're more than welcome. Uncle E is upstairs. He knows everything and it's all good," Deedee smiled.

"I guess Sophia was your ideal ally, huh?"

"Yes, two heads are always better," Deedee laughed. "But she was fantastic. She did such a good job convincing Uncle E, he proposed to her," she continued.

"Really now?"

"They seem very happy. But how's your first semester as a college student?

"So far soo good. I miss y'all though, yo."

They hugged again and walked inside the building. Inside the lobby, Eric and Sophia were sitting and waiting for them. He walked to them and hugged Coco.

"Thanks, Uncle E," she said.

"I'm with my favorite ladies. Let's go to dinner," Eric announced.

The limousine left them outside a popular eatery. With the holidays rolling in, the mood was festive and the group enjoyed themselves. The feast went down well and Coco saw the loving reaction between the couple. It couldn't be a better homecoming for her and she enjoyed every moment. When Eric made his toast she was so choked up, Coco felt the tears.

"To a number-one selling album—welcome home, Coco, we did it," he raised his glass.

"No, we all did it, Uncle E," Coco said, raising her glass.

"Here, here," Deedee and Sophia chorused.

Long-stemmed champagne flutes clinked, then they drank. Coco smiled at Deedee when Eric said, "Be easy, Dee. You might damage the baby's liver."

"Oh, one won't hurt, Uncle E," Deedee said.

"Tell her Soph..."

"One glass of champagne will not hurt Dee or the baby," Sophia smiled, kissing Eric's lips.

His concerns seemed to fade into a loving smile. Coco watched and couldn't help but think that this was the family she always wanted. There was genuine love to replace what she never experienced within her real family. The warmth she felt melted her heart. Suddenly Coco opened up, echoing her feelings.

"You guys make me feel soo good to be here, right now," Coco said. "I don't even wanna think about leaving to go back to college. I mean you guys are like family, and I miss you soo much when I'm in Mass... I don't think I wanna go back," she blurted in tears.

Coco's sudden outburst drew stares of concern from all around. Not only did Deedee, Eric, and Sophia look on with raised eyebrows, but so did the servers and waitresses along with the maitre D. Eric saw the tears in Coco's eyes and knew the sadness she felt. He realized that as tough an outer shell as Coco possessed, she missed her mother, and needed the comfort of friends.

"We'll cross that bridge when we get to it," he smiled softly. "When your mother was in the hospital, she told me that you must finish college. She was soo proud of you, Coco. She really wanted you to finish. And you'll always have a family right here," Eric smiled.

There was a long pause. Coco felt all their eyes on her, and held her head high, in a futile attempt to hold back the tears. It was a joyful moment, but Coco cried. Deedee hugged and comforted her while Eric and Sophia smiled looking on. It was a special occasion. Coco sighed and said, "I will, yo."

There were no dry eyes. Their tears flowed as Deedee, Eric and Sophia all hugged, and embraced the sobbing Coco.

New movies opened every week, but Gold Crest Studios decided to pull out all the stops. The movie studio threw an old-fashioned, full-blown special screening of *Angels at the Gate.* It was quite a sight outside the Lincoln Center. High-intensity searchlights crisscrossed the night sky. The police roped off the area, and makeshift barricades were set up for crowd control. Movie stars and rap stars arrived in stretch limousines.

Most of the celebs stopped and chatted with the crowd before walking up the red carpet and going inside to see the film. Dazzled by the stars, an adoring swarm of fans waited outside, and applauded loudly as Coco, Eric, Deedee, and Sophia stepped onto the red carpet.

Photographers shot photos of Deedee and Sophia slipping off. While a news reporter interviewed Eric, Coco tried to walk away, but was immediately met by TV reporters. Even though the experience was a bit exhausting, Coco was gracious. She handled the all attention and questions with humility mixed with grace.

"We're here at the world premiere of her new movie, *Angels At The Gate*, with Coco Harvey, America. And I just have to say congratulations."

"Thank you very much," Coco said, politely nodding.

"Coco, everyone knows your story by now... All the obstacles you've been through, but you've managed to complete a top-selling music album on the charts, headlining sold-out shows and concerts, and now what appears to be a blockbuster movie. How do you feel?"

"I feel really blessed. And I just want to show my gratitude, and appreciation to everyone who helped me along the way."

"Is there anything you want to say to the people who've helped you?"

"Yes, I'd like to thank them all, Miss Katie for her words of inspiration, my producer, Eric Ascot, for believing in me. My BFF, Deedee, Sophia. My girls, gone but not forgotten, Da Crew, Danielle and Josephine, my girl, Bebop, and Madukes..." Coco's voice trailed for a beat. She became emotional when she said, "Rest in peace, Madukes... To all my ghetto girls everywhere going through your struggles, one love. Just know that there's a light at the end of the tunnel. And shout out to Kim and Tina. Get better soon, Tina..."

Propped up by several pillows, Tina sat in her hospital bed with tubes connecting her to life supporting machines. There was a tube extending to her mouth, and tubes running from her nostrils to assist her in breathing. Tubes extended from the veins in her arms. She had survived six surgeries over the past six months to repair her damaged lungs. Tina's body was ravished. She was weak and tired. The emaciated woman was facing the possibility of not being able to speak again. Her recovery from the severe stab wound was beginning to show some signs of progress.

Although she was in some physical discomfort, Tina could not hold back her feeling of gratitude. Amidst the tears streaming down her face, her smile was also prevalent. The emotion was caused by what Coco had done. She reached out and grabbed the hand of her best friend.

Kim sat next to the hospital bed, beaming like a city lamppost giving light to weary travelers in a dense fog of bad memories. Her smile cleared the deluge of underlying feelings that once clogged the relationship with the talented teen. They smiled triumphantly, sahring her success while watching the entertainment channel.

"Shyt ho! I told you Coco would shout your ass out. She and Deedee look really fly up there on TV!" Kim said, and Tina nodded in appreciation. "Hurry up and feel better soon, bitch. We gotta go catch that flick before everyone else sees it. Your ho ass already made me miss the red carpet. We don't wanna be the last one to see *Angels At The Gate*, bitch!" Kim said, tears of joy streaming down her face.

She felt Tina's grip tightened on her hand, and Kim smiled, looking at her. Then they continued watching the live interview and broadcast.

"Coco, what would you like the public and your fans to take away from all this?"

"I just want everyone to be inspired, and to know that sometimes things may seem difficult, and may not always go your way. No matter what's thrown your way, just keep believing in yourself. Keep doing your thing, cause anything's possible. Sky's the limit... Frank White said that, yo." Coco answered with a soft smile.

The talented teen had grown up, and moved on. She was able to put her past behind her. She flashed a wink at Deedee and Sophia. They were standing in a corner watching, and pumping their fists. Coco stopped to pose for the paparazzi. She smiled elatedly as camera bulbs continued flashing. Then she walked away to join Deedee and Sophia.

"You did it, Coco," Sophia said.

"Yes, you most certainly did," Deedee said.

"No, we did it," Coco said, wrapping Sophia and Deedee's hands in her own.

Coco had come of age, and was well on her way to becoming a star. Later, there was nothing but smiles as they all walked proudly inside the theater to watch the film.

THE END

GHETTO GIRLS

THE SERIES

ESSENCE BESTSELLING AUTHOR

ANTHONY WHYTE

The most electrifying young adult series ever.

GHETTO GIRLS SERIES is drama at its best. Talented teen, Coco Harvey and her privileged, best friend, Deedee Ascot are teamed up with Danielle, and Josephine. They are students from the same high school, but all are from very different background, and see life from different point of view. The girls live out a dramatic existence resulting in death, deceit, and betrayal. Life in the ghetto can be soo rough, and the chance of surviving is virtually nonexistent. In a deadly background of violence, can Coco step out of the shadows of her mother's drug influence, and create a life of her own?

GHETTO GIRLS is an invigorating series with mind-bending twists and suspenseful turns taking the reader on a dramatic journey from junior year in high school to an electrifying end. The GHETTO GIRLS SERIES is irrepressibly stimulating, must-read drama at its best.

PAPERBACK BOOKS

MAIL US A LIST OF THE TITLES YOU WOULD LIKE INCLUDE **$14.95 PER TITLE** + SHIPPING CHARGES $3.95 FOR ONE BOOK & $1.00 FOR EACH ADDITIONAL BOOK. MAKE ALL CHECKS PAYABLE TO: AUGUSTUS PUBLISHING 33 INDIAN RD. NY, NY 10034

DEAD AND STINKIN'
STEPHEN HEWETT

A GOOD DAY TO DIE
JAMES HENDRICKS

WHEN LOVE TURNS TO HATE
SHARRON DOYLE

IF IT AIN'T ONE THING IT'S ANOTHER
SHARRON DOYLE

WOMAN'S CRY
VANESSA MARTIR

BLACKOUT
JERRY LaMOTHE
ANTHONY WHYTE

HUSTLE HARD
BLAINE MARTIN

A BOOGIE DOWN STORY
KEISHA SEIGNIOUS

CRAVE ALL LOSE ALL
ERICK S GRAY

LOVE AND A GANGSTA
ERICK S GRAY

AMERICA'S SOUL
ERICK S GRAY

SPOT RUSHERS
BRANDON McCALLA

**THIN LINE:
A CHILD'S EYE NEVER LIES**
ANTHONY WHYTE

NAKED CONFESSIONS
TRACEE A. HANNA

PURE BRONX
MARK NAISON PhD
MELISSA CASTILLO-GARSOW

IT CAN HAPPEN IN A MINUTE
S.M. JOHNSON

HARD WHITE
SHANNON HOLMES
ANTHONY WHYTE

STREET CHIC
ANTHONY WHYTE

BOOTY CALL *69
ERICK S GRAY

POWER OF THE P
JAMES HENDRICKS

STREETS OF NEW YORK VOL. 1
ERICK S GRAY, ANTHONY WHYTE
MARK ANTHONY, SHANNON HOLMES

STREETS OF NEW YORK VOL. 2
ERICK S GRAY, ANTHONY WHYTE
MARK ANTHONY, K'WAN

STREETS OF NEW YORK VOL. 3
ERICK S GRAY, ANTHONY WHYTE
MARK ANTHONY, TREASURE BLUE

SMUT CENTRAL
BRANDON McCALLA

GHETTO GIRLS
ANTHONY WHYTE

GHETTO GIRLS TOO
ANTHONY WHYTE

GHETTO GIRLS 3:
SOO HOOD
ANTHONY WHYTE

GHETTO GIRLS IV:
YOUNG LUV
ANTHONY WHYTE

GHETO GIRLS 5:
TOUGHER THAN DICE
ANTHONY WHYTE

GHETO GIRLS 6:
BACK IN THE DAYS
ANTHONY WHYTE

LIPSTICK DIARIES
CRYSTAL LACEY WINSLOW
VARIOUS FEMALE AUTHORS

LIPSTICK DIARIES 2
WAHIDA CLARK
VARIOUS FEMALE AUTHORS

  nook _by Barnes & Noble._   amazonkindle   **READ ALL OUR BOOK ON YOUR COMPUTER, TABLET, SMART PHONE OR OTHER MOBILE DEVICES**